CHAR

A STEEL BONES MOTORCYCLE CLUB ROMANCE

CATE C. WELLS

Thanks for reading! Like what you read? Please do me a solid and leave a review.

Want more? Visit www.catecwells.com.

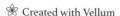

For Becca, Julie, and Louisa

1

KAYLA

A bearded biker with a man bun is checking out my ass.

If today wasn't already the worst, it'd make me kind of uncomfortable. As it is...of course, there's a pervy old biker ogling my ass. The way my life has been going, I'm surprised he doesn't have his whole club sitting next to him like the ice skating judges at the Olympics, scoring my ass as I haul boxes up this rickety iron staircase. Which I'm pretty sure is actually a fire escape? And that has to be out of compliance with all kinds of codes.

I hope Jimmy doesn't notice this guy—shit. Where's Jimmy?

My eyes fly to the Corolla.

No surprise. He's not where he's supposed to be, *guarding* the open trunk. I should've known that ploy wouldn't work. Not now that he's a *big six*. The other day he woke up in the middle of the night and caught me crying over the checkbook. He gave me this stern look and flipped the book shut.

"Mama, go to bed," he'd said. "I'm a big six now. You don't have to worry anymore."

Right.

He can't have gotten far. I picked this place in part because it's like a zoo for kids. Lots to look at but no real danger. We're at the bottom of a cul-de-sac next to the shallowest, laziest stretch of the Luckahannock. The railroad runs on a trestle two stories overhead.

I do a quick scan. The swampy mud bank where the river must've risen during the spring thaw. The wall of cattails thick enough that even Jimmy at his stubbornest couldn't get through them without a scythe and more upper body strength than a *big six* can muster. The squat pre-fab house with a handicap ramp and pier next door where the biker sits on the front stairs, swigging his beer and leering.

Then I check out the main reason I signed the lease: the big old patch of green behind our new place with its swingset-without-a-swing and droopy weeping willow. And there he is. Swinging from the willow branches, frowning and muttering to himself.

That's my Jimmy. Can't stay put. Won't stay still. Doesn't care to smile, not even when he was a baby. He's the crankiest old man of a little boy you'll ever meet. And I love him just the way he is: grumpy and perfect and mine.

And I'm taking care of him. Even if this all doesn't really feel much like *taking care of* a lot of the time.

A few weeks ago, I realized we needed to downsize from our one bedroom in town with utilities. I was two months behind on rent, and I didn't need Dad and Victoria finding out about an eviction. So I found this second-floor studio without utilities on the outskirts of Petty's Mill. Rent is three hundred less a month, but no utilities included means my electric can get cut off.

Can and will. If I don't pay the electric on time.

Which has a good chance of happening eventually because—math. Basic addition and subtraction. I've only got a GED, and Petty's Mill doesn't even have a mill anymore. I've got a decent thing going as a picker at the General Goods warehouse, but that's all contingent on the Corolla not dying on me.

And a few weeks ago, along with the rent being late and Jimmy's teacher calling about how she caught the other kids teasing him about his dollar store backpack, the Corolla contracted a bit of a death rattle. It shudders a little each time I turn it off now as if it's saying, "That's the last time, lady. Seriously. I've had enough."

I know the feeling.

After all, the Corolla and I have been knocking around about the same amount of time. It was my mom's before she passed, and it sat around in Dad's garage until I turned sixteen and Victoria figured it was either get it working again or keep driving me places. Anyway, it's almost twenty, and I'm twenty-one. If I've made it this long, a Toyota should sure be able to chug along a few more years.

Right.

My arms full of a box of dishes, I swing the door open with my hip, maybe harder than strictly necessary because life kind of sucks. I'm sweating under my boobs, my thighs are rubbing, and my shorts are riding up. And an unemployed biker is taking it all in like I'm the damn nature channel. I bang my hipbone good on the knob, and I can't stop the whimper.

"Oh, baby, don't hurt it. Ain't nobody want a bruised peach."

Oh, good. The biker's decided to step it up to catcalling. I drop the box and rub my hip. He's right about one thing. That's gonna leave a mark.

I kick-scoot the box to the far wall, the one that serves as a kitchen with a sink, a stovetop, no oven, and a yellow-green fridge from the seventies. There's a smell coming from the fridge, but I can't worry about that now. I have half a Corolla left to unload and Jimmy's not going to be content swinging on the willow tree forever. He's going to get bored, and a bored Jimmy is the devil's plaything.

I don't think he can climb a railroad trestle, but he can start making plans. And gathering equipment.

I turn to make another trip, but before I take two steps, boots on the iron stairs sets the metal clanging. Big boots.

Shit. Shit, shit, shit. I dart my gaze around the apartment, but I've got nothing. The kitchen knives are in a box in the car, so are the standing lamp and Jimmy's tee ball bat. The furniture I reassembled yesterday isn't much help; it's more cardboard than anything.

It's broad daylight though, and everyone's windows are open. Besides, it's ten o'clock in the morning on a Tuesday. It's fine. I'm fine.

My heart's still in my throat, though, and my skin goes hot and clammy.

At least Jimmy's out back.

The screen door flies open.

"Where you want these, Peaches?"

His voice is normal. Casual. He's carrying a box on each shoulder, the heavy ones I'd marked *hold from the bottom*.

"There." I nod toward the bathroom. When he saunters over, all six-feet-four of him, I take the opportunity to duck out the door.

The weight bearing down on my chest lifts, and I can breathe again. I wipe my hands down my slacks.

And I start to feel dumb.

Like my friend Sue always says, not everyone has nefarious intentions.

He's probably your average guy just trying to be neighborly. It's not like I don't know his type. The places Jimmy and I've lived since I got him back...guys like him are par for the course.

But that's not what this guy's seeing when he comes back out and rakes his eyes down my front, making the weird, cold sweats come back big time. This guy thinks I'm something I've never been. A sorority girl maybe. The girl next door.

He's eating me up with his eyes. And it's one part creepy, and another part amazing. Like I'm amazed this is happening. This never happens. My body's okay—my tits are on the big side and I'm the kind of curvy that makes a number eight when I lay on my side—but I know my face and hair are nothing much. And I'm short.

You wouldn't know it by how long this guy is taking to give me the once-over.

And, yeah, I was totally wrong about his age. He's not old enough to be my dad. More like thirty or so. And now that he's close enough to touch, my stomach starts flipping like a dog doing tricks. The face behind the beard...dude is gorgeous. Movie star, chiseled jaw, freakin' twinkling sky-blue eyes—gorgeous. Full lips and thick, shiny hair and veiny, muscled forearms like an Italian sculpture. Bright white teeth. He smells good, too. Kind of like molasses.

Oh, shit. He's grinning. He noticed me staring. Of course he did. The landing's narrow, but several feet long, and he's standing close, not giving me space. He's ducked past me, and he's leaning against the siding, all James Dean. He's probably noticed the sweat above my upper lip. And the dried milk in my hair from the mishap with the straw this morning.

This isn't awkward. Not at all.

"Like what you see, Peaches?"

"My name's not Peaches."

That's what I went with? Not thanks, but no thanks? Get lost? Hard pass?

Damn, I need to get tougher. The biker isn't deterred. Not in the least. His grin widens.

"I know, babe. It's a nickname. On account of your ass being shaped like a peach."

I drag in a breath. That's right. Dude's definitely a drop-dead-gorgeous, Italian-marble asshole biker.

"I gathered that, pervert. Let me pass?"

I hadn't meant it to come out as a question. A tough chick would tell him to move. Push past. She wouldn't stare at his thick, beautiful brown hair with the caramel streaks and wonder why God always makes pretty things bad for you.

"I ain't a pervert. I'm a—what d'you call it—an aficionado."

"Of fruit?"

He laughs. Oh, Lord. Even his laugh is gorgeous. Deep and raspy, but warm and easy at the same time. Like fingers tripping down a piano at the low end of the octaves.

"Yeah. Sure. Whatever you want to call it."

"Can I get past?"

"I don't know, Peaches. Wouldn't you rather sit up here? Feel the breeze while I bring the rest of the boxes up? Then you can get me a beer and tell me all about where you're from and what your interests are and—"

"Oh, yeah? You want to have a conversation with me? Get to know me?"

Why is it the hottest guys have the worst lines? Besides, dude is a grown-ass man. Aren't grown-ass men supposed to be smoother than this?

"Nah, let me finish, woman. You can tell me all about your stressful moving day while I cup that perfect peach of an ass and work the kinks out of your achin' back."

He...wha—?

"Don't look so shocked. You tellin' me ain't nobody ever remarked on that perfect ass before?"

Nope. Sure haven't. Not this specifically.

God, I wish I had a comeback. I know I'll have one at two in the morning when I wake up with this dude's gravelly, playful voice in my head. And a picture of what he's describing burning in my brain.

Damn, I need to get him gone before—

"Mama! Look what I found!"

Before this.

What happens next happens in slow motion, and it's so clichéd, it'd be comical if I weren't so worried that the biker will say something in front of Jimmy, and I'll have to push his enormous smoking-hot body over the railing.

Jimmy bounds up to us, a cattail in his fist. The biker looks at Jimmy, looks back at me, stares back at Jimmy. Understanding and then horror dawn on his impossibly handsome face. He raises his hands like I've got a gun pointed at him and takes two big steps back, his impossibly blue eyes searching for an escape route.

He's stuck between me, my apartment, and forty-eight pounds of filthy, scowling, scabby-elbowed six-year-old with an instinctive dislike of people. Especially men talking to his mama.

The biker is scared shitless. Forget me pushing him. If we weren't a full story up, he'd leap.

"Uh..." He realizes he has his hands up like it's a stickup, and he tries to play it cool and rub the back of his neck. He's got no sleazy lines now.

It'd all be funny if it didn't kind of suck. Yeah, a lot of guys don't want a woman with a kid. Especially not a twenty-one-year-old with a kid in kindergarden.

The biker is doing the math in his head, and I can tell the exact moment when he borrows from the two and gets something like fourteen or fifteen. His eyebrows go up, and there's some serious judgment going on behind those blue eyes.

Nothing like getting judged by a long-haired, tattooed dude who's just hanging out and having a beer at eleven o'clock on a workday. Really reminds you that all things are relative.

I want to say something smart, clap back like my best friend Sue can, but I've never been able to speak up for myself in the moment.

Lucky, I guess, that I have Jimmy with me. He has none of my limitations. I'm making damn sure of it.

"What you doing up here, mister?"

The biker looks desperately at me like I have the answer. I shrug. I don't know. Pervin'?

"Nothin', little man. Just helpin' your ma with a box."

"Mama don't need your help."

"Doesn't," I correct. It's a habit. My mom did the same.

It's funny hearing her voice come out of my mouth these days. Funny and sad and wonderful. All these things I thought I'd forgotten about her have been coming back to mind since I got Jimmy back.

"My mama doesn't need your help." Jimmy says *doesn't* like *fuck off mister*.

"I'm sure she don't, little man."

"Doesn't," Jimmy says.

In a normal situation, I'd lose my mind to hear him sassing a grown-up, but I'm feeling like making an exception. Maybe I don't have the temperament to talk back, but I'm not raising the kind of kid I was. That kind of kid doesn't have a chance in this type of world.

"I'm sure your mama can take care of herself just fine."

Right.

Jimmy is glaring a hole in the man's forehead, but he's so tall Jimmy has to cock his head all the way back to do it. My little guy has a hand fisted on his hip and a black scowl on his face, cattail forgotten and dropped to a step.

I should grab his hand, go back to the car. Put some distance between us. But Jimmy's in the way, and he's got something on his mind. I'm making the *let's leave* face like crazy, but he's not even looking at me.

"What's your name?" Jimmy squints at the patches on the man's vest as if he can read them. He can't. Not yet. He's a little slow with letters, but Mrs. Garner at school says not to worry quite yet. Just keep reading to him and taking him to story time at the library.

"I'm called Charge."

"That your bike?"

Jimmy points to the Harley pulled up in front of the house next door.

"Ayup."

"What kind is it?"

"Harley Davidson Fat Boy with a Milwaukee-Eight Big Twin engine. One-fourteen displacement."

Jimmy nods like he knows what any of those words mean.

"You ever crash it?"

"I laid it down a few times."

Jimmy only has eyes for the bike now. Please, Lord, don't let him ask to sit on it. I don't know much about bikers besides what I've seen on television, but I'm sure there's something in their code about letting grubby little boys climb on their ride like a swing set.

"You live here?" Jimmy asks.

The man—Charge—shakes his head no.

"My pops lives over there." He jerks his chin at the little house with the pier and the long ramp next to the side door. "I'm over here a lot. Taking care of him."

Jimmy nods solemnly. "I take care of my mama, too."

Charge smiles, and damn, but it's half blinding. Even knowing he's an asshole, my tummy does a squishy flip.

"I bet you do, little man. Help me with the rest of the boxes?"

I want to say there's no need, but before I can make my stupid tongue work, Jimmy nods, and then they're both off down the stairs, Jimmy interrogating him in that slightly hostile tone he uses with strangers he deigns to speak to— which he rarely does—asking about what fish is in the river and if Charge has a fishing pole and if he doesn't, does Charge's pops have a fishing pole and—so on and so forth.

I make a mental note to pick up one of those plastic fishing poles at one of the big box stores near Gracy's Corner the next time I visit my dad.

And then the three of us carry up the rest of the boxes, Charge hauling three to our one, and many hands make for light work, as my mama used to say. Charge keeps his eyes anywhere but on my ass, and I guess I'm grateful for that.

It'd be really messed up if I wasn't. If the attention was kind of intriguing. If I wanted to know—just once—what it feels like to be a normal good girl brushing off a normal bad boy.

I should have higher standards for myself. That's what Sue would say.

Anyway, it's not like it matters. When that last box is upstairs, Charge can't get away quick enough. He mumbles something about his pops, and then he tosses his beer bottle into the trash can under the stairs and disappears next door.

I'm not sure what I should be more offended by: him talking to me like he did or him running off like his shirt was on fire after he saw I had a kid.

But honestly, I'm not really offended. And I sure don't have time to be wistful about men.

I've got to unpack, scrub the bathtub so it's clean enough to give Jimmy a bath, go down to the Rutter's to pick up some beef jerky and snacks for his packed lunch tomorrow, and call Victoria so she doesn't get hysterical because she hasn't heard from me in a few days.

Oh, and find out why the fridge smells.

I'm a busy woman. With apparently one peach of an ass.

2

CHARGE

"You strike out with the babysitter?" Pops is sitting at his table by the bay window, making lures and laughing his ass off at me.

"She ain't the babysitter."

"No? Strike out with Teen Mom, then?"

I don't dignify that with a response. I just snag up Pops' half-full beer bottle and take it into the kitchen.

"Wasn't done with that!"

"Oh, my bad," I say, makin' sure he can hear me drop it in the recycling.

He cackles. The burnt idiot. My mom must've been smart. I sure as shit didn't get my brains, such as they are, from the old man.

Of course, after that fucking fiasco just now, I can't claim much in the way of brains. Maybe Harper took my common sense along with my house and my dignity and my fucking dog.

Yeah, I'm blaming my ex for my problems. Time-honored male tradition. I didn't make an ass out of myself on my own accord. Being with Harper has made me a moron.

Why else would I think it's a good idea to dog on some barely legal chick, stone cold sober and right in front of my pops? And using my best lines, too. Double the cheese.

Did I ever have game? Or was it always my face, my bike, and the fact I run with Steel Bones? I ain't gonna lie. I'm pretty as shit.

Anyway, I shoulda noticed the car seat in the back of the beater, but I only had eyes for that ripe, juicy ass. I gotta adjust my dick, remembering her bounce up those stairs, that ass so tight it only jiggled the littlest bit. Two perfect globes, more than a handful, the kind of ass you want to slap to watch it bob while she's bent over on all fours in front of you, staring at you over her shoulder—

Shit.

I'm not an ass man or anything; I'm more into the total package, but you'd have to be dead or blind not to want to take a bite.

Tragic really, about the kid. I don't do kids. I like 'em and all. If they ain't brats. But a female with a kid ain't lookin' to get plowed and get gone. And I ain't interested in playin' daddy until it's time to bail. I'm an asshole, but not that kind of asshole.

Harper and I agreed on that from the start. No kids. Kids weren't on my radar, and she wasn't looking to set aside her career for nothin' or nobody.

I wonder if she still thinks that way. Now that she's fuckin' a civilian shot caller.

Is a dude a civilian if he's neck deep in shit but keeps his hands clean? If he runs game from a downtown office with a view?

That's a philosophical fuckin' question, and one I don't

need to be ponderin'. Harper made her choice. Flushed seven years down the shitter. I don't get a choice. I get to get over it. Or leave town and lose my club.

In retrospect, it was a dumbass move to make the prez's sister my old lady. Shittin' where you eat and all.

Maybe I take after Pops more than I like to admit.

Speakin' of...I take down the bin with his meds from the top of the fridge.

"Where's the weekly pill thingy?" I holler into the living room.

"Up my ass!" He turns up the game so he can pretend he can't hear me.

It's missing in action. Again. Which means he probably hasn't been taking his pills since he lost it. I was last here two days ago, so maybe he missed one dose, maybe he's missed six.

Maybe Shirlene moved 'em. She comes around a lot since her old man passed. I don't think she's got a thing for Pops; she's just the kind of old lady who needs shit to do.

"Shirlene been here?"

"I got beers, don't I?"

Guess she has since she's the one keeps him stocked. I'll ask her about the pills next time I see her. In the meantime, I ain't gonna worry about his old stoner ass. I got enough on my plate.

The Rebel Raiders have been sniffing around the Paton-quin site for one. Can't figure out why. They got a plan or they just kickin' up dirt, trying to see what crawls out? Could always be fuckin' with us on principle. We got old, ugly beef with the Raiders. Fact is that the men who founded the Raiders were Steel Bones once upon a time. Like a fuckin' rebellious kid, they don't need no real reason to start shit with us.

Since I'm on *project management*, I gotta worry about that and still make time for the prick who's fucking my ex-fiancé when he drops by to *supervise*. Then, instead of going home to my La-Z-Boy and my big screen, I'm stuck crashin' at Pops' or the bunk room at the clubhouse like some prospect. And I need to get my dog back.

If Pops wants to keel over from a case of the dumb fucks, I can't tear myself up over it.

I check the crack between the fridge and the counter, and then I check the catch-all basket on the kitchen table.

I ain't going to buy his ass another one of those weekly pill organizers. This is like the fifth one he's lost. I swear he throws 'em in the trash. Or he—

Oh, I know where that little fucker is. I lope back into the living room to his workbench. He makes lures, mostly spinner baits and flies. He gets Shirlene to help him sell some online, but mostly he trades 'em with brothers for weed.

I rummage around on his bench while he bitches, and then—there it is. He's got his metal bobbers stored in it.

"Where are the meds?" I wheel him away from the bench, check the floor underneath.

"I don't know what you're talkin' about, five-oh."

"Pops, that shit is expensive, man." I sift through his tins of feathers and safety-pin spinners.

"Ain't in there, officer."

He grins at me with his messed-up jack-o-lantern face, and all I can think of is how much I love the dumb fucker. I ain't sayin' he was father of the year. He wasn't so good about rememberin' to feed me and never made me take a bath or go to school. But not many kids get to have all their growin' up memories be laughing their asses off, watching

Looney Tunes with their old man and ridin' bitch up to the mountains to score kush.

And then it occurs to me. "You sellin' 'em, Boots? You sellin' your pills?"

"I plead the second."

"You plead the right to bear arms?"

"Hell yeah. I'm an American, ain't I?"

Fu—u-u-u-u-ck.

Pops cackles. "Chill out, ossifer. I dropped 'em in the sink by accident. Almost out anyway."

God, this was all so much easier with Harper. She helped look out for Pops, handled the money. And she worked, too. A gorgeous, smart, classy lawyer who got the MC lifestyle and loved to fuck dirty.

And when we were together, I had it together. I wasn't some white trash ex-con with no diploma. I was the guy with the four-bedroom house in Gracy's Corner. The guy fucking the hot-as-shit lawyer.

Now I'm the guy hittin' on teen moms. The guy about to wash his pops' dirty chonies. The guy who's seriously thinking about breaking into a gated community to steal a Corgi.

I gotta get down to the clubhouse, throw some back, throw some punches, get the taste of loser out of my mouth. Maybe fuck some strange until I don't feel like such a fuckin' pussy.

I don't though. I call in a refill at the pharmacy, and I put in a load of laundry before I ride into town to pick it up. On my way out, I see the kid—Jimmy—squatting beneath the willow tree I used to climb when I was a scrub. He's scowling as he digs in the mud with a stick.

He's one bitter kid. Reminds me of Nickel. When we was kids, Nickel got us into a crap ton of fights with his hostile mug and his dumb mouth. His face got my nose broke for the first time, and his mouth played a key role in my first incarceration.

God, I love that guy.

Too bad this kid doesn't have a crew like we did back in the day. When you're that mad at the world, you need brothers at your back to help cash the checks your mouth writes.

As I roll the throttle to give the kid a cheap thrill, I think maybe I'm not so unlucky. I got my wheels; I got a way out. And I'll always have brothers at my back.

Ain't so bad, even if I did never get anywhere further than the right side of the tracks in pissant ol' Petty's Mill.

3

KAYLA

I figured out what the smell was: a carton of rancid milk. I also figured out why it smelled so bad. The fridge is busted.

And I'm figuring out something else. The rent is so cheap because there's not exactly a landlord.

There's a number you can call. It's on the lease, and it's on a sign above the laundry machine in the basement. But no one answers. Not in the morning, not at night. And after I left two voicemails, I get a message now that the box is full.

It's not like I can go to the offices of South River Property Management, Inc. A man met me at the apartment with the keys and the lease after I set everything up by phone. I mail my check to a post office box, and even though the internet is supposed to know everything, it thinks SRPM is located at the post office. Where the post office box is located.

When no one picks up or calls me back after three days, I only panic for a little while. This is a vast improvement from when I first got Jimmy back and moved out on my own. Something would go wrong, and my first instinct would be to call my dad, but I had to remind myself that that's what got me into trouble in the first place.

So I'd call Sue instead. She didn't know any more about hand-foot-mouth disease or failing an emissions test than I did, but she's smart and bossy and cool-headed. We'd talk through it. She'd make me lay out all the information, and then she'd ask me to tell her the possible solutions, and we'd make a plan.

A lot of times, the plan was *life sucks, if the kid's fed and safe, live with it.*

It's not like I don't need my best friend. I can't imagine life without her—but now I can do it all on my own. More or less.

So I think it out, make a plan. I drive down to Rutter's—again—and buy a bag of ice for my cooler. At least Jimmy'll have cold milk. Then I see if the downstairs neighbors have a different phone number for the landlord. They don't. What they do have is a hoarding problem and a severe mistrust of strangers. Which is cool. I don't much like strangers either.

Especially ones who've ogled my ass. And indecently propositioned me. And then decided they were too good for me because I've got a kid.

I'm getting desperate, though. I can't afford a fridge. And maybe Charge's dad knows the landlord. Based on the rusting car hull in his side lawn and the various other pieces of what could either be tractor parts or lawn art, Charge's dad has lived here awhile.

I hope against hope that Charge isn't there. I don't see his bike. It's drizzling though. I don't know if bikers ride in the rain. Maybe if they're real badasses?

Before I go over, I face the single mom's conundrum.

Take the kid into a possibly sketchy situation or leave the kid alone?

In the end, I split the difference. I take Jimmy with me, but I tell him to wait at the bottom of the porch stairs.

I don't know why my stomach's so flippy. All I need's a number. A quick conversation.

I knock, and there's a lot of banging and clattering, as if my knocking started a chain reaction like that board game Mouse Trap. I can hear whatever's in the house making its way to the door, so I'm not startled when it's thrown open by an old guy in a wheelchair with the biggest snaggle-toothed grin I've ever seen. His long grey hair is tied in a braid, and so is his long grey beard. His face looks like a friendly pumpkin.

This is the smokin' hot biker's dad?

"Hey, girlie! Whatcha doin' out there in the rain? Where's that boy of yours"

He's peering around me, and I can tell when he sees Jimmy because his big grin grows impossibly bigger, like a fat, happy Cheshire cat.

"There he is! Get up here, boy."

I'm totally taken by surprise when Jimmy dashes up. He is not a friendly, chatty type of kid.

I'm struck even more dumb when he opens his mouth and asks, "Where're your legs at?"

My face flames as I hush him, but the old man cackles, wheeling backwards, and gesturing us in. "One's in a place called Vi-et-nam. The other's mounted on a wall at the Steel Bones clubhouse."

I wrap an arm around Jimmy's chest before he can follow this jolly biker into his surprisingly neat house. From what I can see over his shoulder, it's really cozy. A plaid couch with wooden arms from the seventies, a worn leather recliner with scratches that say a cat used to live here.

"I'm sorry, sir."

I make note to have a talk with Jimmy about being nosy. He's usually so reticent, I don't need to worry about him being rude. I guess he's growing out of his shyness. Victoria'll be happy. She's been talking about him *becoming more extroverted* since he took his first steps.

"We don't want to bother you. I just wanted to know if you have a number for the landlord next door."

"Why's it hanging on the wall?" Jimmy's staring at the man's legs, covered in sweatpants folded and pinned below the knee.

"Conversation piece." Charge's dad is wheeling backwards, and Jimmy squirms out of my arms to follow him.

I have no idea what's gotten into my boy. He won't even look my dad in the eye, but he runs right up to this grizzled biker.

"What's a conversation piece?"

"Somethin' to talk about. When you ain't got nothin' to say."

"Why would you talk if you got nothin' to say?"

I resist the urge to correct Jimmy's grammar. He's never this open with other people.

"Good point. Want to see my lures?"

I try to interrupt, politely decline, but Jimmy's too quick. "Yeah."

He follows Charge's dad to a cluttered work table in front of the bay window. It's covered in containers of hooks and feathers and spools of line. There's a magnifying glass and a fancy vise.

Jimmy is entranced. "You fish?"

"Do I breathe, son?" Charge's dad roots around on his desk until he finds a fluffy bit of fur. "Know what this is?"

Jimmy shakes his head.

"It's an elk hair caddis. Good for trout and steelhead."

"What's a steelhead?"

"Kind of trout."

"What's it made of?"

"The elk hair caddis?"

Jimmy nods.

"Elk hair mostly."

This all should sound like who's on first, but it doesn't. Jimmy is as serious as he always is, and Charge's dad isn't humoring him like most adults do with kids. He's not shooting me any winking smiles. These two are having an honest-to-God conversation.

I back off and look around.

Snoop, really.

Everything in the little house is at least thirty years old, but clean. There's a few fish mounted on the wall, a deer head, and a mirror with a beer logo, but other than that the walls are bare. No family pictures. No books. There are crates of records along one wall, and a wood stove. I can see through to the kitchen, and it's clean, too.

I have to admit, I'm surprised.

I sit on the sofa, and it's so worn, my butt sinks a good few inches. It's comfy. My flip-flops slip loose, and I don't bother wedging them back on.

The boys are chatting like old friends. Who are both six.

"What's your name?"

"Jimmy. My mama is Kayla. You can call her that. What's your name?"

"Boots."

"How come you're called Boots? You don't have legs."

"It's a joke."

"That's mean."

"Nah. It's funny."

"Kind of."

"Yeah."

Their patter is so natural, so easy, I exhale a bit, relax into the sofa, let it wash over me.

Is this what it'd be like if my dad wasn't so uptight? If he wasn't so worried about Jimmy being athletic, and Jimmy being smart, and Jimmy being extroverted because *now more than ever, it's not what you know, but who you know?*

As soon as I had Jimmy—hell, even before, when we found out I was pregnant—it was like my dad dusted his hands together and said, "Whelp. Done with that one. Failed." All his high expectations moved on to Jimmy.

I figured out what sucks more than being a disappointment to your father. It's your kid being a disappointment to your father.

I wish I could protect Jimmy from it, but I can't. Because of, you know, math. Jimmy and I are on my dad's health insurance. Victoria buys Jimmy clothes. She pays for his tee ball and summer camp and field trips. And there have been many times that their money has been the difference between Jimmy getting fresh fruits and vegetables and him getting his vitamins from fortified generic Captain Crunch.

I'm only twenty-one, but one thing I've learned: everything's a tradeoff. Everything's a catch 22.

I shake myself, tune back in to the conversation. No sense in dwelling on crap I can't change. It's all going to be okay because it has to be. That's my mantra.

Boots is showing Jimmy how to make a lure, answering his hundred questions.

"How many kids do you have?" Jimmy asks.

"Just one. Charge."

"Where's his mama?"

"Couldn't say. Maybe California."

"I've never been to California."

"Me neither."

Their conversation loops around and meanders, soothing me again. I suppose I should interrupt, ask about the phone number, get going. There's always a million things to do. Get more ice from Rutter's. Do laundry. Find a place for the boxes I can't unpack because I ran out of space.

But the rain on the roof and the warmth from the wood stove is lulling me—not to sleep, but somewhere else. My stomach, which is always in knots, eases up, unfurls. I feel floaty, boneless. I pull my legs up and sit cross-legged like I used to when I was a kid at home.

This is the most comfortable sofa ever.

"What about you, girlie?"

Huh. Boots is talking to me. He has Jimmy sorting all these bits of foil and feathers and metal beads, and he's leaned back in his wheelchair, smiling at me.

"What? Pardon?"

How embarrassing. I come over to ask him a question, and I decide to veg out on his couch instead.

"Jimmy says he likes it here. What about you?"

"Oh." I hadn't thought about it. I'm too busy trying to keep it together to think about whether I like it or not. "The river's real nice."

"That she is. When Charge was a kid, I couldn't get him out of it. Always messin' with the crawdads."

I try, but I can't imagine the chiseled biker with movie star good looks as some off-brand Huck Finn. He's too...stunning.

"What's a crawdad?" Jimmy pipes up.

"A mudbug."

Jimmy takes this as a good enough answer and goes back to his sorting.

"Where you grow up, girlie, that he don't know what a crawdad is?"

Boots says this like it's a real shortcoming.

"Gracy's Corner."

I wait for the judgment. Everyone in town hates Gracy's Corner. It was built by the mill owner, Gracy Petty, so he didn't have to live near the men who worked in the mill. It's the only gated, McMansion development in the county. When I moved out with Jimmy, I learned real quick that no one has kind feelings toward people from Gracy's Corner.

"Oh yeah? Charge lived up that-a-way."

"He did?"

"Yup. Till his woman kicked him out."

Oh. I feel kind of bad listening to this, but if I were a rabbit, my ears would be perked straight up. The biker had a rich wife? I could kind of see it. He is freakin' gorgeous. Maybe he was a kept man. Some kind of roughneck gigolo. My mind is swirling at the thought.

"Oh, that's rough." I remember my manners. I shouldn't be gleefully imagining that man, shirtless and mowing a lawn on Gracy Lane while a lady who looks like Victoria gives him orders as she sits on her porch, sipping Chardonnay. I really shouldn't.

"Sure is. Had a mind to get me some grandbabies, but the female heart is fickle."

I guess I wouldn't know. I've never been in love. I can't imagine it. I mean, I know in my head that there are good men in the world. Reliable, kind, decent. After all, I'm raising Jimmy, and he's a great kid, so he's definitely going to be a good man. But when I think of the men I know—the guys down at General Goods, the boys from high school before I had to drop out. Good is not the word that comes to mind. And how can you love a man who isn't good?

Curse this couch. I'm drifting off into my head again. I shake myself to clear my mind, and as I do, I hear an engine out front.

"Speak of the devil," Boots says.

And just like that, my stomach clenches again. I try to straighten up, but the couch is nothing but give. I don't want to spring up like I'm guilty of something, but I'm thinking about it when Charge comes through the door, hair down in a dripping wet braid, saddle bag in hand, his leather jacket slick with rain.

"God damn pouring out there now."

He stamps his feet at the door, drops the bag and squeezes out his braid on the welcome mat. It's like he takes up most of the room and makes the ceiling seems lower.

And there are raindrops in his beard. Then he sees me. His eyes blaze, his expression turning from mild irritation to something...hotter. I'm still sitting like a kid, and I can feel him rake his eyes down my splayed thighs and crossed ankles. A wave of heat blossoms in my belly, turning my palms and behind my knees damp. I clasp my hands in my lap, aware too late that I'm wearing shorts, and even though you can't see anything, you can still see a lot.

And then he tears his eyes away and looks for Jimmy.

"Hey, bud." He scoops up the bag from the floor and tousles Jimmy's hair on the way to the kitchen. "Boots put you to work?"

"I'm organizing."

He grunts, unpacking groceries. "And what are you doing? Supervising?"

He gives me a look over his shoulder. It's not friendly. But it's not exactly unfriendly.

"I came by to ask if your dad has a number for my landlord."

"You don't have your landlord's phone number?" He raises an eyebrow, and his look turns decidedly too friendly. Aggressively, suggestively friendly.

And then I can see what this looks like.

This looks like I came up with an excuse to come over here.

Like I made myself comfortable waiting for him to come home.

Oh, no. He thinks I'm creeping on him. And when he walked in, filling the doorway, bringing in the scent of leather and rain, so help me my nipples got hard when a very twisted part of me thought, Daddy's home.

I *am* creeping on him.

Oh, no. We need to go.

I ignore him, forcing my eyes away and willing my cheeks to cool down. "Do you have a number for South River Property Management?" I ask Boots. "Nobody answers the number I have."

"Something broke? My boy's good at fixing stuff."

An image of a shirtless Charge, on his back, under my sink...oh dear Lord.

I don't want to look at him because I'm convinced he knows what I'm thinking. Lord knows my face must be bright red.

"No. That is—the fridge is broken. I just need a replacement. I'm sure if I can get ahold of them, they'll get a new one."

Boots snorts. "Doubt it, girlie. Ain't no such thing as South River Property Management."

I must look really pitiful because Boots' kindly face wrinkles up and he rolls over to me. "South River whatever is some dude named Irvin. Gunderson maybe. Or Gunnerson? He only comes around when he rents a place out. He don't even mow. Prospects do it when they do mine."

My stomach sinks like a stone, and all the weird things my body has been doing—floating and blushing and sweating—the stress comes sweeping in like a broom and all those feelings are gone.

I need a fridge. Jimmy needs milk and yogurt, and yeah, maybe I could make do with the cooler for a while, but I have to buy in bulk, and you can't store bulk in a cooler. And a bag of ice at Rutter's is five dollars, and I'd need maybe three bags a week, and that's fifteen dollars a week and sixty dollars a month and math—I hate math.

I need to breathe. Think. This is a problem, and problems have solutions.

I force the panic down.

"Woman?" Charge stares down at me, his face severe, his beard still wet.

Boots is staring at me too, his brown, crinkly eyes warm and worried.

"Kayla," I croak. My throat is totally dry.

"Kayla," Charge repeats. "You okay?" I glance over, and I see Jimmy is staring at me too.

I nod.

I'm okay. I have to be okay.

"Do you have a number for Irvin Gunderson?"

"That I don't," Boots answers.

I stand on shaky legs and gesture to Jimmy. Thank the Lord he doesn't argue.

"Well, thank you anyway." My voice cracks, so I clear my

throat and keep going. "And thanks for letting Jimmy help you. Jimmy, what do you say?"

Jimmy mumbles his thanks, and usually I'd make him try again, speak up, but I just want to get out of here and go home. I know Charge is still staring at me, from the kitchen now, all tall and strong and badass, while Boots smiles at me with pity in his eyes.

It puts a pit in my stomach.

"Why don't—"

I don't wait to hear the rest of what Charge is going to say. "Well, see you around," I interrupt, a little too loud and way too cheerful. And then I drag Jimmy behind me out the door and across the yard between our places.

It's raining buckets now, and we're both going to be drenched by the time we're up the stairs, but I'm not so worried about that. It's bath night anyway.

I peel Jimmy's wet clothes off as soon as we're through the door, wrap him in a towel and then run the bath water extra warm. His forehead's furrowed, and his lips are screwed down.

Uh, oh. He's thinking.

"Do we need a new fridge, Mama?"

"Sadly, yes. I think we do."

He thinks about this. "Do refrigerators cost much money?"

"Some," I say. I don't know how much a used fridge might cost. I don't know if this is an *I can't afford this* emergency or an *I hella can't afford this* emergency.

"We don't have no money."

"Any," I correct. "Any money." Because what else am I going to say to that?

I try not to talk about it in front of him. But Victoria and my dad...whenever they see me in a new outfit, they ask, "Can you afford that?"

When I tell them I'm thinking about taking Jimmy down to Harrisburg to the science museum, they ask, "Do you have the money to spare for that kind of thing?"

No, I can't, and no, I don't, but I need to cover my nakedness with something. Victoria's hand-me-downs only kind of fit up top; the bottoms don't fit at all unless they're elastic —and Jimmy's only going to be a kid once. So I rob the hell out of Peter to pay Paul.

"Maybe Charge can fix this one. Boots says Charge is good at fixing things."

"I'm sure he is, baby, but I think this old gal is beyond repair."

Besides, this is real life. No one swoops in to save the day. And if they do, you can be sure there are strings attached.

I'm real familiar with strings.

While Jimmy sails his amphibious assault vehicle through the tub, I have some time to think this problem through. I can't afford a fridge, but my dad does have a largish mini-fridge in his garage. It's got a freezer compartment.

He'll probably let me borrow it. I'll just have to let him and Victoria yank my strings a bit.

I'm sure they'll be very gracious about helping out. They won't use it as an in to drag us back. Victoria won't gossip about me to my old friends' mothers, letting them know how proud she is of how independent I am, even though I do need a lot of support, like I didn't even have a working fridge so of course, she had to step in because even when they have babies of their own, they're still just babies themselves. Right?

Right.

I hold up the bath toy net and tell Jimmy, "Drive those bad boys into the garage."

He beeps and revs pretend engines until all the bath toys are accounted for.

"Read me the bulldozer book tonight, Mama?"

"Sure thing." I pat him dry and help him into his pajamas, being careful not to mother him too much. He gets prickly if you love on him unless he's really tired.

When he's almost asleep, though, he cuddles up to me, tucking his head into the crook of my neck.

Yeah, I can grit my teeth and smile at Victoria for a mini-fridge. I tuck a stray curl behind Jimmy's ear. I can do anything for this guy. I have before, and I will again.

Giving up is not an option.

4

CHARGE

I swear, that ass is haunting me. Right now, it's boppin' up the cul-de-sac to the school bus stop. Kayla's holding her kid's hand, and it feels dirty, thinking these thoughts about someone's mom, even though she's ten years younger than me, easy.

And the thought's I'm havin'…ain't right. I can't sleep for shit, never could, so last night I stared at the ceiling and pictured her sittin' on the sofa in her shorts, her legs crossed and those sexy fuckin' seams where her calves pressed into her thighs, her flip-flops on the floor and her little bare feet tucked up.

I want to tickle her sweet, chubby middle until she squirms and spreads those legs, and then hitch one up so I can bury my face in that sweet pussy while she watches me go to town.

I bet her eyes would get all big and round. She don't strike me as the type who's had a lot of men between her thighs.

There's the kid and all, but something about her screams

innocent. She ain't like the sweetbutts or the girls down at The White Van. She blushes.

She blushed yesterday before she ran like a dog was chasing her.

I'm so tempted to make her blush again.

What is wrong with my head?

Even when I was a young buck, I wasn't into the girl-next-door thing.

Those chicks in the eighties videos, the ones with the tight black dresses and killer heels, bright red lips, and pantyhose with the line up the back. Man-eaters. Females who know what they want. That's what does it for me.

Well, did it for me.

Maybe this is some kind of rebound thing, a reaction to Harper bailing.

Whatever, I can't resist. When the bus pulls away and she heads back down the hill, I duck walk my ride to meet her. She's holding herself tight. I bet she thinks her face is guarded, but you can read every worry there. Makes her eyes dull and turns her mouth down a little at the corner.

It's cute as fuck, but it bothers me. Couldn't say why.

"You get that number?" I call out and pull to a stop next to her.

I can tell she doesn't know if she should give me the cold shoulder or be neighborly. Hell, part of me wants to yell at her to hustle her ass back to her apartment and lock the door. She has no business talking to men who look like me. What's wrong with her that she can't tell trouble when she's looking at it?

Oh, yeah. Pops said she's a rich bitch. From Gracy's Corner. That's what's wrong with her. Someone taught her being polite was more important than exercisin' her damn common sense.

Also, my face has turned plenty of ladies reckless before. Not braggin', just truth.

She blinks at me and stops walking. "No. I looked up Irvin Gunderson on the internet, but I didn't find anything."

She's decided to be neighborly. It's what I want, but it irritates me a little, too. Again, can't say quite why.

"Don't mail the rent check. You'll hear from him."

She gives me a thin, worried smile. "I'll hear from the sheriff."

I shrug. "Doug Baker's good people. He'll hear you out."

"You know the sheriff?"

I grin wide. The smile that drops panties at the clubhouse. "I get around."

She doesn't know what to say to that. Pink circles show up on her cheeks. Like little lollipops. I don't think this girl's been flirted with much. The idea's strangely satisfying.

"Yeah?" She crosses her arms, tryin' to look tougher. Less innocent. It ain't workin'.

"Yeah. People like me. We tend to run into people like him."

"People like what?"

"You seriously need to ask, little girl?" No one's that innocent.

"Oh..." She's takin' a step back now, tentatively, her gaze ducking over her shoulder, checkin' to see if we're alone. We are. There's no cars along the curb; everyone's at work.

So now is when she decides to start showin' some common sense. When if I were a different sort of man, she'd already be in a mess of trouble.

The thought worms into my head, does somethin' strange. My body gets all tight. Ready. Now I got a picture of her standin' by the side of the road, all wide-eyed and friendly like she is now with Bucky or Creech or fuckin' forbid one of the Rebel Raiders. My fists clench.

And I kinda lose my grip for a second.

"Oh." I mimic. She cocks her head, confused. A little pissed at my tone.

I should drop it. Ride away. I'm the one who started this. I'm the one who pulled over.

But I'm an idiot because even though I know I have no business fuckin' around with her—and no right givin' her shit for being friendly—that irritation is ridin' me and nothin' in me wants to drop it and roll off. Besides, she smells like vanilla body wash. I love that fuckin' smell. Harper wouldn't wear it, said it made her smell like a cheap soap store.

I guess I kinda like the way a cheap soap store smells.

"I guess it's none of my business." She can't look at me now. The blush on her cheeks has spread, and her whole face is bright red.

"I guess it isn't."

Her eyes search me. She's puzzled, and holy hell, she's so damn young.

"You got your phone on you?" I ask.

Her forehead wrinkles. The question throws her for a loop. "I don't—not right now. No."

"You don't have a phone?" The irritation is burrowing down, spreading. Like when I see an asshole leave his ride out in the snow. Just the thought of someone not taking care of somethin' nice.

"Of course I have a phone. Just not on me right now."

Not the right response.

"How can you be walkin' around alone with no phone? You got a kid. You can't have no sense of self-preservation and no phone."

"Are you lecturing me? It's eight in the morning in broad daylight."

She's confused. Offended. I don't blame her. I have no idea where I get off either. I ain't never been the preachy type. And she's right. This ain't a good neighborhood, but it ain't a war zone either.

"Lecture'd be longer. Said my piece."

She's good and pissed back at me now, those brown eyes flashin' and that stubborn chin up. Damn but you can read every single thing this girl is feelin' on her face. Is this what growin' up in Gracy's Corner does? Cause Harper sure as hell doesn't have this...whatever it is. She'd been bangin' Des Wade for months before she told me, and I had no clue.

"Fine," she huffs. "Point taken. Don't talk to people like you."

She flounces off, over the curb and through an over-grown vacant lot, takin' a short cut so I can't follow. Not that I would. I did what I did. I'm not sure why, but I ain't gonna go regrettin' it. I don't need to be pantin' after some barely legal pussy, and I sure as shit don't need to be dippin' my dick where a kid's involved.

If I did some good runnin' her off, make her think twice about talking to men who look like me, curlin' up on their sofas like Goldilocks...it's all to the good.

The rest of my day only underlines the point.

As soon as I roll to the Patonquin site, shit starts. Boom found a hole cut in the chain link. We've had visitors, and since Garvis, our contracted security, sucks, not a single asshole on payroll can say for sure how long the breach has been there.

Some dude named Dan, the ranking Garvis guy, swears that length of fence was secure after the last shift. Asshole shows me all these initialed forms like that's proof. I seen that shit hangin' in restrooms before. It's bullshit there, and it's bullshit now.

In fairness, though, it's a huge site, and it's nowhere near secure. Garvis and the MC are in a pissing contest about who's taking lead on the perimeter alarm, so shit's been hectic.

Don't really matter, anyway. If someone's pokin' around in our shit, it's the Rebel Raiders. We got a grudge goes back aways. Led to blood, ugly shit. Heavy's brother Hobs losin' a piece of his frontal lobe to a baseball bat. Worse. We've mostly moved past it during the day-to-day—business keeps us busy—but fuckin' with us is still their life's mission. And selling meth and pussy. They don't got a lot going on.

I'm goin' to have to go to the clubhouse, talk to Heavy. Let the prez make the call.

I need another crew of men and a workin' perimeter alarm, and that means paying double to Garvis or pullin' brothers from the garage, maybe tappin' a few of the bouncers at The White Van.

Both solutions are going to cut into the bottom line. Patonquin has us stretched thin, and Heavy's gonna be a raging asshole until the client takes the keys. It don't help that the client on this one is Des Wade, the white-collar Mafioso motherfucker balls deep in Heavy's sister.

My ex-old lady.

I shake it off as I get back on my ride. "See anyone who ain't Steel Bones, bleed 'em," I tell Boom.

This is the best part of my job—the commute.

Since Steel Bones Construction has made itself a name now, we're workin' sites all up and down the interstate.

Some days I get to ride an hour or two both ways, and you know I take the back roads, let the wind part my beard and bliss out.

Today though, there ain't enough wind and sunshine to settle me. I can get free of Rebel Raiders and disloyal bitches, but...I can't find the bliss.

I've got that ass in my mind, and now it's connected to those thick thighs and delicate little feet with the bright pink toes. Who the fuck wears shorts and flip-flops in late March anyway?

Kids, that's who. And little boy or no, Kayla ain't grown. Just thinkin' of her in the same room as Harper...Harper would eat her alive. Kayla got flustered by me givin' her the once over.

Harper, though...I've seen Harper step over a sweetbutt getting a train run on her on the clubhouse floor without batting an eye. Woman was damn careful not to get any jizz on her high heels though.

I wait for my chest to tighten like it does whenever my mind goes down this path. Wait for the feeling that I'm lost, that everything that made sense has been torn up like a tossed room.

Harper and me was meant to be, man. The prez's best friend and his big sister. The lawyer and the criminal. The bitch all the brothers get hard for and the brother all the bitches want to fuck.

And we were so fuckin' good together. She liked my kind of rough; I loved her class. She didn't give a shit about the time I spent with my brothers, and I didn't give a shit about her workin' all hours and the constant drama.

Bein' with Harper was winnin' the poor white trash lottery; she knew it, and I knew it, and I really honestly believed it didn't matter.

But I guess it fuckin' mattered.

My chest should be a vise, and I should be twistin' the throttle and temptin' fate to put me out of my misery—which is what I've been doin' for goin' on six months now—but I guess maybe there's enough sun today and enough of a breeze to keep the worst of it at bay.

And then there's Peaches.

I pull up Kayla's round ass flouncin' away from the spank bank, and I spend the rest of the ride picturin' her kneelin' on the stairs, propped on her elbows, while I thrust into her with my knee lunged on a step for leverage.

And then I mix it up and I'm sitting on the stairs, and she's riding my cock, buckin' like she can't get enough, hair stuck to her face with sweat, eyes glued to mine so I can watch every feeling she has as my dick bottoms out.

Why does that picture suck me in so hard?

It does, though, cause my dirty mind spends the last ten miles just thinkin' about her face. What she looks like scared, what she looks like belly-laughin'. What she'd look like comin' all over my dick. Would her eyes fly open or would they scrunch shut? Would she keep those brown eyes on me and let me see or would she be too shy, tuck her head into the crook of my neck?

By the time I get to the clubhouse, I have a raging hard-on, and I'm more than a little annoyed with myself. Girl's off limits. I saw to that myself this morning by being a total asshole. I shouldn't have to keep remindin' myself. She's a kid with a kid. She's in a bad situation, and she don't need me addin' to her problems. And I don't need to be the pathetic fuck who got curbed and makes himself feel better with barely legal pussy.

Speakin' of...Harper's Audi is parked in the side lot. And so is Des Wade's Maybach.

Well, my dick just got soft.

I kick down the stand and throw the keys to one of the prospects. Wash, I think. Or Bush. Four of 'em came in at the same time, and they're all named after presidents. Or are now since Heavy can't be bothered to come up with no decent road names no more.

I can't tell 'em apart, regardless. They're scrubs, and I swear one of 'em's voice is still changin'.

I bet they're Kayla's age. Maybe even a little older. They might've gone to school with her.

Could be one of them knows what she looks like when she comes.

Pure break-a-face-with-my-fist adrenaline streams through my veins.

Shit. I gotta get my head straight. Focus.

How does Nickel walk around feelin' like this twenty-four seven? It's fuckin' stressful.

Maybe once I'm done with business, I can get back to normal with some no strings pussy. Could be fun, especially if Harper's still around. Maybe have Jo-Beth suck my dick. Harper fuckin' hates Jo-Beth.

Whatever I do, I got to stop thinkin' about the girl next door.

Can't ride my bike with a stiffy much more without breakin' it off.

"What up, Charge?" Pig Iron hails me from behind the bar, raising a bottle of Jack to me, half offer, half toast.

The two sweetbutts he's got bellied up to the bar turn and giggle. They arch their backs, thrustin' their tits out.

"Hi, Charge." They smile wide and eager. Ever since Harper bailed, the sweetbutts have been laying it on extra heavy.

And no lie, the girls are gorgeous. Pig Iron might be half-blind from the glaucoma, but he can pick 'em. Danielle, a sweetbutt from all the way back when, and Story, a girl from The White Van. Danielle's made it known she'd risk a throw down with Harper for a ride on my cock. Maybe now that the way is clear, I'll take her up on it.

Danielle sidles over and runs her hand down my chest, cups my jock.

"You got a little somethin' for me?"

I brush her hand away, mouth *later*, and slap the bar for a beer.

"Cookin' the books, old man?" I bump fists with Pig when he slides me a cold one.

It's a runnin' joke. Pig Iron has been the club treasurer since Heavy's dad was prez, but everyone knows it's Pig's old lady Deb who keeps the books. Pig Iron definitely didn't go to school much past eighth grade.

Not many of us did from my crew, and none did back in the day when the mill was hiring at fifteen.

"Cookin' up a little somethin', maybe. Want a Pig Special?" He sets two cocktail glasses in front of the sweet-butts, filled with bubbly pink and blue shit, umbrellas and straws and all.

"Got a dick, Pig Iron."

"So do I. And I'm thinking after one or two of these, my wrinkly old pecker is gonna be lookin' mighty tasty. Right ladies?"

The girls titter.

"Ain't going near your dick, Pig Iron." Danielle flicks her straw wrapper at him and shoots me an appraising look. I catch what she's laying down. She's up for it.

"You afraid of what I'm packin'?" Pig Iron's not givin' up easy.

"I'm afraid of Deb."

"Smart girl." A plump lady with big silver hair stalks past and swats Story on the ass. "Drink one for me ladies." She gives me a nod and jerks her chin toward the back. "You here for the powwow?"

"Don't know nothin' about that, Deb. Just some trouble at the site I need to run past Heavy."

"You gonna have to interrupt him pouring the champagne. He's got high class company in his office. I gotta put out the good towels."

"He run you out?"

Deb's prickly most days, but she can't stand when Heavy pulls rank. She points out she changed his diaper more than once, which is true, if not pertinent. Past is past. Heavy's the club's future.

Even though his old man was prez back in the day, Heavy earned his patches the old-fashioned way. Paid more for it than most. He saved Steel Bones, and every day I wake up free without bill collectors nippin' at my heels, it's a direct result of his hard choices.

There's no man I respect more. Even now, when I can't hardly understand where he has us headin' or what the fuck he's doin' day-to-day.

You'd think Heavy'd ease up now that we have so much work. Our legit cover projects could keep the club whole. Finish the beef with the Rebel Raiders and retire. But Heavy don't go in a straight line. He's always pushin' us somewhere new, aimin' bigger. Takin' risks.

It's like he wants to know how much he can get away with.

I can only guess that's why he has the club mixed up with Des Wade.

Heavy and I don't talk about Des and Harper. Heavy tried a few times, but whatever he's got to say, it ain't gonna go back in time and take that fucker's dick out of her mouth. Not gonna change the fact that she saw his Maybach and his slick suits and decided her days slummin' were over.

Speaking of...I guess I could wait at the bar, but I ain't sittin' in my own club like it's a waiting room. I grab a beer, walk into Heavy's office like it's any day, and let myself go Zen.

I got a special skill with that. It's why I always pulled the decoy jobs when I was younger. I'd get into it with some meathead civilians, throw some punches, piss on a cop car, whatever was needed to create a diversion. As soon as I was in the paddy wagon, I'd be joking with the five-oh. Representin' my charming and remorseful ass in court was how I got tight with Harper.

My rap sheet is a few pages long, but it'd been a book if I hadn't been the most chill motherfucker at Gracy County Courthouse—and if Judge Greta Doyle hadn't loved my Irish eyes and pulled at least half of my cases.

PBJ wasn't just my favorite sandwich.

Anyway, I've had a lot of practice, so I don't lose my shit when I see Harper now, sitting thigh-to-thigh next to that lizard Des Wade, ice on her wrists and neck, and the red bottoms of her thousand dollar pumps flashing at me as she swings the leg she's got crossed over her knee.

"Charge," she purrs, her face a perfect mask: smoky eyes, bright red lips, her hair perfectly shellacked back into a fancy bun. She's fuckin' flawless, and she knows it, and somehow her knowing it makes her even more stunning. When we went out, even women had a hard time not staring at her. And it's plain truth to say the females usually only have eyes for me.

"Harper." I flash her a big ol' smile, lettin' my eyes linger on her tits. Give her the appreciation I know she eats up like one of those dementors from those kids' movies.

Hope it pisses off the asshole with her.

Her new man might be rich, but I'm the kind of pretty that even men check out. She ain't never been immune to it, and the way she straightens up says she ain't now, neither.

"Is there a problem with my site?" Des Wade stands. No time for the pleasantries, I guess.

Heavy shoots me a guarded look. I can speak, but I gotta watch my words.

"Someone cut through the chain link last night. Nothing's disturbed; nothing's missing. Probably kids looking for a place to party."

Red seeps up from Wade's starched collar. He's the kind of thug born to wear a suit, and you can tell he don't like dealing with roughnecks. He's probably wonderin' where Becky is with his latte.

Heh. We ain't got no Becky with a latte, but we got a Starla with crabs.

"How did this happen?"

His face shifts from *concerned* to *righteously pissed*.

I shrug. "Wire cutters. Or garden shears?"

His face goes totally red.

Heavy clears his throat and stands, emerging from behind his desk. I like this dynamic better. Heavy's a big fucker, not fat but solid, and I ain't a small man. Des Wade might have his finger in all the pies in Gracy County—legit and not—he might own the only building with an elevator in town, but in this room, he ain't a big man.

Heavy raises his eyebrows. He's askin' was it Rebel Raiders. I give a slight nod.

"Where was Garvis?" Heavy asks.

Good question. Walkin' just far and fast enough for

eight bucks an hour is my guess. Garvis, Inc. is chickshit. It's one of Wade's outfits, so that ain't surprising or anything.

"On a half-hour rotation. The intruders got in through the fence at the tree line. We've got our guys posted to the east and west where there's road access."

"How did this happen, Heavy? I was assured that security would be airtight."

Wade is all CEO now. He stalks to a window and leans, looking out. Probably checking his Maybach, making sure no one's white trash ass brushes too close. How does Harper tolerate this prick?

She's standing now, resting a perfectly manicured hand on his forearm. "Steel Bones is the best. This can happen on any site. You know that."

"This can't happen again. Not after the foundation is laid. I'm paying for discretion. If you can't deliver..."

"Understood." Heavy's lookin' the way he did before we jumped Alonso Arrington in the seventh grade. He wants to punch this motherfucker as bad as I do, but I guess there's more money ridin' on this deal than I thought.

"Add bodies?" Heavy asks, doesn't tell.

Wade's face hardens. He doesn't like that the hired help gets to make a call.

Good. Pissing Wade off almost feels as good as breaking my knuckles on his face. Almost.

I nod. "Either Garvis or our own guys. My preference is our own."

"You should call my man Dan. At Garvis," Wade interrupts. We ignore him.

"How long would it take to gather some brothers?" Heavy asks.

"I can muster them now. Cost is the question."

"I'm not paying more for what you assured me you had

handled when we signed the contract." Wade jerks down his jacket.

It's beyond me why Heavy lets this fucker talk. He's got to be workin' an angle. Heavy leads more with his mind than his fists, but he ain't averse to using the latter. And he ain't in the habit of letting civilians talk to him like he's a bitch. 'Specially not in his own clubhouse.

Heavy smiles, though. "Of course Steel Bones will absorb the cost. Security is our responsibility. We'll handle it." He opens the door, smooth as shit, ushering Wade through. "We'll discuss it. Call you with the plan."

He walks Wade out, and Harper lingers behind. I knew she would. Bitch is a succubus. She can't resist the opportunity to feed off drama. I guess after years of writing it off each time she fucked with the sweetbutts and the dumber brothers, it's karma that I get to deal with her now.

"How you doin', Charge?"

Her voice is all fake concern. She stops in front of me, looks up from under her thick black lashes. I wouldn't know they were fake if I hadn't watched her glue those caterpillars on for the past seven years.

"Good, babe. You?" I give her my laziest smile. She don't need to know that until recently, I haven't even been able to rub one out cause I couldn't stay stiff from thinkin' about what a pathetic fuck I am.

I'd thought I was a man. I provided for my woman, satisfied her in bed, had other brothers lookin' up at me for gettin' my ass out of a shithole on the wrong side of the tracks and into a fuckin' two-story colonial with a three-car garage.

And then she fucks me like a cowgirl, and after, when I'm strokin' her hair, thinkin' I'm the shit, she tells me we need to talk. She just can't do this no more.

The worst is when she looks at me, I can tell she's gettin' off on it. She knows me well enough that she can read me, and she loves seein' the damage she's done.

"I been missin' you." She makes her eyes all wide and blinks. "You gotta come around sometime. See Georgie."

Yeah, she named our dog "Georgie." I wanted a Great Dane named Killer, and I got a Corgi named Georgie.

"Seems like you got enough to keep you busy." I nod after Wade's retreating back.

"Doesn't mean we can't be friends. We go way back, Charge."

That we do. She was Heavy's hot older sister when I was a scrub with a voice like a strangled duck. Shit, I can still remember the first time I sunk into her perfect pussy. She'd been wearin' a black suit, fuck-me heels, and she'd just gotten me off on a bullshit assault charge. I'd backed her against a wall in a courthouse bathroom, and she'd dug her nails so deep in my back she left scratches in my leather cut.

I thought I'd won the fuckin' lottery.

And I had, in that I was enjoyin' shit I hadn't earned, the kind of good luck that ruins a good life.

"I don't know, Harper. Not sure I'm down with the crowd you runnin' with these days."

Her eyes flash and then narrow. She never did like being questioned. I'm laid back and give few shits about anything outside my ride and club, so it worked for us. Then.

Now? Not so much, I guess.

"I don't 'run with a crowd,' Mark."

Oh, she's pissed. She used my government name.

"Nah, you fuck old-ass white collar criminals." Damn. I didn't mean to go so hostile, but it was out of my mouth before I could call it back.

"Are you fucking kidding me?"

She goes from zero and purrin' to a hundred and murder-in-her-eyes in a second. That hit too close to home. She's got to hit back harder, keep her pride. I used to love that about her. Now it makes me fuckin' sad.

"How many times have I defended you in court, Charge? I've never known you to be a hypocrite. Of course, you've always been happy to let everyone else do the real work, haven't you?"

"What the fuck are you talkin' about, Harper?" This is new. Usually, if we fought, it was over me failin' to get as pissed as she was at some petty bullshit.

"You've ridden Heavy's coat tails since we were kids, and then you rode mine. And now that I don't want to carry you anymore, you're all judgmental? You aren't any better than Des Wade, Charge. You're just dumber, poorer, and you're willing to play bitch."

"I ain't a bitch, Harper."

My nerves are jumpin', and everything's tense—my shoulders, my fists. I'm not used to this feeling, and even as part of me realizes she's getting' to me, the rest of me is itchin' to do...something.

Pissed twice in one day. This is a record for me.

"Yeah, what's your rap sheet then?" She grabs her purse from beside the sofa and shoves it over a shoulder like a shield.

I don't know what she's talking about, and I try to let it go, make my fists relax, open the door wider for her so she walks out.

She stays put.

"Your rap sheet, Mark David Denney, is a list of all the times you were Heavy's bottom bitch. How many times have you been arrested that Heavy didn't put you up to?"

Ain't gonna lie. Not many. If it wasn't Heavy, it was Nickel or another brother draggin' me into something.

"You're not a badass, you're a fall guy. And you want to turn your nose up because I'm with a man who earns? A man who isn't anybody's bitch?"

I can't say nothin' because nothin' wants to come out of my mouth. My fists, yeah. But I ain't never hit a woman, and the wall ain't never done nothin' to me.

"Yeah, you don't have anything to say for yourself, do you? You never did. I have no idea what I was doing for so long with some sad sack piece of shit who plays stooge for my brother. I guess it was the pretty face and the big dick."

She pretends to think a minute, cockin' her head and pressin' her glossy red fingernail to her lipstick coated lower lip. "Of course, big dicks aren't that hard to come by. If you catch my drift."

She struts out of Heavy's office now, swishin' her ass, like I got told.

I guess I did.

'Cause as bad as it's been losin' the house and the dog, my pride and my woman, it's worse knowin' she's right.

I been playin' bitch for years.

Not for Heavy. There's plenty between Heavy and me that Harper don't know. If I'd gone down for him fifty times, that was nothin' to what he done for me and the club. I'm not his bitch; I'm his brother, something I thought Harper understood.

Hell, I thought there was loyalty between Harper and me. I should have known. In the club, we talk like there's two types of females. Old ladies and sweetbutts. But in my experience, it don't really go down like that. There are those rare females like Shirlene and Deb who are ride-and-die, and then the rest of them. The club whore who squeezed me out and bailed, Harper. Bitches makin' time until somethin' better comes along or shit gets inconveniently real. That or growin' bitter when somethin' better never does show up.

Really, I'm the bitch for expectin' something else. They don't make ride-and-die no more. Or hell, maybe we don't deserve 'em no more.

Ain't like my pops offered the bitch who birthed me anything but a roof, and I bet that shit leaked. And it ain't like I brought anything to the table with Harper except a pretty face and a big dick.

And I'm told a big dick ain't that hard to come by.

MY PRIDE IS STILL SMARTIN' when I roll up to Pops' and see a kid havin' a worse day than me. Peaches' boy—Jimmy—is out by the willow, just wailin' on it. Bark's flying. Shit, you can hear the stick whistle in the air.

I look around for Peaches, but he's all alone. His face is beet red, and his little body is wired tight like he's about to blow. Reminds me so much of Nickel. Right before he punches someone in the face.

I should skip up the stairs, see to Pops. Kid probably doesn't want anyone up in his business.

When Nickel got like this, we'd send Heavy in cause he could take a punch better than the rest of us, given his massive fuckin' girth. Besides, Heavy's the only one who could talk him down. Sometimes, though, he'd be too far gone, and we'd just sit somewhere and wait for him to wear himself out.

Thwack. Thwack. This kid ain't slowin' down. And he's got no crew waitin' on him.

I glance over at Peaches' place, and then back at the kid. I walk over. Not really sure why.

Hope the boy don't fuckin' swing on me.

"What that tree do to you?" I call out.

He startles, turns on me.

I take a step back.

Don't need no piece of that stick.

The kid's thin chest is heaving, and his button-down shirt is open like that dude from Saturday Night Fever. Someone's ripped it.

"You gonna tell my mama?" The kid's voice is tight, mean. He's holdin' back tears by a thread. I got respect for that.

"Not a snitch," I say.

"So what do you want?"

"I dunno. Save a tree. I'm a nature lover."

The kid freezes a second, his body tightening up like he's gonna blow, and then his face falls. He lowers the hand with the stick. Thank the Lord. Don't need to lose no eye to some pissed off six-year-old.

"I'll leave it be," he says, defeated.

Shit. Didn't mean to make it worse.

"You want to hit something, Pops got a punchin' bag hanging up in the garage."

The kid frowns deeper. "I want to hit Cal Porter."

"What'd he do?"

"Ran his mouth." The kid presses his lips together and narrows his eyes, darin' me to give him a lecture about resolvin' things with words.

"You shut it for him?"

That surprises him. I ain't no civilian, though. I know there's times when a man has to use his fists.

"Tried."

I cock my head.

"He's bigger than me. Faster."

"If I know anything about assholes, he'll give you another shot to get it right."

The kid's lip sneaks up. "Yeah," he says. Then he just collapses to the ground, back against the tree, like a puppet that got its strings dropped. Poor kid. He's beat. Tired.

Hell. Me, too.

"He won't stop," the kid says.

I figure the patchy grass under the willow's big enough for two. I lower down, and damn—been a while since I popped a squat in dirt after a long ride. I'm sittin' now, though. Ain't fixin' to get back up soon.

"What's this kid sayin'?"

Jimmy starts drawin' in the dirt with the stick. "About my clothes. And my mama."

I raise my eyebrows. Give him some time. Been down this road a few times when I was a scrub. My groupie ma was a hell of an easy target. Kayla, though...she's young and all. But she's got the *cuts the crust off* vibe goin', hard.

"Cause I don't have no daddy. Cal Porter says she's a...she's a—"

Kid's face is gettin' hot thinkin' about it. I tug the stick from his hand and start my own doodle.

"He calls her names. That aren't right." Jimmy spits this out as hard as I say fuck.

"He's tryin' to fu—" I correct myself right quick. "Git a rise outta you. Y'know?"

His old-man scowl tells me he does know. This little dude has been around this block a few times.

"Still not gonna let them say things about my mama," he mumbles.

"Nope," I agree. I think back on all the run-ins I had with

little shits like Cal Porter. It wasn't ever a thing though, cause I had Heavy on one side, Nickel or Scrap or Forty on the other. I'd take a few hits, deal out a few more, then go down the river and hunt mud bugs.

I realize the kid's lookin' at me like I got an answer or somethin'. Wish I did. Don't though. Kids can be assholes. Adults too, as a matter of fact.

"You find any mud bugs down over that way yet?" I ask, changin' the subject. Just in time, too. I hear a screen door slam and quick steps down metal stairs.

"Yeah. Pops showed me how. He gave me a bucket."

"Catch many?"

Kayla's roundin' the corner of her building now. Her eyes get wide, and she crosses her hands, squishin' together those magnificent tits. She stops a few feet from us and cocks a foot sideways like a stuck-up cheerleader. She's fuckin' adorable.

I stand, brushin' the dirt off my jeans. Jimmy hops up, too.

"Jimmy?" Kayla's chin is up. She's obviously still twerked at me from earlier. Which is good. That's what I wanted.

I guess.

Now I'm kind of regrettin' my choices.

"Yeah, Mama. Me and Charge are just talking about catching crayfish."

I check out my partner-in-crime. His face is still red; his shirt's still hangin' open. Hope Kayla don't jump to any conclusions. Could get hella awkward.

"I told you to change that shirt before you went out," she says.

Little dude looks down, guilty. "Sorry, Mama. I forgot."

"He fell at recess," Kayla explains, arms tightening across her chest. Why's she's tellin' me? It's like she's daring me to say somethin' about the kid's shirt. Don't make no sense. I ain't the type to judge. My pants got more holes than the kid's shirt.

"Off the monkey bars," Jimmy adds. "That's where I fell."

Hah. Hope that kid's good at school, cause he's shit at lyin'. Kayla don't seem to notice, though.

"Well, go in and change it now," she orders. "Besides, dinner's ready."

"Catch you later, little man." I give Jimmy a chin jerk, and he gives me a stare that promises death if I open my mouth. It's hard, but I don't crack a smile until he leaves.

When I do, I get a miracle.

Kayla's glarin' at me, but then, it's like she can't help it. I grin, and her sweet lips curve up, her whole body losin' that uptight vibe, and I love it. I know my smile has been known to drop panties, but I never got this high off it before. Her big, brown eyes go soft and warm, and my boots take me steps closer to her before my brain can have a say.

And then the moment's over. She must remember how I was a dick, and that chin goes back up, and she turns and flounces off like some chick in a Western.

God damn, that ass.

There is an upside of pissin' off a woman like her. And it's a hundred percent her backside as she walks away.

5

KAYLA

I need a fridge. There's no way around it. So I need to go to Gracy's Corner.

I don't need to be thinking about a hot biker sitting with my son, deep in conversation as if they were friends, almost.

Nope. I need a fridge.

I try to time it so Victoria's at the gym when Jimmy and I drop by my dad's, but no, like always, she makes sure I never get to speak to *Vern* without her around.

When she moved in a few months after my mom passed, she had all these rules. Her and *Vern* make all decisions together, no locks on doors, and the passwords to all personal electronics had to be "f-a-m-i-l-y." At the time, I thought she was worried my dad and I were so tight that she'd be the odd man out, which was hilarious since my dad and I are in no way, shape, or form tight.

Later, Sue pointed out that more likely, Victoria had been the *other woman* before my mom passed, and so she was paranoid *Vern* would replace her with a healthier model if she ever got out of shape and sick.

I guess I could have gotten mad about it, but I think my mom liked that my dad was never around at the end. He made her tense. He's got a gift for stressing people out.

I know my stomach's all knotted up as I walk Jimmy up the front walk to the enormous wrap-around porch. When I was a kid, we always came in the back, kicked off our shoes in the mud room, and grabbed a snack from the kitchen. Victoria has a thing about always wearing shoes or slippers in the house, and she keeps the back door bolted.

It's weird knocking on your own front door.

Victoria answers, as always, and immediately makes over Jimmy.

"My baby!" She reaches down to gather him up, and he goes stiff. "You're getting so tall! And you're all bones." She feels his arms like she's checking livestock. "Are you eating?"

She finally looks at me.

"Is he eating?"

"He's eating," I say as Jimmy wrestles out of her grasp. He reaches back for my hand, which is something he doesn't usually do.

He doesn't really know what happened when he was real little, but I think somewhere deep down, he remembers. He's always really clingy after we visit my dad and Victoria.

"Well come on in!" Victoria says, as if she hasn't been blocking the doorway. "Your father's in his office. Of course."

She tries to keep it light, but her eyes are hard, checking me out from head to toe. She wears so much makeup, every expression is too big, fake like a clown or an actress, so I figured out a long time ago to watch her eyes. Her eyes are frustrated. She wants to find fault, but I wore her hand-me-downs in case she was here. She can't accuse me of looking too slutty or too slovenly without dissing her own taste.

I've out-smarted her. There's nothing she can criticize.

"Well, you look healthy!" she says.

Oh, I know you mean fat, Victoria.

"Did you eat before you came?" She asks Jimmy, not me, but he's not answering. "Do you want dinner? I left the casserole in the oven on low heat just in case. And we had salad. I found the best no-calorie vinaigrette—"

She wanders into the kitchen, assuming we'll follow. And, of course, we do. Victoria is an amazing cook. She talks a lot about how she replaces the vegetable oil with apple sauce and uses yogurt instead of sour cream, but behind the scenes, she uses the good European butter, and she puts an extra dash and pat into everything *for the pot*.

"For my baby." She puts a pre-made plate shaped like a dinosaur in front of Jimmy along with a sippy cup of milk. Jimmy'd kick a fuss if I tried to feed him on a *baby* plate, but maybe it's her cooking—or how uptight he gets in my father's house—but Jimmy doesn't complain.

"On your fa-vo-rite plate!" Victoria flashes a theatrical smile, and pinches Jimmy's chin. Her eyes fill with tears.

"Did you miss me, baby?" She smooths his hair, sinking into the chair next to him. "I miss you to the moon and back."

I grab a plate and help myself. It's a taco casserole, real cheesy, only a little spicy. Delicious.

I bliss out on meat and carbs while Victoria coos at Jimmy, and Jimmy gives her careful responses between bites. Somehow, even though I don't push the issue, he knows he has to be on his best behavior with my parents.

"How's school, baby? You working really hard?"

"It's good. Teacher said I'm catching up."

She did? She didn't tell me that.

"Says I'm going to be reading real soon." Jimmy sniffs, like he does every time he tells a bold-faced lie. Oh, crap. He lied for me. He knows how Victoria and Dad ride me about his reading.

My heart breaks. It's such a familiar feeling; I know where each of the pieces is going to land. I never wanted anything to be hard for Jimmy, but it seems like nothing's easy. School, making friends...the kid doesn't even have his own bedroom anymore.

Victoria widens her eyes at me. Oh, I'm in trouble. I'm supposed to keep her apprised of Jimmy's progress in school; that was part of the agreement when I got Jimmy back, and we moved out.

"Well, that is great news! Why didn't you call and tell me, Kayla? I've been looking into tutors, but I haven't found anyone I like. But if Mrs. Garner says he's doing better, well..."

I shrug, noncommittal. If Victoria pays for a tutor, I'll get him there. Somehow. I'm not going to out my kid as a liar, though. And who knows? Maybe Mrs. Garner did say that, trying to boost his confidence.

I'm thinking about what to say when I hear my dad's steps on the basement stairs. Instantly, whatever shabby little high I had going from taco casserole and the prospect of a tutor for Jimmy disappears, replaced with the usual stomach-gnawing anxiety.

I will never forget. When they kicked me out and took Jimmy, it might have been Victoria's idea, but my dad was the one who made it happen.

He pours himself a cup of coffee before deigning to say hello to either Jimmy or me, and then after haphazardly tousling Jimmy's hair, he sits at the head of the table.

Even though it's seven at night, he's still wearing his suit from work. No jacket, but the tie's still on.

I used to think he was too busy to change when he got

home, but then I figured out he doesn't want to relax. That's why even though this house is huge: five bedrooms, media room, pool, three car garage, home office and a home gym...it's totally uncomfortable. The seating is designer with sleek lines and stiff backs, and the art is modern and cold.

He couldn't wait to turn my mom's sewing room, stuffed to the gills with leaning towers of dress patterns and heaps of fabric, into the home gym. If he could have traded me in for an uptight honor roll student-athlete at the same time, he would have.

"So you want my fridge," he begins. It's not a question.

Yeah, this is going to suck.

I nod. "Just until I can save up for a new one."

"Have you called your landlord? As a renter, it's your landlord's responsibility to repair or replace appliances."

I take a deep breath. "I can't get ahold of him."

My dad shakes his head. "Ridiculous." He pulls out his cell phone. "What's the number? I'll call now. Petty's Landing is a GP Property Management Company. Doug Jenner's over there as I recall."

Doug Jenner must be a friend from the club. Basically, everyone in Petty's Mill who's anyone is a friend of Dad's from the club.

"We're not at Petty's Landing anymore."

It's like someone scratched a record. My dad's jaw sets, and Victoria's black-winged eyelashes fly up. They exchange a look, and Victoria hustles Jimmy out of the room.

"Come on, baby. Let's let Mommy and Pop Pop talk. I'll show you the new workbench Daddy—I mean Pop Pop—got for your playhouse. Want to see?"

Jimmy's eyes light up, and he races for the back door. He loves the playhouse Victoria had built for him; he's more at ease there than anywhere in this house where he spent his first four years.

I try to check all the ugly feelings swirling in my chest and put Jimmy at the center of my thoughts. Nothing matters more than doing the best for him. Certainly not my pride.

I squeeze my hands together under the table. I'm about to be lectured like a twelve-year-old.

"Explain yourself, Kayla."

Same thing he said after I passed out during mod four American History, first quarter of ninth grade, and ended up at Patonquin Medical Center with a positive pregnancy test and an ultrasound saying I had a five-month-old bun in the oven.

Not "I love you."

Not "It'll be okay."

But "Explain yourself."

It used to hurt. I can't afford hurt feelings anymore.

"I couldn't keep up with the rent at Petty's Landing," I explain, keeping my voice calm and even. "I moved to a smaller place, further away from downtown. It's real nice. It's by the river."

"There's nothing but trailer trash down by the river."

"Garret Rodgers lives by the river." I throw out his best golf buddy's name like it'll change his opinion. I know it's futile; my entire life, he's never changed his mind.

"The Rodgers live on the bluffs. Is your new apartment on the bluffs?"

He knows it's not.

"We're down past the Rutter's on Coventry Road. It's districted for the same elementary as Petty's Landing, so Jimmy didn't have to switch schools."

"Well." My father leans back in his chair and steeples his

fingers. Now we're going to get down to it. "Good to see you're at least thinking a little bit about Jimmy's well-being."

My entire body stiffens. This is dangerous ground. Whenever he starts talking about Jimmy's well-being or his health or his development, I know what he means. He means tread carefully or else. He means I better shape up, act right, watch myself. Or he'll have no choice but to call his good, personal friend Denise Edgerton at the Department of Child Services. To counsel me. Help me make good choices.

The taco casserole turns to a rock in my stomach.

"What kind of living situation doesn't have a service on-call for emergencies? This is basic sanitation, Kayla. I mean, don't you think Jimmy deserves basic sanitation?"

The question hits me right in the gut. Jimmy does deserve a working fridge. And a swing set with a swing and a tutor and a freakin' father. There was a time I'd let it pile up in my head, all the things Jimmy deserves that I can't give him, overwhelming me until I couldn't do anything but lie in bed and cry. But not anymore.

I channel Sue's voice: Jimmy deserves a mom who loves him more than life.

I force my hands apart and out of my lap, resting them on the table.

I'm not a confused and terrified fifteen-year-old with a guilty conscience anymore. I'm a mom.

"Look. Dad. I think it's just a mix-up. The new landlord is probably on vacation, and he probably told me, but in all the chaos of moving...I just need to borrow the fridge for a little while until I can get it straightened out."

He takes a long sip from his coffee and then sits it precisely at three o'clock in front of him.

"I have to be honest, Kayla. This all seems fishy to me. If

you were struggling with the rent, why didn't you talk to me? Did you lose the job at General Goods?"

He's staring at me speculatively.

"No. I'm still working first shift. Tuesday through Saturday."

"Then where's the money going?" He asks like he thinks the answer is meth and not the grocery store.

I snort on the inside. My dad's the CFO of Gracy Industries, the import business the Gracy family started when they sold the mill. He should know how math works.

"Rent. Groceries. Daycare. Gas. Co-pays—"

"I didn't ask for a smart response."

He didn't get one either. Life costs money. It's the second big life lesson I ever learned. The first was the strong prey on the weak, and there is virtually nothing anyone can do about it.

I take another deep breath. "I'm sorry, Dad. I just need to borrow the fridge. Just for a little while."

He takes a long time, *thinking*. He doesn't fool me. Not anymore. He's a negotiator by profession. He already knows what he wants from me. He's waiting so I'm more likely to crack.

"You know, Kayla, Victoria really misses having Jimmy around the house."

I nod. I don't like where this is going.

"She has graciously offered to watch Jimmy overnight on Fridays and Saturdays. You can pick up overtime, and Jimmy can have weekends here. We have the backyard, the playhouse. And he'll get the benefit of having a man around. A boy needs a male role model. Plus you won't need to pay for childcare. Weekend rates have got to be steep."

Oh, they are. Mrs. Jenner charges her normal hourly rate plus half for Saturdays and double for Sundays.

And if things were different...Jimmy deserves loving grandparents and room to run and play. He deserves a bedroom with his name on the wall like he has here, and a long driveway where he can safely ride his bike in circles for hours.

But he also deserves me. I'm not going to lose sight of that again. And we've been down this road before. Best interest of the child. Fitness. Consistency. Primary caregiver. Temporary custody. Supervised visitation.

"I don't feel comfortable with that." I keep my face calm. Non-confrontational. That was one of my mistakes before. Not being able to control my emotions. I mean, what fifteen-year-old can? But you learn quick when you're motivated.

My dad glares down the table at me, his expression all parental disappointment. He's not necessarily disappointed I've turned him down; his face says he's fundamentally disappointed in me, what I am, what little I've managed to make of myself. His next words don't surprise me in the least.

"It shouldn't come as a shock that you'd put your needs above Jimmy's. Again."

I press my sweating palms into the table. The jumble in my head—the old guilt and shame and fear and betrayal and panic—all of it threatens to spill out of my mouth, onto the long table between us, ruining the tentative peace I've built by pretending they didn't steal my baby and send me away like some family disgrace.

I won't let it though. I worked too damn hard for all of this. For Jimmy.

"Dad, I just need the fridge. For a couple weeks."

"How is it that you think you're fit to raise a child, and at the same time, you ask Victoria and I to bail you out time and time again?"

Does he think it's my choice? More than anything, I want to cut them off, take Jimmy away from them like they took him from me. But that's spite. And it's not in Jimmy's best interest. And maybe I am a little afraid that one day I'll fail at this whole being a mother thing, and I don't want to leave Jimmy alone in the world.

I can't keep looking at my dad and keep the calm I've got hanging on by a thread. I let my gaze wander around the dining room, the strategically arranged black and white photos of great grandparents interspersed with professional shots of my dad's wedding to Victoria and Jimmy when he was a baby. I'm in a few group shots of my father's family, taken when I was little, but my mom's nowhere to be seen.

I guess that's not so strange. No one wants a picture of your husband's first wife hanging up in the dining room. But for at least one of the group shots—a reunion at Patonquin State Park—I remember my mom was there. Victoria must have cropped her out of the photo before she framed it.

If I hadn't gotten Jimmy back, would she have cropped me out too?

My throat's tightening. I have to get out of here.

"Can I have the fridge, Dad?"

He sighs. He's about to double down; I know the expression. He's going to tell me that he's concerned, that maybe I need to check in with Dr. Hewitt, make sure I'm well, but before he can, the backdoor slams and Jimmy comes trotting into the dining room, an out-of-breath Victoria on his heels.

"Hey, bud." I make myself smile, as real as I can make it. "How's the workbench?"

He slides a glance at my dad, and then he wriggles up under my arm until he's half on my lap. "It's cool."

"Did you say thank you to Victoria?"

"Thank you, Victoria." He's eyeing me. He knows something's not right. "Is Pop Pop letting us borrow the fridge?"

And I swear. I did not prompt him to ask. But Lord, I could kiss the boy.

Victoria and my dad exchange a look. Yeah, they're not happy. Jimmy just ruined their leverage.

"Sure am, son," my dad says, rising. "Back the Corolla up to the garage."

I do as he says, and then I help him maneuver the fridge into the trunk. It takes two of us to get it in, and I'm a little worried about how I'm going to get it up the metal stairs to the crane's nest, as Jimmy and I dubbed our place by the river.

I'll cross that bridge when I come to it.

When we're all ready to go, my dad walks up to the driver's side and gestures for me to roll the window down.

Whatever he wants, I'm not going to like it. At least Jimmy is already drowsing in his car seat. It's a late night for him. He's going to be a grumpster in the morning.

"Are you going to be able to get that into your new place by yourself?"

Uh, no. An image of Charge flashes in my mind, his muscles bunching as he hauls the fridge up the stairs, sweat beading on his—

Nope.

"N— Yes. I can manage."

He scores me with his hard eyes. Victoria hovers over his shoulder, her face all fake concern, her eyes harder and colder than his.

"Can you, though, Kayla? You agreed. When we allowed you to—when you moved out with Jimmy, you agreed to certain conditions."

My stomach is clenching tighter and tighter, tears

welling up behind my eyes. I'm too afraid to let them out, but my nose is tickling like when a cry is unavoidable. I'm starting to panic because how am I going to get out of Gracy's Corner before I need to pull over and bawl? I can't drive in hysterics; it's not safe. But if I pull over somewhere nearby, some busybody will definitely call my dad or Victoria and let them know their prodigal daughter is having a nervous breakdown on the side of the road.

"Yes, Dad." I keep it short so they can't hear my voice break.

"You agreed to maintain a certain level of agreed upon support, and that certainly includes working refrigeration."

I wonder if any other parent in the world talks to his daughter like a lawyer. Conditions. Agreed upon. Refrigeration.

"Yes, Dad."

"I would be remiss if I didn't remind you that if you fail to meet those conditions, Victoria and I will have no choice but to—" He pauses for a minute and checks the back seat. Jimmy is conked out. "Pursue all avenues available to us in the best interest of our grandchild."

I learned another lesson pretty early on in life. If you're afraid enough, there's no room for anger.

So my white knuckles gripping the steering wheel? The blood pounding through me, whooshing in my ears? That's not fury. That's pure, unadulterated terror.

"Yes, Dad," I whisper as I roll up the window and ease the car into drive.

I make it five miles away from Gracy's Corner before I have to pull over and cry silently into my fist while Jimmy snores softly behind me.

I can't keep doing this. I can't run myself ragged at work and at home, and then rake myself over the coals every other week when I see Dad and Victoria. I can't keep being so afraid all the time. I can't keep living with this dread hanging over me that everything is going to fall apart, and I'm going to lose everything.

But I don't have a choice.

I have a Jimmy.

And Jimmy is everything.

CHARGE

"**Y**ou gonna help our girl or you gonna keep sitting here mopin' with your head up your ass?"

Pops and I are out on the pier, night fishin' by the full moon. Well, Pops' got a line in, and I'm coolin' my feet in the Luckahannock. I was on 'em for hours after the run-in with Harper. In the end, I passed on sweetbutt. Instead, I went back to the site and walked the fence, makin' sure the Rebel Raiders ain't breeched the perimeter elsewhere.

After, I didn't want to go back to the clubhouse. Club pussy climbs on me like I'm a damn swing set, and I need a break, so I headed here. Shirlene'd been around all day, makin' a roast, so I ate well before Pops and I headed out to drop lines.

The river in spring is freezin' fuckin' cold, but it's a good cold. Bracing.

We been out here a few hours, passin' a flask, not catchin' anything, but not bothered. Pops is talkin' like he does, goin' from one subject to another like he's high as shit, but really, he's just an old head who never was much for makin' logical sense.

So at first I don't know what he's talkin' about when he mentions the girl. Then I see he's lookin' back at the neighbor's.

Kayla has come home, and she just half-carried, half-dragged her sleep-walkin' boy upstairs. Now's she's wrestling somethin' out of her trunk.

It's hard to make out in the moonlight. Looks bulky.

"Go give her a hand. I'm tired of lookin' at your miserable ass."

"You ain't raised no Boy Scout, Pops."

"Well, she ain't gonna jump on your dick if you all the way over here, boy."

I ain't lettin' that image in my head. Not with Pops' pumpkin grin leering at me in the dark.

"Not interested in fuckin' someone's mom, Pops."

"I fucked your mom. Wasn't too bad." He's cacklin'.

To be honest, I've seen pictures of her. My mom. She looked like a model, like some eighties rocker-chick Marilyn Monroe. I have no fuckin' clue how Pops got a piece of that. I can only assume there was alcohol involved.

There's a thump and a crack from over by Kayla's Corolla and a soft little cry. Instantly, my cock's hard.

"Sounds like a damsel's in distress." Pops chuckles.

Shit.

Don't I know it. She's the definition of trouble waiting to happen. She's ripe, all alone, not enough sense to leave that shit for morning when it's light out.

That irritation creeps up on me again. Whoever's been careless with her has made her careless with herself.

But I ain't that guy. There's a reason I'm not a club enforcer. I don't get off on serve and protect.

Besides, females come to me.

I don't do this. I don't stalk over to them, makin' sure to clear my throat as I come up so they don't startle and clutch their fuckin' pearls.

Oh, fuck. Now I got the image in my mind of Kayla's open face, flushed and drowsy from fucking, with my cum sprayed over her peachy skin and dripping down her throat onto the top of her bare tits. My kind of pearl necklace.

When I speak, it comes out harsher than I mean it to. "Need help?"

She stands over the mini fridge she's wrangled out from her trunk. Her chest's heavin', and there's a little line of sweat above her lip. I don't know why that's the hottest shit I've ever seen, but it is.

She's got her hair up in a ponytail, and she's wearing an old lady top, the knit kind with a collar and three buttons, all buttoned up.

Of course I check out lower, and damn if she ain't wearin' slacks. With an elastic waistband.

She looks like she's wearing her mother's clothes.

I didn't know MILF was my thing, but I want to work my hand down past that elastic waistband and cup her, let her juices slick my palm.

Fuck.

She ain't thinkin' what I'm thinkin'. She's clearly still cold on me. As well she should be.

She huffs to get a wisp of hair out of her eye and tries to make her face mean. She fails fuckin' miserably. For one, you can read every thought she has. She's a little freaked out, and a lot irritated. And she must have had a rough night. Her cheeks are tear-streaked, and her eyes are puffy.

And it bothers me. Her being out here in the dark, upset,

temptin' fate being alone at night in this part of town. Ain't right.

She sticks her chin up and sniffs. Can't blame her. I wasn't exactly a gentleman earlier.

"No, I've got it."

She looks away and edges the fridge toward the stairs, using that luscious ass to shove it along. Ain't no way she's gettin' it up the stairs alone. It probably weighs sixty, seventy pounds.

"Don't think you do."

She stops, her breath coming quickly, and she glares at me. "I don't need your help."

She thinks a minute. Looks like she's screwin' up her courage. "I don't need help from people like you." She throws my words back at me.

Yeah, guess I was a real asshole earlier. It wasn't like me, and I don't know what good I thought it'd do. But like now, it got me twisted, her trompin' around alone, that kid in tow, as if half the fuckers around ain't tweakin' or lookin' for a mark and the other half ain't happy to shut the blinds and ignore whatever big, bad ugly is creepin' around outside.

"You're lookin' for trouble if you try and push that up the stairs alone."

I go to pick up the fridge, but she leans her palms down hard on the top. "I can do this myself."

Her voice wavers. She's tired, and this close, I can see her eyes are bloodshot. She ain't had an easy day, neither.

"Nope. You cain't."

I say it simple, a statement of fact, but I guess no woman likes hearin' that.

"Get out of my way."

She's pissed now. She's breathin' so hard, her tits are straining at the buttons on her mom shirt.

I've never wanted a button to pop worse.

Her brown eyes flash, and she clenches that jaw, makin' the least-scary, most-scrunched pissed-off face I've ever seen.

I want to laugh, but I ain't that stupid. "Let me help you."

"No. I'm supposed to steer clear of your type."

The thought of her stoppin' to chat with any of my brothers like she did with me this morning makes my blood run cold again. She's so fuckin' ripe. None of them would pass up a chance to try and get his dick wet. Rebel Raiders wouldn't be very particular as to whether she was willin'.

"Yeah. You are." I make my face serious. Usually civilians shut up and brothers back off. Not Kayla.

She's so in her head about whatever made her cry, she don't notice or care.

"So I'm supposed to not speak to strangers, get this, this...*fucking* refrigerator up these stairs, get it all taken care of and not let on that it's, it's—"

She slams to a stop, realizing her mouth got away from her. She drags in a breath.

"Hard," I finish for her. She swallows, and I can tell it's not that she's out of words, but that she's afraid that if she says anything else, whatever shit's eatin' at her is going to spill out.

I respect the fact she's not down with that.

I got to be honest. I can't imagine what's goin' on with her. I ain't never known her kind of hard. But maybe it's two people sharin' one shit day, but I'm kinda feelin' her. Somethin' in me wants to take over, wants her to let me.

I ain't never had that kind of instinct. I know brothers who do. Heavy's one domineering motherfucker, and so's Forty, but I've never been the one.

Except in this moment. Her arms crossed, her sweet face all tight, her eyes narrowed and wary.

"Back up." I make it an order. "Now."

This time, she listens.

She paces me while I lug the fridge to the bottom stair, and then we both stare up. Yeah. They're steep. She looks to me, and my chest swells.

She's askin' if I got this.

Of course I got this.

"Get up two stairs and hold under. I've got the weight; you just need to guide it. Okay?"

"Okay," she murmurs. She's havin' trouble meetin' my eye. Her tiny breakdown musta turned her shy.

She backs up the stairs slowly, and we work together, steppin' at the same time, not talkin'. Once we're at the top, she eases open the screen door, and I carry the fridge the rest of the way, past the bed with the boy passed out on it, to the kitchenette.

I put it by the outlet since there's no real place for it to go. She's got this place packed. It's organized, but there's a lot of shit. Tubs of kid's toys stacked all along one wall, two bikes—a woman's and a kid's—mounted on the wall, a futon and television stand. Besides a small table with two chairs, there's nothin' else in the way of furniture but the bed.

My room at the clubhouse is bigger. And I've got a closet. I can't even see where she keeps her clothes.

I plug the fridge in, and then I walk out with a soft tread.

The kid's half under a quilt, his foot hangin' off the side of the bed. Damn, he's small.

I kind of expect her to shut the door after me, but she follows me out to the landing. She's got her arms crossed, and her face is still shut down.

"Thanks," she says, grudging.

And I don't know what gets into me—I really fuckin' don't—but I lower myself down till I'm sitting at the edge of landing, my bare feet danglin' down. I pat the ledge next to me.

She sighs, makes me wait a long minute, and then she sinks down, leanin' forward so her forehead presses into the iron railing.

We both look out to the river where the moon's reflected all smooth and white except for every so often when a frog or a dragonfly sets off tiny ripples.

Pops is still out at the end of the pier, but he's got his rod wedged in the spokes of his chair, and he's clearly nodded off. I'm gonna have to remember to wheel him back inside before I head out for the night. He ain't that good with the three-point turns even when wide awake and sober.

"That your dad?" She nods towards him.

"Ayup."

"That why your pants are rolled up?"

I look down. I'd forgotten I'd rolled my jeans past my knees to dip my feet in the river. I got nothin' else but a white tee on, and my hair's down. I must look like one happy hippy.

"We was fishin'."

She sighs again, and it's such a sad little sound.

"Jimmy really wants to go fishing. I have to buy him a rod."

"Don't bother. Pops'll lend him one of my old ones. Probably a dozen of 'em out in the shed."

"Really?" She turns to me, searchin' for somethin'. Ulterior motives, I guess.

"Sure. Pops always got worms in the fridge out back."

Her eyebrows go up. "You've got a fridge out back?"

"Rednecks, ain't we?"

She laughs, but I don't like the sound. It's bitter. Tired.

"What?"

She shakes her head. "It's just funny. I have to bend over backwards for a mini-fridge. You've got one out back for worms. Really feels like there's a metaphor there."

"A what?"

"A...nevermind."

"You know a lot of big words, don't you?" I eye her up. Especially dressed like a Stepford wife, she don't look like the women I'm used to. "You a college girl, Peaches?"

She snorts. Huh. Sensitive subject.

"Nope. I dropped out. Got my GED."

"Juvenile delinquent?"

Her lips twitch up, a hint of a smile, and it goes straight to my dick.

Her face ain't nothin' to Harper's, plain most would probably say, but damn, I can't stop watching it. Every feeling flits across clear as day, and it's like I'm a Peeping Tom, seein' shit I shouldn't, but I can't tear my eyes away.

A little lip lift ain't enough; I want to see her laugh.

"I'm not one of those types of people." She sniffs and looks down her nose at me, teasing now. "Not like some."

"You're still young. You got time," I tease back, and I get another one of those lip lifts. Damn, but my girl is tired. I can tell. If she weren't so beat down, she'd have told me to get gone already.

I slip my flask from my pocket, take a swig, and pass it to her.

She eyes it a minute, and then she takes it, sniffs. "What is it?"

"Whiskey."

I watch her debate, and I can tell the moment she says fuck it. She takes a small sip and grimaces. And then she sticks her tongue out, airing it. Her pretty, pink tongue with the pointed tip.

Oh, damn, but I want to suck on that tongue. I want to watch that tongue lick up and down my dick, dip into the tip, lap up the bead of pre-cum.

I groan. Out loud.

"What?" She frowns at me. "I'm not used to hard liquor."

"Take another sip. Goes down smoother the second time."

Not gonna lie. I want to see that tongue again.

She takes another little sip, and this time, she only grimaces. And then the thought occurs to me. "Shit. You even legal?"

"You mean legal drinking age?" Her eyes light up a touch, and she takes another sip.

"Yeah. You twenty-one?"

Oh, she finds this amusing. She tips the flask, playing like she's taking a deep swig but not really, and then she pops her lips. "Yes sir, I am, Mr. Charge. I've been twenty-one for two whole months."

I groan, taking the flask back since she seems disinclined to pass it. She grins at me, teasing, and it's so tentative, so unpracticed. This ain't like Harper or one of the sweetbutts, playing a game they got down cold. Peaches don't know what she's doing; it's so fuckin' clear. I wonder if this girl has ever flirted before.

It's heady shit. More than the whiskey.

I want to urge her on, watch her find her feet.

"I like it when you call me that." I pitch my voice lower. See if she follows.

She replies all breathy, "What...Mister Charge?"

"Umm humm." I lean down, and she tilts her head up until we're inches apart. I've got her eyes glued to mine. I'm going to taste her; I have to fuckin' taste her, but I can't break myself out of this moment. Her breath is coming out in soft pants, her brown eyes are swirlin' with wonder, and that smell of vanilla turns every sharp edge in the world fuzzy.

"Okay, then, Mister Charge."

I watch her lips form the words, and I can't stop myself. Don't even know why I'd ever wanted to.

"You gonna do what I say, Peaches?" I reach for her ponytail and wrap it around my hand. Damn, even her hair is soft and fine.

"Yes, Mister Charge." Her voice is playful, flirting, but her eyes are hungry.

I pull her in, done waitin', and take that pretty mouth. And hot damn, but she is sweet. She draws in a sharp breath, and one of her hands lands on my chest by instinct. She clutches the cotton, and lets out the softest whimper of surprise. I lap at the seam of her lips, try to get her to open up. She don't know what she's doin' though so she keeps them lips closed, but she sways closer, holdin' onto me with tight hands.

My dick is so hard I can feel the zipper diggin' in. My body's yellin' at me to lay her back, take off that ugly shirt, find a place between her legs, and I struggle to think of why I shouldn't. She wants this, and I want it, and I had reasons not to, but I can't begin to remember what they—

The screen door creaks open, and a sleepy voice calls, "Mama?"

She leaps up so quick I can't get my hand out of her hair in time, and she ends up yanking it loose, a little yowl escaping. Shit. That's gotta smart.

"Hey, baby. What's up?"

The kid pokes his head out the door. "Who's out there with you?"

I swear if this don't feel just like the time in high school when my girlfriend's dad busted us in the back of my ride.

"It's Charge," I call out, shiftin' to hide my lap. "Hey, bud."

"Hi," he shuffles out, yawning. "Can I have some water, Mama?"

"Of course, baby." She tousles his hair and turns him back into the apartment. I stand so she can get past me.

"Thanks for your help," she says, breathless, as she shuffles her boy back inside. Her chin's down; she's not meeting my eyes. Every inch of her exposed skin is flushed bright red. The moment's gone.

And it's a good thing.

Right?

I mean what the fuck was I thinking?

I adjust my aching cock in my jeans. That's what I was thinking.

I get Pops and wheel him inside, reminding myself of all the reasons Kayla's a terrible idea. She's a civilian, and she's a kid with a kid. I live at the clubhouse out of boxes, and she lives next door to my Pops.

I shit where I eat with Harper, and now I'm livin' the fallout. I don't need to do that again.

It's just too complicated.

Besides, what am I gonna do with a single mom? My ride don't have no sidecar.

Peaches is ripe, but she ain't the only pussy out there. I need to steer clear, work this shit out with a warm and willing bitch who knows the score.

I'm clearly fucked up from Harper. And whatever else I am, I ain't the asshole who takes advantage of some innocent piece of ass to make himself feel big.

When I ride out, I make sure Pops' meds are set out for

the week, and I put chicken and potatoes in the slow cooker so he'll have leftovers for a few days. I need to sort my shit, and it ain't gonna happen if I'm hidin' out at my Pops' place, creepin' on the girl next door.

She'll be fine.

She's a big girl.

Twenty-one and two whole months.

Fuck.

7

KAYLA

"**N**o sign of the hot biker?" Sue pants.

"Nope." I pop a cotton ball between each toe, holding the phone with my shoulder as I keep an eye on Jimmy. Just like he has been every free minute since we moved in, he's hanging out with Pops. This morning, they're sorting through fishing poles in front of his shed. I'm also keeping an ear open for the washing machine buzzer.

What can I say? I'm a mom. I'm one hell of a multi-tasker.

"How long's it been?" Sue asks on an exhale. She always calls me from the gym. She's a multi-tasker, too. She has a paid internship at one of the biggest tech companies in Philly, her freelance work, at least two boy toys at any given time, and an obsession with cardio.

"Almost two weeks."

"Oooo, he's really scared."

I snort. "Because I'm so intimidating."

"Tell me how it went down again," Sue prods. I can hear her feet pounding the treadmill.

I sigh. I should have never told her about that night with

the fridge. I had no idea she was so invested in me finally kissing a guy. Or doing other stuff.

Sue's not interested in men for more than fun, so we don't do typical *girl talk* very often. Ever since I mentioned Charge, though, she's been all Sex and the City.

"So he carries his heavy package up your stairs, and then," she prompts.

"It was my heavy package. And then we sat on the landing and shared a drink."

"Did you gaze deeply into each other's eyes?"

Did we?

We kind of did.

"Yeah. It was awkward."

"Why awkward?"

It's hard to explain. I guess mostly because I'm not used to that kind of attention. Definitely not from such a beautiful man. Such a grown, badass man. Who throws mixed signals like he's pitching wrong-handed, getting all up in my space one minute and disappearing the next.

It's the exact kind of bossy male bullshit Sue won't tolerate. She'd be pissed at me for even thinking about him if she knew.

I say, "I'm not exactly used to it."

"To what? Flirting?"

"Yeah. That and...everything else. It's a non-issue though."

"He hate kids?"

Sue says that like she'd say, "He kick puppies?" which is totally ironic. Sue hates kids. She has no interest in ever having one, calls them rug rats and ankle biters, but when I got pregnant, she developed one huge Jimmy-sized exception. Half of Jimmy's toys are paid for out of the money Sue makes on her freelance coding work.

"I don't know if he hates them, but he bails whenever he sees mine."

"See? He's scared."

"Of Jimmy?"

"Of responsibility."

I roll my eyes while I start brushing pink polish on my toes. "Isn't that a little tired? The man-child who's scared of responsibility?"

"I don't know. Being a little scared seems smart to me. A kid's a big deal."

Don't I know it. A few guys have asked me out over the years, and I'm always up front that I have a kid. I'm always nervous about telling, though. It can be bad. One guy asked me whether I'd *kept it tight*.

I don't really know what a good thing would look like— let alone how to get a good thing going—so I focus on work and Jimmy. Most days I don't have any time to wonder what it would be like. To be with a man.

There's a little longing in me, though. I'm human.

"Sue, do you think I'll ever do it with a guy?" I can be wistful with Sue. Nothing's off limits between us.

I hear a beep. She's paused the treadmill. "Oh, of course, Kayla-cakes. You're going to do it with a guy and go out on dates and bring a guy home to meet the Jimmy and tell a guy you love him and hear him say it back."

"How do you know?" My voice is a whisper. I usually don't let myself think about the future. My dreams. But ever since she moved to Gracy's Corner in the fifth grade, Sue has had a way of making me feel like my life could be different. Better. She's the one who helped me get Jimmy back. I'm damn lucky a girl as smart as her decided I was her best friend.

"Because there's nothing wrong with you, Kayla. And in

ten years, everyone's going to have kids. You're not going to be the weird one out. But you're still gonna have a bangin' ass."

"Ten years?" She's got a point, but it's still depressing.

"Or tomorrow. Or next week. I'm not a fortune teller, Kayla."

"No, you're a systems engineer."

"That's right, baby." She's quiet a moment. "It's going to be okay, Kayla. I know it."

"Okay, Sue. But what if—"

I don't have to say it. Sue and I have known each other half our lives. I know her worst fears—wolf spiders and an apocalyptic event that destroys the electrical grid—and she knows mine.

"There's nothing wrong with you, Kayla-cakes."

"Yeah?"

"Yeah."

"I'm not ruined?" The question is hardly even a whisper.

"Nope. Not at all."

Another beep—this time on my end—interrupts our conversation. Over by the shed, Pops is showing Jimmy how to cast a line. He seems to be having as much fun as my boy. Shirlene is on the front porch, shucking corn. She waves. I check my phone, and it's General Goods.

This can't be good. It's Sunday. My day off.

"Sue? Work's on the other line."

"Okay. Call me when the hot biker comes sniffing back around."

"I don't think he will."

"Oh, I think he will, *Peaches*."

The phone beeps again.

"Gotta go. Love you."

I press the button a second too quickly, and end up

telling Greg, my team manager, that I love him. He thinks this is hilarious.

"You're gonna love me even more in a minute. I got you another shift. Time-and-a-half."

Greg's the type who makes a big deal about being *cool*, but he makes you clock out and then return a cart of go-backs before you can leave.

Plus he calls us *his girls* even though there's at least two guys on our team.

He can call me whatever he wants for time-and-a-half though.

"When?"

"Right now. The ten to six. The Mother's Day orders have started rolling in and corporate didn't staff up enough."

Oh, that sucks. I'd already mentally banked that time-and-a-half. The Corolla needs a tune-up. Maybe some new used tires.

"I can't do it, Greg. I have my son."

"Call a sitter. We need you."

I wish. Sitters are like unicorns in my world.

"I can't Greg. Maybe next time?"

"Not gonna be a next time. I can't rely on you in a pinch, I can't keep scheduling you on the plum shifts. It's scratch my back; I'll scratch yours. You know that."

I do know that. Usually scratching Greg's back means doing double go-backs or getting him a Coke from the staff room. But I've seen the way he schedules people on his shit list. Different days each week, rotating shifts, cutting hours. I can't lose my schedule.

My chest tightens. I can't call Victoria. It's Sunday. Victoria and Dad have church and brunch at the club. I can't ask Sue. She'd do it, but she's at least two hours out. If I'm lucky enough that Mrs. Jenner would take Jimmy on a

Sunday, she charges double for drop-ins, and that would be the grocery money.

"Greg, I'm between a rock and a hard place here. I'd come in if I could—believe me, I need the money—but I don't have anyone to watch Jimmy."

"Reliable transportation and child care are requirements of the job, Kayla. You knew that when you applied."

"I have—" No. Arguing is not going to help. Maybe flattery? "Greg, I know you understand how it is. I can't make it this time, but next time—"

"Not going to be a next time, Kayla. I don't need girls on my team who aren't reliable. I do need someone on second shift."

I can't do second shift. I'd never see Jimmy. Mrs. Jenner can't watch him until midnight.

Oh, God, I'm starting to hyperventilate. I need to pull it together. Think. Solve the problem.

A peal of Jimmy's laughter pulls me out of my spiral. His laugh?

He never laughs.

Pops is casting a line across his yard, and one of the feral cats that roam the cul-de-sac is chasing the red bobber.

I take a deep breath, force myself to go over the facts. I can't lose my schedule. The grocery money can be diverted this once. I have spaghetti and a half jar of peanut butter, and I can take Jimmy to visit Victoria a couple times this week. Get dinner there.

"I'm coming in, Greg."

"That's my girl. See you in an hour."

"Okay, Greg."

"And Kayla?"

"Yes?"

"Any longer than an hour, and I'm gonna have to start dialing my other girls."

"I'll be there, Greg." I pluck the cotton balls quickly out of my toes and screw the top on the nail polish. I guess I'm going to have three pink toenails.

I call Mrs. Jenner, and thank the Lord, she takes pity on me. Then I holler at Jimmy that we have to go. He isn't too pleased at that, but when he starts to complain, Pops says something and Jimmy falls silent.

I'm inside tugging on my work khakis, grabbing my shoes and keys when I hear a bike pull up.

My stomach does a weird drop, like when you speed over a bump on a back-country road.

He's ba-ack.

When I hurry down the stairs, Charge has parked his bike, and he's striding up to Pops and Jimmy. Damn, that walk. So cocky. Like music should be playing along.

Even though it's a weekend, he looks like he's coming from work. His boots are mud-crusted and there's red dust caking his jeans. He's wearing the vest with the patches, a ratty black T-shirt under it, and his hair is up in the man bun again. When he walks, his beat-up jeans mold to his butt and thighs, and I don't want to stare, but I can't not.

He squats next to Jimmy and picks up a rod, spins the handle of the reel. They talk low, heads together. I can't hear until I'm up next to them.

"—always sticks, this one." Charge spins the handle again.

Jimmy's listening so intently. His chin is tilted up, his big eyes stuck on Charge, while his fingers reach for another rod.

I don't want to drag him away, but...I sigh. Louder than I intended.

"Jimmy, honey, Mama got called into work. I need you to hop in the car."

"But—"

Charge cuts him off with a pat on the back. "I'll catch up with you later, little man. Pops and I will check out this reel while you're gone. See if some oil will help."

Charge and Jimmy exchange a look, and then Jimmy nods. It's like they understand each other without words, and I'm baffled. Jimmy stonewalls everyone. And it's not like he knows Charge that well.

Charge stands, his eyes dragging down my front. I feel myself turn red, and I try desperately to ignore the butterflies that start beating like crazy in my stomach. He's a neighbor. He's clearly not that interested. This isn't a big deal.

I give him what I mean to be a chill, pleasant smile. I'm pretty sure it comes off like I'm baring my teeth for the dentist.

I'm so not any good at this.

"In the car, Jimmy," I say, managing a real smile for Pops and a wave.

It takes little time for him to belt himself in, and I can exhale a little. I have forty-five minutes to drop Jimmy off and get to General Goods. I'm going to make it. I turn the key.

And nothing happens.

No sound, no shuddering complaint. The engine doesn't turn over at all.

I try again.

Nothing.

Oh shit.

"Mama?"

I break into sweat, all over my body. What do I do? What

do I do? My gaze darts around, as if help is somewhere if I can only find it. A magic key that'll start my worst-possible-timing broke down car.

I barely register Charge returning the rods to the shed.

"Mama, what's wrong?"

"The car won't start." It comes out a whisper.

My mind is racing—Dad's at church, I can't afford a tow, let alone repairs, there's no money, call Greg and tell him I'm stuck, reliable transportation is a requirement for employment, I'm going to lose my schedule. If I tell Dad, he'll say I should've gotten the oil changed but I do get the oil changed, I just have to space it out more than you're supposed to because of math...my body moves of its own accord.

I pop the hood, get out, and stare down at the engine. I have no idea what I'm looking at. Vaguely, I hear Jimmy get out and join me.

"What's wrong with it, Mama?"

I have no idea.

I can't afford this.

I don't have time for this.

"What's wrong with it, Charge?" Jimmy asks.

I startle. I hadn't heard Charge and Pops come up, but Charge is beside me now, and Pops has rolled up next to Jimmy. All four of us are staring under the hood.

"She turn over at all?" Charge leans over the engine.

I shake my head.

I'm numb, trying to think of what to do next, when Charge carefully takes off his vest with the patches and hands it to Pops. Then he pulls his holey T-black shirt off. He unscrews the dip stick, wipes it on the hem, and then checks the oil.

His bare chest, damp with a sheen from his long day, is

inches away from me. I can see the tan line on his biceps where his T-shirt ends. The man is built. His sides, his shoulders, every plane of his body ends in a hard ridge. He's strong. Not gym rat strong, but like he uses his body. Like he spends his days lifting and climbing and hauling. Working.

I've got to think of a plan, and his bare chest is messing with my ability to reason.

I'm going to lose my job because I'm ogling a biker's obliques.

"Well, you got oil." Charge leans further, looking closer. "Battery cables don't look corroded."

"Do you know what's wrong with it?" There's hope in my voice. Something's gotta break my way at some point.

Charge shakes his head. "I'd need to get it in the shop."

The shop?

I can't think about taking it to a shop. I have to get to work or Greg will call Sheila, I'll lose my shift, I'll have to quit General Goods, after moving I have nothing saved so I'll miss my first rent payment, Victoria will take Jimmy...

"Peaches?"

I suck in a breath. I realize I'm just standing there, my hands gripping the hood for dear life, knuckles white, and everyone's looking at me. Charge is staring at me, intent, his face...worried?

He lays a calloused hand on mine, pries my fingers loose. Gently moves my hand to my side.

I force myself to relax the other.

"What's going on, Peaches?"

We're standing there together in a line, and they're all waiting for me. Jimmy expectant, Pops patient, Charge with his impossibly handsome face dark with concern. It strikes me as so crazy then. The boy and the two men, looking to me. As if I'm in charge.

I can't be in charge. I don't know what I'm doing.

My eyes search out Charge's. "I have to get to work."

"Can't you call out?"

I shake my head. "I'll lose my shift."

Charge looks to Pops. "Truck's gassed up," Pops says.

And then everything moves fast. Charge heads into the house and comes out in another black T-shirt. Then he gets me to explain how to take Jimmy's car seat out. He carries it like it weighs nothing to the truck parked behind Pops' house. It's a big one—real nice—the kind with a back-row seat.

Pops reminds me to shut the hood, and I follow Charge, holding Jimmy's hand—for once, he lets me—and clutching my purse.

A part of me wants to say no, I don't need the help, I'll call a ride. But I do need help. And I can't call a ride. I don't have the money. Not if I'm paying Mrs. Jenner.

So I just sort of numbly follow along as Charge boosts Jimmy into the back seat and then gives me a leg up into the front. I clutch my purse tight in my lap, and I jump when Charge reaches an arm across me.

"Seatbelt," he says, pulling it forward from where it was tucked behind the seat.

His hard arm presses against my chest, and shivers skitter across my skin like ripples.

I suck in a breath and try to hide it by grabbing the belt and jamming it home.

Charge gives me a side eye. He noticed. He starts to grin, but then he's distracted by Jimmy in the rearview.

"Ready, bud?"

Jimmy nods.

"Where to, Peaches?"

I give him directions to Mrs. Jenner, and then I fall quiet.

I don't know what to say. I'm embarrassed that I need help—again—and my body is being weird. I feel small in the big truck, next to Charge. I can smell him—he's kind of earthy from work and sweat—and my stomach is fluttering, and I don't know what to do with my legs. Cross them? Lean toward the door?

I'm startled when Charge speaks.

"Roosevelt," he says.

"Ayup," a young man's voice rings out in the cab. Oh. Charge made a call on his Bluetooth.

"Swing by Pops with the tow truck. There's a tan Corolla there. Take it to the garage. Ask Big George to check it out. When he figures out what's wrong with it, gimme a call."

"Ayup." The calls ends as abruptly as it started.

I turn my head to look at Charge. He's staring at the road, his perfect face unperturbed. Calm.

I can't let him have my car towed. I can't afford it. None of it.

My cheeks heat, this time with embarrassment. I have to speak up.

"Charge." I take in a breath. "I can't afford a tow."

He glances at me quick and returns his eyes to the road. "No cost."

I don't know what to say to that.

Of course there's a cost.

I squirm in my seat. Check Jimmy in the rear view. He's contentedly fiddling with two plastic soldiers he must have squirreled away in his pocket.

"I can't let you do that," I say. I keep my voice low, even.

Charge doesn't even look at me. "I don't know about that, Peaches. You said you'd do what I say. Remember?"

Heat blossoms in my cheeks.

Oh. He's actually mentioning the other night. I thought

we were going to pretend it never happened. That's what I've heard most boys do.

I take in Charge's beard. His big, work-busted hands. He's not a boy.

"You can't just take a person's car without their permission."

"Just did. Gonna fix it, too. Though really it needs to be taken out back and shot."

He's not wrong. But it's all I have. I feel panic rising in my throat. What is he going to want for helping?

Nothing's free.

Sadness rises up amid all the worry. I guess he's going to be like all the men my dad and Victoria and Sue and the vast amount of my limited experiences have warned me about. Taking advantage. And it's so damn disappointing.

"What do you want for the work? I don't have any money." I almost don't want to ask because I don't want to hear what he says. I don't want him to turn out to be a real asshole.

He's quiet a long minute, and then he says, "Can you check up on Pops? Maybe when you get home from work? Shirlene gets up there a lot, but there's days she cain't make it."

I let out a breath I didn't know I was holding.

"Yeah. I can do that."

"Just, you know, make sure he's still breathin' and shit."

I nod. A big feeling wells up in my chest, smoothing out all the bad and making me feel a touch stronger, more awake. I don't know what it is, but my eyes burn, tears threatening.

I cannot cry in front of this man. I already feel too young and too hot of a mess. I try to breathe deep, and I end up sniffling.

"You cryin', girl?"

Charge presses a rough thumb on the edge of my eye. A quick touch, there then gone.

"Ain't no call for that." He frowns. Drums his fingers on the steering wheel.

I can't say anything, because if I open my mouth, I'm going to sob like a baby. I check Jimmy in the rearview again. He's still playing, not paying any attention to the front seat. I don't want him to worry. I try so hard to stuff it down, but it's like I'm shaking it up.

Charge lets out a sharp sigh. "Big George'll get it runnin' again. Even if it is a piece of shit."

"Okay."

He's quiet a minute. "You gonna stop crying now?"

"Okay." I don't though. Not until we get close to Mrs. Jenner's. I have to wipe my eyes with my forearm. I walk Jimmy in, and he gives me a big hug and no grief like he does sometimes when I have to go in on a day off, and that almost makes me lose it again.

We're silent on the ride the rest of the way to General Goods. Charge pulls right up front, and he leans over me to push open my door. Before I can hop out, he stills me with a heavy hand on my knee.

"Pick you up here when?"

I hadn't thought that far ahead. I usually think ten steps ahead. I never wallow when I have to figure shit out. Damn, but I'm off my game. My brains flips through possibilities until I realize I'm out of choices. I'm stuck. I've got to trust the bearded biker.

"Six."

"Six," he repeats. "I'll text if I'm gonna be a few minutes late."

"My cell doesn't work inside. There's no reception."

"Then I won't be late." He smiles, all bright and white, and I jump from the cab, my cheeks still hot and my stomach flipping and a pulse starting between my legs, turning my legs to jelly.

As I walk into the warehouse, I know he's watching me. He doesn't pull off until the door closes behind me.

My step is light as I go to clock in. Everything's wrong, just like always. But for some reason, the smallest part of me feels lighter. Like I don't need to worry quite so much. I feel...

Right.

8

CHARGE

It ain't right.

After dropping Kayla off and watching that sweet ass swish into that ugly fuckin' box, I decide to drive down to the garage. Check on the Corolla.

I guess I could head down the clubhouse, have a few beers. It's what I'd usually do on a Sunday with no ride planned. But that not-right feelin' is fuckin' with my day off.

No part of me wanted to let her out of my truck, her eyes still red. Hell, I couldn't hardly take my hand from her knee.

All I wanted to do was lift her into my lap, peel off those ass-ugly khakis, and stroke her until all that weight lifted off those small shoulders. Yeah, my cock got hard thinkin' about it, but it wasn't like that.

My truck is always my second-choice ride, but today... her boy in the back and her beside me...well, the truck's got its good points.

Ain't right some asshole left those two alone in the world. And when she dropped the kid off...fuck. He stared after her like he was watching the sun get up and leave.

I kind of understand the feeling. I just let all that sweet

walk off sad and scared, and I can't do anything about it. I mean, what am I gonna do? Take Peaches out on a date? Kids don't even date these days. They Netflix and chill. And how the fuck does that work with a kid?

And ain't no takin' her back to my place. Where would that be? My room at the clubhouse? The storage unit I rent over in Ferndale? My old bedroom at Pops'? Fuck. I got no business even thinkin' down this road.

Which is why I'm bent over the most rusted-out, road-unworthy, busted-up engine I've ever fuckin' seen inside Steel Bones Autowerks. Scrap's at my shoulder, tinkerin' with a valve. He picked up some automotive training when he was upstate, and now he's out, he's spendin' most his time here with Big George.

Hidin' from a piece of pussy that frequents the club-house, some might say. If they was the type to get in other motherfuckers' business. Which I am not.

Usually.

"Why ain't we towin' this piece of shit up the junkyard?" Scrap spits.

"Ain't mine."

Scrap eyes me. "You actin' like it is."

I ain't got nothin' to say to that. "Gonna have to replace the whole engine." I knew it before we opened the hood.

"Like puttin' fake tits on my grandma."

"Missus Raylene? She fine as shit as is, brother." I snort as Scrap punches my arm. He don't play around much since he got out, on edge all the time, so it's nice to see him relax when I bust his balls. Makes some of the wrongness in the day fade.

"You payin' for this?"

I nod.

"Pissin' away good money."

Yeah. It is. I nod and walk over to the office to order the parts. It ain't like I don't have the scratch. Back when we got together, Harper was the one with the cash, but the past few years, the dividends on the legit operations have put us about equal. Now that I don't have half a mortgage to pay, I'm damn near flush.

Instead of ordering vintage fuckin' Corolla parts online, I should be heading down to Hanover. Lookin' at a new ride.

Kayla needs a mom vehicle. Like a Highlander but American made. Maybe an Explorer. Something with a video screen so the little man can watch cartoons and shit. They never had that when I was comin' up. We just had the view up Shirlene and Deb's shirts when the wind got 'em as they rode bitch.

I shake my head. What the fuck am I thinking? Kayla got stiff as hell when I had her car towed. Probably thought I was gonna ask for payment in pussy.

I know quite a few men who wouldn't have hesitated to take payment in kind.

But that ain't what this is.

This is—

I have no fuckin' clue. But all day, I keep checkin' the clock. Six o'clock is takin' its good sweet time rollin' around.

I head out so early, I have time to stop for sodas on the way. I put Jimmy's in the back in the cup holder next to his car seat. It's weird as fuck seein' that seat there. I tug the straps to check the fit. It's snug.

I'm sittin' in my truck out front of General Goods for a good half hour before the workers start coming through the turnstile gate, one at a time, opening their purses for the loss control guy. The sense of wrongness creeps up my neck again. I don't want some smarmy fuck checkin' Kayla up and down, puttin' a stick in her purse after she comes through a gate like she's livestock.

Without thinking, I get out of the truck and stand next to the passenger door, leanin' with my arms crossed. I will that rent-a-cop to look up and see me eye-fuckin' him, but he's too busy being a general dick to the ladies as they go past him.

And then Kayla comes through, and I don't have eyes for anyone else. She's untucked that ugly red collared shirt, and she has her purse clutched to her belly. Her hair's springin' loose from her ponytail, fine and shining, and I can tell she's tired. Her steps are slow, shuffling.

I do it without thinking. As soon as she comes close, I pull her into my arms, rubbin' up and down her back, whisperin' whatever dumb shit comes into my head into her ear. About how she looks tired, how was her day, how I gotta get her off her feet.

She's so fuckin' surprised, she lets me cup the back of her neck, take her hand, and lift her up into the truck.

I want to take her home, lay her out on a bed, explore every fuckin' idea I've been toyin' with all day long about what I want to do with her ripe, sweet body.

But I also want to get her to her boy. Take in the smile that I know's gonna brighten her face when she sees him. I want to give her what she needs, and I'm so fuckin' out of my depth, I can only turn on the radio and twist open a bottle of Coke, pushin' it into her hand.

"It's still cold," I say.

She sighs, a happy little sigh, and sinks back into her seat. I feel more like a man than I've ever felt before.

And I'm scared shitless.

9

KAYLA

I can't believe Charge gave my kid a twenty-ounce Coke. Luckily, I saw it before Jimmy did and acted like it was mine. If that kid had gotten ahold of it, he'd be up until three in the morning, bouncing on the bed, going *boom* and *whoosh* against some invisible enemy soldiers.

My tummy does a little flip thinking about the sodas, though. And how Charge folded me into him after work—how I let him—and murmured in my ear. I can't hardly remember what he said, but I can still feel his soft lips glancing over my earlobe.

I shiver, and Charge gives me a look. Then he turns up the heat.

It's quiet in the truck cab and getting dark. We're on a long stretch of back country road, hills making black outlines against the almost purple sky.

"Did you fish today?" Jimmy asks Charge out of nowhere.

Charge shoots him a look in the rearview. I can't read it. Charge isn't overly friendly like a lot of guys are with other people's kids. But he's not cold. Or awkward.

"Nope. Went into the garage."

"Pops' garage?"

"The MC's garage. That's where we towed your ma's car.

"Did you fix it?" Jimmy's real curious now.

"Had to order parts."

"Are you gonna fix it?"

"Ayup. Once the parts come in."

"Can I watch?" Jimmy looks at me when he asks. I stiffen, shake my head no a little, but Jimmy doesn't notice. Or he pretends not to notice.

Lord. I don't want to be any more obligated to Charge than I am. But do I want to push him away? I mean, if I'm not cool with Charge being in our lives—in this way or whatever way—I need to call it. Put on my big girl britches and call my dad to bail me out.

Ugh.

All I ever wanted was to be an independent woman— like at the beginning of the Kelly Clarkson song. But here I am. Just ugh.

Stuck in my head, I almost miss Charge's reply. "Ayup. You can help."

And Jimmy's face breaks into the widest, happiest grin, and I can't help but smile back like I made this happen. And now I'm afraid Charge'll let him down. Or I'll mess this up. Or I'm making bad choices.

"Can I watch TV when we get home?" Jimmy asks. He must figure he's on a run. He's right. After that smile, I have no will to tell that boy no.

"One show. Thirty minutes. Then it's bedtime."

"Is tomorrow a school day?"

"Yup." I try to sound upbeat, but I'm not a little pissed that I lost my weekend with Jimmy. I have tomorrow off, but he's in school. I should use the time to drive around and look for a—nope. The Corolla. I'm not going anywhere to look for a new job. At least I can walk to the Rutter's for milk.

Charge looks down at me. Even though his face is shadowed, I see his lips turn down. Somehow he can read me real easy.

"Can you drive stick?" he asks.

"Yeah. Why do you ask?"

He nods. There's respect there.

"My granddad taught me before he passed. He had an old Chevy truck. The kind with wood side beams."

Charge's gorgeous smile flashes white in the dark. "You a Chevy girl, then?"

"I'm not really particular. But I've always liked a manual."

"Just like the feel of a stick in your hand?"

Did he just—? Did he mean—?

I glance over, and he winks.

Oh, Lord. Yes, he did.

I kind of shrug and find something real interesting to look at out the window. I don't know what to say when he flirts. My mouth goes dry, and my tongue gets stupid.

"I'm gonna leave you the keys to this truck. Registration is in the glove box."

"You are?"

"Ayup."

"I—I don't understand."

"In case you need to get Jimmy or somethin'."

"I— I couldn't—"

"Corolla won't be ready for a week or two. You need a ride in the meantime."

This is too much. No one—not anyone in my life *ever*—

has helped me out like this. Well, except for Sue. But Charge is not at all like Sue.

He seems to sense my reluctance. "If Pops needs something when you check on him, you need a way to get it. Yeah?"

I relax back into the seat. I hadn't realized how rigid I'd gone. "Yeah."

"Plus, can you pick up his prescriptions this week? At Walnut Drug? Downtown."

"Of course." I forgot. This is business. Or friends doing each other favors. My nerves ease up as we pull up to a stop light.

"Kayla?"

I glance up, catch his eyes, and I'm stuck. They sparkle in the dark, and his lips are curled up in the corners, soft and so close. My breath stops, and my thighs clench together.

I nod.

"Don't wreck my truck."

"Okay, Mister Charge." I mean it playfully, but my voice catches halfway through. It becomes something else.

"Whatever I say, right?" His voice dips down, low and gravelly.

"Right." I exhale. He reaches out and gently tweaks my chin with his calloused fingers and something in my belly unfurls.

He drops his hand to the seat, inches from my thigh, and that's where he leaves it for the last twenty minutes of the drive home. It drives me crazy. So close, but he doesn't move it. Doesn't reach over. Doesn't grab my hand or squeeze my thigh. And I'm too shy to inch my hand over to touch his.

And I want to so bad.

Because I'm a total idiot. A guy's nice to me, and I want to jump his bones.

Or hold his hand.

When we pull into the parking area between my place and Pops', Charge takes the keys out of the ignition and starts wrangling one off the key chain. Jimmy leaps right out of the truck.

"Bye, Charge. Keys, Mama?" He sticks his open hand in my face.

"You got it by yourself, kiddo?"

He nods, and I give him the house keys, watching him bound up the stairs and let himself in. A few seconds later, the light of the television flickers in the window.

"Kid has places to be." Charge's voice is low, amused.

I smile and shake my head. "By the time I get up there, he'll have a bowl of snack crackers in the bed and crumbs all in the covers."

"You not gonna kick him out, are you?"

"Not for eating crackers." I smile. It's getting a little easier. This flirting thing.

"He gonna be occupied awhile?"

I think about how many times I have to say his name before he looks at me if Robo Rangers is on.

"Yeah."

"Kayla." Charge's voice is rough. Needy. He unbuckles me in one move, dropping the truck key in my purse.

"Yeah?" My voice is so breathy. I'm watching him, and I know he's going to touch me—he's pushing his seat back— and I don't know what to do. Where to put my hands. What to say.

But I know I want this. Whatever it's going to be.

"Come here," he growls and lifts me, drawing me onto his lap, facing him. My knees are propped on the seat on either side of his ribs, kind of tucked under his armpits. I gasp. I can feel him. Hard. Between my legs. The seam of my khakis dulls the sensation, but it's there. Big. Demanding.

I freeze.

He holds my face still between his hands.

"Just a kiss, okay?" He waits for my answer, stroking my cheeks with his calloused thumbs.

"Okay," I whisper.

And then he ghosts his lips across mine. I moan. I can't help it. My cheeks heat instantly, and I screw my eyes shut. I can't look at him.

He must know I don't know what I'm doing.

He chuckles. "Fuck, I wish the moon was out. I want to see your face. Watch your eyes get all dopey for me."

He does?

He takes my bottom lip and tugs, then eases his tongue into my mouth, teasing, gentle. I part my lips, let him in.

"That's right, Peaches." He moves a hand to cradle the back of my head, and like the other night, I can tell he's done this before. A lot. He's tender, and then he's insistent, exploring my mouth, nipping my upper lip, and I imagine this must look like a movie kiss, but it's dark, so I can only feel.

My body's going all weird on me. My stomach's swooping, and there's a pulse between my legs where his hardness is notched. I wiggle, testing; I can't help it. It feels so good. Not exactly scratching an itch, but close. I rock, slow, and Charge wraps his arms around me, moving his hands to the small of my back, keeping them light. No pressure.

Charge laughs low in his throat. "That's it, baby. Do what feels good."

Do what feels good? Okay. I grind down harder, loving

the groan that escapes Charge's lips. I did that. His breath goes ragged, and I want...I want more.

But Jimmy's upstairs. Waiting for me. And how long have I been lost in this kiss? An episode of his favorite show is eighteen minutes. I know this because that's how long I give myself to shower in the morning.

It's been—

Oh. I moan again. Charge's hands have moved, cupping my ass and pressing me more firmly against him, making that longing grow. My hips grind down on their own, seeking more of the hardness.

"Like that," Charge urges. His breath speeds up, and I peek up to see him looking down where our bodies are connected. He rests his forehead on mine.

And I want to keep going, block out everything, but I can't. I can't.

Jimmy's waiting for me.

I drag in a deep breath and push my palm against Charge's chest.

"I gotta go in."

His hands tighten on my hips for just a second, and then he lets go. Tucks a stray hair behind my ear.

"Yeah," he rasps. "Okay."

He sets me back down in my seat, and while I'm scrounging on the floor for my purse, he comes over and opens my door. He helps me down, and then he walks me up the stairs.

I don't know what to say. Thank you?

It feels weird to thank the guy I've been riding like a cowgirl.

There's light on the landing, and I want to study his face. See if his mind is blown like mine. Probably not. He's probably made out with a hundred girls. In that truck. That same seat. My stomach sinks.

Oh, damn, I'm that girl. The one who fools around with boys in cars.

The girl my father thinks I am.

"Goodnight," I rush and through the door, flipping the deadbolt after me. I don't dare look up, see if it's true, if there's a leer on Charge's too pretty face. Gloating.

I'm shaking, and I feel like I'm going to throw up. For a long moment, I stand, bent over, propping myself up on the kitchen counter. Inhale. Exhale.

Think about what Sue would say. Ignore the voices in my head. Especially the ones with nothing nice to say. Focus on putting one foot in front of another.

I pull myself together and stare around the shadowy room.

Jimmy has fallen asleep with the television on and his hand stuck in a pack of fruit snacks. I've got to brush that kid's teeth and get him in some pajamas.

I have things to do.

Really, it doesn't really matter if the world thinks I'm a slut or a fool or a piece of trash. At the end of the day— every day including this one—I am a mom. Fact, not opinion.

I've gotta keep my eye on the prize.

No making out with boys.

And no freaking out.

10

CHARGE

Kayla's freaked out. Which is fair. cause I'm freaked the fuck out too.

I knock on her door the next morning, and she acts like she isn't home. Her car's at my garage and my truck was still parked out front. She ain't gone nowhere.

At least she takes the truck the rest of the week. And she checks on Pops mornings and after work. He calls me each time she visits and tells me what she's wearin' and whether she looks good. So far, she's been hot, damn hot, and pretty hot for a lady wearin' elastic slacks.

I've been ridin' around all week with a boner you could pound nails with and the craziest fuckin' ideas. Like askin' Shirlene to babysit the kid so I can take Kayla to one of those hotels with the tubs shaped like champagne glasses. Or just sayin' fuck it, sign over the house in Gracy's Corner to Harper, and buy a place in town with the kind of neighbors a kid can play with.

Pop's been keepin' Jimmy busy fishin', but it's only a matter of time before he falls in with those delinquent punks who run wild round here, poppin' wheelies on their dirt bikes all hours.

The irony doesn't escape me. Nickel, Heavy, and me could pop some badass wheelies back in the day. And I don't think Jimmy's weak. Besides that Cal Porter business, Pops told me that he seen the kid buck at that little red-headed shit who lives up the way. Kid took the fishin' pole Pops had given him. Wouldn't hand it back. Jimmy stepped up and pushed back hard. I wonder if Kayla knows her little boy's a scrapper.

I guess we was lucky bein' raised in the club. You did something you shouldn't, your pop heard about it at the clubhouse. We had a long rope—hella longer than the kids you hear about today—but we had men killin' themselves to put food on the table and more than happy to take a chunk out of our asses when we acted stupid.

Jimmy is a smart kid, but rule of nature—all boys get up to some dumb fuckin' shit. And Kayla can't be around all the time.

So, yeah, along with the boner, I've had worry ridin' me. And I ain't used to it, and I don't fuckin' like it.

By Friday, it's been a long week. Dan, the asshole from Garvis, Inc., gave us the runaround with upping the guards so I've spent the past three nights on the fence at the Patonquin site. It's only because Nickel relieved me with his crew that I'm now kicked back on Pops' porch with a beer in my hand.

If I'm jiggling my knees, it's cause of the Rebel Raiders. It's been too quiet. They don't wave a red flag and then go back to boozin' and chasin' tail. They're either fuckin' with Patonquin cause they're makin' moves elsewhere, or this ain't what it seems. Or, hell, maybe it was kids lookin' for a place to party. In which case I'm doin' Rebel Raiders' work for 'em, psyching myself out over a little harmless tresspassin'.

If I'm strung tight, it's that bullshit. Not cause I'm waiting on a pretty little thing to drive up in my truck and make my week all better. A peach of a girl whose shivers and sighs been playin' in my head all night, every night.

I made her feel good, and she's so untouched, she didn't know what the fuck to make of it. My dick feels twice as big every time I remember that.

Anyway, it ain't her got me wound up, so I don't know why everything unwinds when she drives up.

Shit, she's so short, her chin barely clears the steering wheel.

I hop up quick to help her down. She's bashful, eyes down, cheeks pink, and her hand trembles a little.

My blood heats and my cock throbs.

She's so shy. So nervous.

I want to gentle her like a wild thing, tame her to my hand.

Her boy hops down, bumps knuckles with me, and tears off for the garage. Pops says he's made himself comfortable, banging doors in and out, lettin' in the flies, like we use to do. I'm happy his mama lets him. Something inside me settles when I know they're both with Pops.

"Hi," Kayla mumbles at me, chin down.

That won't do.

I tilt it up. "Hi back." I swipe my thumb over her lower lip and it quivers. She inhales sharp and presses those lips together. Tryin' to play cool.

I don't want her cool. I want her burnin' hot like she was the other night before she let her brain get in the way. Tuckin' her sweet pussy into my cock, partin' those soft lips, cryin' quiet little cries into my mouth, her eyes filled with marvel like I'm pullin' rabbits out of fuckin' hats.

How do I get back there with her closed up tighter than a drum?

Liquor and a ride.

That's what my brothers would say.

Jimmy calls from the pier. "Wanna fish, Charge?"

Yeah. I gotta come at this a different way.

"In a minute," I call back.

I catch the flash of disappointment in Kayla's big brown eyes. She ain't immune to this. Not at all.

"You two eat yet?" I jerk my chin toward Jimmy.

She shakes her head no. "Just got home."

I reach into her messy bun and work out the tie. This close, I can't help but put my hands on her. I run my fingers through her hair, and she sways forward. I lean in to whisper in her ear. Not cause what I have to say is a secret, but because I want to smell that sweet vanilla that clings behind her tiny ears.

"I'm gonna fish with the boy awhile. You take a shower. Once you're done, we'll go to Broyce's. Get some steaks."

Her hazy brown eyes spark with confusion, and a little wrinkle appears on the bridge of her nose.

"I can't afford—"

I growl. Not much. Enough to nip that shit in the bud.

"It's a date, Peaches. You don't pay for no date."

She's real confused now.

I have to admit, I'm surprising myself a bit here, too.

"But." She nibbles her lip. "I can't. Jimmy—"

"They got crayons and menus you can color."

She blinks. And there's a knot in my stomach because I got no control over the situation. And I'm findin' that I really, really care whether this little slip of a thing will bring her boy to go get some damn steaks with me.

"Okay," she whispers.

I nod. Like there was no doubt. She turns to go up to her place, but I keep my hand on hers.

"Peaches?"

She cocks her head.

"Wear a dress." She worries this for a second, the corners of her lips turning down, but then she nods. I think my girl likes bossy.

And damn if I ain't surprised to find I like bein' bossy with her. Not my usual laid-back, that's for sure.

"I'll send Jimmy up in an hour to get cleaned up."

She nods and scampers away.

I join Jimmy and Pops on the pier. Jimmy's good at hookin' worms by himself now, and he can cast a good ways. Learns quick. Ain't nothin' bitin', though. I set back and watch, listen to Pops and the boy yammer at each other. It cracks me up.

"How's school?" Pops asks. He didn't never ask me that. Then again, I wouldn't have had anything to say. I talked to girls, kept my head down, and stopped goin' as soon as I could get away with it.

"Good," Jimmy says. "We got a new class hamster."

"Yeah? What happened to the old hamster?"

"Teacher says retired, but I think that means dead."

"I know many a man feels the same," Pops opines, tipping back his cold one.

I lean back on my hands and let it all go, enjoying the conversation and the silences, filled with the river lappin' its banks.

I got a crick in my back from sleepin' leaned against the

fence at the site, and blue balls for damn days, but this is peace, man. The water. The sunset. Lookin' forward to spendin' time with a pretty girl. And her kid ain't bad company either.

Peace.

Feels nice. Different.

I ain't never felt it before, I guess.

"**K**ayla, slow down." Sue's laughing at me.

"I can't. I have a date. I have to pick a dress. I have to paint my nails. All my nails. I have to—"

"You have to explain to me what's going on. Are we at DEFCON five? One? Which is the worst DEFCON?"

"Sue!" I shouldn't have called her. I mean, I am a great multi-tasker, but I can't get ready for a date and catch her up. Not when I have an hour. And nothing to wear. "I have nothing to wear!"

"Wear your graduation dress."

"You mean the one I wore when you took me out to Sawdust on the Floor to celebrate my GED?"

"That's the one."

"It's at least two sizes too small now."

"It's Lycra. And now it's gonna be bodycon instead of frumpy as hell."

I stare into my closet. What it is is the only dress I own that didn't once belong to Victoria. And all Victoria's dresses have weird geometric patterns in electric colors or polka dots. Broyce's has a reputation for great food, but it is a bit of a dive—and a biker hangout late-nights.

I can't wear polka dots.

"Now how is it that we've gone from 'I'm a slut and that's somehow a bad thing so I should never speak to hot biker daddy again' to 'OH MY GOD!' in a few shorts days?"

And that there is Sue in a nutshell. She has a way of making my crazy seem...kind of ridiculous.

I take a minute to answer, because honestly, I don't know.

I hid from Charge when he dropped by Monday morning, and then I didn't see him all week. I was disappointed. And relieved. And I felt I'd messed something up, and I wasn't sure why I did it. By Friday, I'd just gotten to the point where I could think about those moments in his truck when I was alone and not feel panicky. Then, when I pulled up after work, I found him on Pops' porch.

All the feelings came rushing back, so hard I felt it like a rogue wave at the beach. Slammed in the gut.

Since I'd shoved the feelings deep down instead of figuring them out, I'm left here on my cell, frozen in place, naked except for my one pair of matching bra and panties— both white store-brand from the Megamart—nail polish bottle open and hair half-brushed.

I sigh long. "Oh, Sue. He's just—" What? Too beautiful to look at? Wildly inappropriate for a girl from Gracy's Corner? Too good for me? Too old for me?

Probably—likely—trouble and definitely more than I can manage?

"Whatever it is, say it. I'm not a judge. I'm a friend. Always and no matter what." Sue waits, patient, while I find the words.

"I can't say no to him."

She waits. True to her word, she doesn't jump to judge.

"No, that's not right. I don't want to say no to him. I know I'm supposed to be strong and independent, and I'm supposed to value myself and focus on being a mom and...I just want to go out on a date with a hot guy who likes me. I've never been on a date before."

"Damn."

I sink to the bed. I feel a prickling in the corner of my eyes. I can see Jimmy and the guys from the window, and my stomach clenches again. They seem so relaxed. Charge is sitting with one knee bent, the other outstretched, leaning back against a wooden pile.

Why can't I be relaxed?

"Why do you say damn?" I ask Sue.

"Because they've done one hell of a job on your head, friend."

"What do you mean?"

"I mean, number one, making out with a dude in a truck is normal. And being jealous that a dude might have made out with other girls in that truck? Normal. Know what else is normal?"

I sniffle.

"Single moms going on dates. And?"

I sniff again.

"Feeling guilty for doing something *you* want to do for a change."

"I want to go on a date!" I'm kind of whining, but it's Sue. She doesn't mind. "I want to order dessert!"

Sue laughs. I love her laugh. It's low and throaty. A worldy-wise laugh.

"Totally normal." She pauses a minute. "So who's watching Jimmy?"

"He's coming with. Charge says they have crayons and a menu you can color on."

Sue laughs again. "He's taking you both? Oh, sweetie. How are you going to get laid?"

"I think it's sweet."

I do. Really sweet. Oh, crap. Or is it?

This isn't the way you're supposed to do this. You're supposed to wait months before you introduce your kid to the man you're dating. So as not to traumatize him, let him get attached to someone who's going to bail. Oh, shit.

"You panicking over there?"

"Yes," I wheeze into the phone.

"What mind worm is squirming around in that noggin of yours now?"

"You're not supposed to introduce your kid to the man you're dating too soon."

Sue hums like she's thinking this over. "Can you go out to dinner with a neighbor?"

Yeah. I guess you can.

"Planning on sucking face with him over spaghetti and telling Jimmy to meet his new daddy?"

Well, no.

Sue takes my silence as an answer. "Then get that pretty dress on and go get you some entrée and dessert."

"It's okay?"

"It's okay," Sue repeats. "And if it goes well, know you've got a coupon for a mommy's night out so you can get laid. Any night there's not a new Doctor Who."

And I get hit by a whole new wave of nerves. Not only do I have to screw up the courage to go, now I have to make sure it goes well.

All of a sudden I'm really, really grateful Jimmy is

coming along. He'll break the tension. It'll be fine. Just neighbors being friendly. Having dinner.

The thought reassures me until I'm ready, and I venture down to the pier, picking my way carefully along the slats in my wedge sandals. I've squeezed my ass into the dress Sue suggested, a stretchy pink knit sheath with three-quarter sleeves and a nipped in waist. My boobs look amazing, all squished up and together, but it hugs real tight to my butt and my middle. If I stop sucking in for a second, you can see a little pudge spill over where the waistband of my underwear cuts in. Good thing I'm a pro at sucking it in.

Charge watches me make my way from the stairs, and by the time I reach them, my cheeks are hot. I've left my hair down and curled the pieces framing my face, so I try to let my hair fall to hide my blushing.

I stand there, holding my purse close to my stomach and my elbows tight to my sides, hiding what I can, and all three just stare at me.

There goes my idea of Jimmy breaking the ice.

Finally, after a really awkward few seconds, Pops whistles, loud and long.

"Pops!" Charge barks.

"Do we have to stop fishing now?" Jimmy asks.

"Ayup." Charge takes his pole. "Go wash your hands up the house. I'll put the tackle back."

"Thanks, Charge." Jimmy bounds off to Pops' place, leaping up the back steps as if he's lived there his whole life.

I turn Pops' wheelchair and push him down the pier, following Charge, his hands full of rods and the tackle box. I can't help but watch him walk, his long stride, his broad back. He's wearing jeans and black boots like usual, but they're not mud-crusted like the other day. He's wearing a tight black T-shirt and his cut, and he has his hair up in a man bun. It's a little damp, like he showered.

Sue hates man buns; she says she's never met a man with a bun who didn't also think he was hot shit and too good for oral.

Sue's really into oral.

I don't know as many men as Sue does, and even though Charge has a confidence to him I've never been around before, it's not arrogance.

As for oral…I trip over the toe of my sandal.

"You okay, Peaches?"

Yeah. A shaky giggle escapes. I'm an idiot.

Pops cackles. "Don't trip and push me into the river, girlie. I ain't ready to go yet."

Charge puts the rods back in the garage, and he takes Pops' to-go order. He gets the truck key and opens the back door for Jimmy and the front door for me, swinging Jimmy up first, and then giving me a hand up to the running board.

"Can I get macaroni and cheese?" Jimmy asks while he buckles himself in.

"Sure baby," I say.

Before Charge gets in, he takes off his cut, folds it neatly, and sets it on the back seat next to Jimmy. I look a question at him, and he shrugs.

Now I can really make out his broad shoulders and pecs tugging at his T-shirt. He drives spread out, long arm dangling so far over the wheel he rests his forearm on it, his left leg kicked out between shifting gears. I feel small next to him. Dainty. I'm short, but I don't usually feel…little.

"You been to Broyce's before?" Charges asks, eyeing me top to bottom. He's been doing this since I came down to the pier in the dress. It's making my skin tingle and my tummy dance.

"No. I've heard of it."

"They got good steaks."

I nod. That's what I heard.

"So where do the boys usually take you?"

He's eyeing me seriously now. Catching my eyes and holding them.

My cheeks heat. "Nowhere."

He chuckles, but he doesn't sound happy. "Oh, yeah. You kids nowadays just talk. Netflix and chill."

"I don't talk to guys. I don't go out. But you're right. My parents have date night. Nobody I know goes on dates."

Charge leans back, his stiff frame eases a touch. A smile curls his lips. "You sayin' I'm old enough to be your daddy?"

No. I don't think so? "How old are you?"

"Thirty."

So not old enough to be my father. But old enough that when he says *daddy*, my stomach flips.

"You're saying people your age go on dates?" Thirty's really not that old.

"I'm sayin' a man's serious enough about a woman, he can pony up for dinner. Hear that, little man?" Charge looks over his shoulder at Jimmy.

Jimmy hasn't been paying a lick of attention. He's got the soldiers he's been keeping in the crack of his car seat, and they're in the middle of a sneak attack on the armrest.

"Huh?" Jimmy blinks.

"Not huh. Yes," I correct.

"Yes," Jimmy repeats.

"Damn, woman. You a stickler."

I shrug. If I don't keep on Jimmy's manners, I hear about it from Dad and Victoria. They say I'm not preparing Jimmy for the work world. That children of teen moms are less successful in life because the home environment isn't up to standards, and I need to be aware of that and do everything I can to *counter Jimmy's natural disadvantages.*

I bite the inside of my lip, try to drive that voice away. I don't want it in the truck with me, not when I'm feeling so excited. Happy.

"Jimmy, you grow up, you like a woman, buy her a damn steak."

"Okay, Charge." Jimmy is quiet awhile, and I think he's dismissing this as weird grown-up stuff, but then he says, "Can I buy her mac and cheese?"

Charge snorts, and I can't help but giggle. "Son, if it's the kind they put lobster in, hell yeah. If not, stick to a filet. Chicks love filets."

When we pull up to Broyce's, Charge opens the back door for Jimmy, and then he gives me a hand, tucking me into his side once I hit the gravel.

He's really tall. My head could fit under his arm.

I hold Jimmy's hand while we walk in, and I know I'm not supposed to even think it, but I wonder if this is what it feels like to be a family with a mom and a dad.

It's heady. The feeling. Like there's a buffer between Jimmy and me and the rest of the world.

Charge opens the door, talks to the hostess, sets me on a bench when we have to wait five minutes for a table.

I feel like I'm floating in a wake. All I have to do for once is let go and go along.

It's nice.

Not nice? How the hostess and then the waitress and then two ladies at a table nearby are eyeing Charge like he's a filet.

When the hostess seats us in a booth, I swear she lingers with a dumb grin on her face, just staring. It's awkward, but I can't really blame her. I stare, too.

Charge maneuvers it so he's next to Jimmy, and I'm across from them both. The boys play tic-tac-toe on the kid's menu while we wait, Charge nursing a beer and me sipping an iced tea. I glance around, but my eyes keep coming back to the man whose long legs are crowding my knees under the table. His broad shoulders. The flash of his smile that heats my insides.

He's too handsome for this town. This place.

For me.

The place is a dive, no doubt. There are beer logo pool table lamps, and as I find when I excuse myself during the wait, the women's restroom is painted black. Clear plastic tablecloths stick to the tables.

The food does smell really, really good, though. I order the filet, and Jimmy orders the mac and cheese. I make him pick the broccoli as his side.

Then, Charge and Jimmy chat—some gentle smack-talking about the game they're playing—and I just listen, running my fingers in the condensation circle left by my glass. I'm nervous—and I definitely feel like an imposter, the plain mom with the hot biker—but I'm also weirdly not on edge.

I guess being alone most of the time with Jimmy...I'm always on high alert. I've got a million tasks: get us up, bathed, dressed, fed, drive the car, make the doctor's appointments and the dentist appointments. And then I also have to keep my eye on the big stuff: balancing somehow between raising him to act with respect and taking care of his feelings. Planning the long term and figuring things out when everything goes to hell. Deciding how much to worry about his reading or his seriousness.

And then all the daily dramas: boo-boos, temper

tantrums, the dropped forks and knives and hundreds of other spills, accidents, and whoopsies.

When Dad and Victoria take us out to eat, I'm the one making sure Jimmy doesn't get bored and cause trouble, rushing through my meal so Jimmy doesn't get finished first and decide to play with the salt and pepper shakers.

But tonight...I can sit across from my little man, let go, and appreciate. He's so serious, so intent and deliberate in how he makes his x's and o's on the tic-tac-toe board, but every so often, a shy smile ghosts across his face. He doesn't wriggle, doesn't climb the walls like I see some other kids doing. He's a calm little dude. He's okay.

And it's such a weight off, realizing this. He's happy. Content. So am I.

I exhale, and Charge shoots me a wide grin at something Jimmy says. I smile back and my insides melt like à la mode.

When the waitress brings the food, I tuck in. I'm a little embarrassed to stuff my face in front of Charge, but this feels like a break. The kind of experience you know isn't going to roll around again soon, so you better grab it with both hands, and save the worry for later. So I ordered the garlic mashed potatoes, and I go to town on the bread basket. It's fluffy and brown and served with room temperature butter.

Charge watches me eat, bemused.

I finish before him, and he asks, "Still hungry?"

I shrug a shoulder. I'm stuffed, but I don't want to say no to dessert.

Dessert's my dream.

Charge smiles, slow. Like he's up to something. He spears a piece of his porterhouse with his fork. "Open up," he says.

I do.

He slips the bite between my lips.

I chew and swallow. He's riveted on my mouth.

The power's heady. I dart my tongue out. Quickly lick the corner of my mouth.

His breath catches on an inhale.

Jimmy spears a piece of broccoli a little wonky, and it goes shooting across the table at me.

I giggle, and Charge snorts.

"You got the broccoli runnin' from you now. Right on, kid."

"Can I have some of your steak, too?" Jimmy asks.

Before I can tell Jimmy he's had enough, Charge drops a hunk on Jimmy's plate, cutting it more or less into kid-sized pieces.

"There you go little man. Don't let this get away."

Later, we order dessert to share. Chocolate lava cake. A drop of chocolate falls on my top, and it's so delicious, I don't even care. Charge can't stop staring at my top, though. And licking his lips.

I squirm in the booth, loving the way he looks at me. Hungry, but with a smile so ready, so bright and filled with humor, I'm not freaked out. I'm completely punch-drunk from his charm. When it's time to go, I don't want to. It's gotten a little louder though, since we came in. The after-dinner crowd is pouring in. I see bikers in doo-rags and cuts like Charge's, and as we walk out, he tucks me close to his side again while I hold Jimmy's hand.

"Charge!" a boisterous male voice calls from the bar area.

Charge raises a hand, half waving, half waving him off. He hustles us out to the truck.

"Don't you want to stop and say hi?" I ask.

I'm not sure if I want to meet his friends. His brothers, I

guess he'd say. I like this fantasy bubble, and from what he's said, his friends are rough around the edges. Still, I want to know more about him. And we're at a restaurant. Not some back alley.

"Nope. I want to get you two home. Get the little guy to bed."

It's an hour past Jimmy's bedtime. Luckily, he doesn't have school tomorrow. He's drooping in his seat though, his long eyelashes fluttering on his cheeks.

"I guess you'll want to go back out. Hang out with your friends."

Charge grins at me in the dark, easing the truck into reverse. "No, Peaches. I want to put the little dude to bed and then sit with you on the porch awhile."

"Yeah?" I struggle, but I can't imagine rocking on Pops' porch swing with Charge, the crazy hot biker.

"You got some things to tell me about. And I got some things to make straight with you."

"Yeah?" A flurry of nerves flutter under my rib cage.

"Yeah."

Do I want to tell him things? Make things straight? I can hardly make myself think about what he means. I'm too excited, too bubbling with hope, too heartsick that when he knows my story, he won't look at me like ice cream anymore. And an ugly voice in my head suggests he wants to let me know this—whatever it is—isn't what I think it is. He only wants a good time.

I mean, when has *let's talk* ever been good?

Jimmy's totally conked out by the time we get home, and I rouse him enough to get him up the stairs, pajamas on, and teeth brushed. I tuck him in, and then I slip off my sandals and slide on my flip flops.

Then I go brush my teeth.

I think about changing out of my dress. That drop of chocolate is still kind of bugging me.

I know I'm procrastinating.

But I'm not a good time. I can't be a good time. I'm a mom.

If that's what Charge wants, then this is over now. Before it's really started. And I don't want it to be over.

I check on Jimmy, tuck him under the blanket. Then I take the tablet my dad got me for Christmas, FaceTime my phone, and set the tablet on the nightstand. It makes a great baby monitor. I'm only going across the parking pad, and I can see the door from there, but still...It makes me feel better knowing I can hear Jimmy if he wakes up.

From the window next to the bed, I can see Charge waiting for me on his Pops' porch. His arm is laid out on the back of the swing, his long legs sprawled. He looks at ease.

He's waiting for me.

And I'm all nerves, sweaty palms, and self-doubt.

But what could happen? On a porch, neighbors all around. Nothing. Nothing can happen.

I steel my spine and flip flop down the steps. And the closer I get to Charge, the more I can make out his eyes gleaming in the porch light, I realize I was wrong.

A lot could happen. He could say anything at all.

"COME SIT HERE, PEACHES." As I approach, feet dragging, Charge shifts to the side of the swing.

I sink down beside him. His stance is so wide, I can't help but press my side to his. I hope he doesn't notice the chocolate lava cake pudge spilling onto his rock-hard obliques.

My feet don't quite touch the ground, but Charge rocks with one boot heel, so we sway gently. The rusty chains creak, and a million crickets compete with the honks of bullfrogs out in the thick rushes along the river. There's a cool breeze blowing up from the water, and I shiver. Charge bends an elbow so his arm is draped on my shoulders, a hand stroking my arm.

"You have a good time tonight?" He fiddles with my sleeve, tucking a finger under the hem so he can touch my skin. Goosebumps blossom where a rough pad grazes my arm.

I nod.

"Don't talk much, do you?"

I guess not. I talk to Sue. Most everyone else—Dad, Victoria, Greg and the others at work—just wants me to listen to them. So I do. It's easier.

I shrug.

"Fine by me." Charge rocks us more, and I stop trying so hard to suck my gut in. Even with the porch light, it's dark out here. And the swaying and warmth from his body is lulling me.

After a while, Charge drops a kiss on my head. "So," he says. A knot twists in my stomach.

I know this is going to be the question. I'm surprised we've gone this long without him asking. Usually, it comes up with guys in the first or second conversation.

I'm sad because I don't get a few more minutes rocking in the porch swing. A little longer before it all gets unfixably awkward. I knew this was coming. It's why I dithered so much coming down to sit on a porch with the hottest guy I personally have ever seen in real life.

"Where's Jimmy's dad at?"

My body tenses, and I know Charge can feel it. He

doesn't stop rocking and stroking, though. He clears his throat a touch and squeezes my arm.

Where is Jimmy's dad?

There's the lie Sue gave me to say. It was a fling. A guy from out of town. He wasn't ready to have a kid.

And there's the truth that only a handful know. Sue and the staff at Patonquin General and a court-mandated therapist. And my dad, Victoria, and Denise Edgerton from the Department of Child Services, although they don't believe it.

I could not tell. Stand up, thank Charge for dinner, go back up to my place. Maybe he'd let it drop; maybe he'd drop me.

Or I could tell him.

He said I shouldn't trust people that look like him.

But I think maybe he's full of crap. I spent a good half hour watching him color in the outlines of hamburgers with two crayon nubs while my kid colored in the buns.

I want to be honest with him. If he can't handle it, he can't handle it. In the end, I have to remember it doesn't matter whether he can or can't. I can handle it. Not all days, not always well. But I can. I do.

"I don't know who his father is," I say.

Charge waits for me to go on. Quiet. Still rocking us.

"There was a party. The summer after middle school. My friend Sue wanted to go. I was fourteen."

"You go to Petty's Mill Middle?"

"Yeah."

Everyone in town went there. Just like everyone went to Petty's Mill High.

"It was a high school party. Some people who were older, out of school. I went with Sue. Sue knew some people. I didn't know anyone."

Charge makes a go-on noise, and he remains still except for his hand on my arm.

"I didn't drink, so I had some lemonade in a red plastic cup."

Creak. Creak. We rock. The moon comes out. Or the clouds clear from in front of it.

"Sue went off with this boy she liked. I told her it was fine. That if I got bored, I'd just head home. It was only a few blocks away. A five-minute walk. It was Gracy's Corner, you know? Super safe."

He nods. He's lived there. He knows.

"So I sat on a sofa. I didn't know anybody. I felt so stupid. Other people were smoking, dancing. I got up to find Sue, let her know I was leaving...and I felt woozy. So I sat back down."

The creaking stops.

I glance up, and Charge's face isn't the chill, confident model-handsome face I've grown used to anymore. His jaw is strained. A tic jumps at the corner of his eye.

He keeps stroking my arm, though. Slow and calm.

"I woke up the next morning outside, by an above ground pool. My underwear was missing. I was...there was blood. And..."

I can't say it.

It had hurt. All over. Not just...not just in front. My chin was scraped, and so were my knees. And a patch of scalp hurt. I was missing a chunk of hair.

"I went home and took a shower."

Charge exhales. And then he tucks my head into the crook where his head met his shoulder.

He starts rocking again.

"You tell the police?" he asks.

No. I told myself I fell. The lemonade must have been

alcoholic, and I was so naïve, I hadn't even noticed. I was embarrassed. I thought maybe I made a fool of myself, and I couldn't remember.

"I didn't tell anyone."

"This girl Sue know anything?"

"I didn't tell her until after...after we found out about Jimmy."

Charge makes a sound then. Kind of a strangled-off snarl. "Your folks go to the police?"

I look down into my lap. I don't want to see his face when I say this part. "I was five months along when we found out. I didn't know I was pregnant. I had no clue. I wasn't regular at all back then. My dad thought I was lying. That I'd been sleeping around, and I knew I was pregnant, and I was hiding it from them."

I don't know why I need Charge to believe this, but I do. "I didn't know. I wasn't hiding it."

There's a long silence, and I don't dare look up. "That's the truth," I say.

And then, suddenly, strong arms scoop me up, and I'm sitting across Charge's lap, and he's tipping my chin up with his forefinger so I can't help but look him in the eye.

He looks pissed. Furious. His face has gone hard, the beautiful turned into something dangerous and scary. I turn my face, but he tips my chin again.

And then he drops his forehead to mine. Brushes kisses on my nose and cheeks.

"Of course it's the truth," he says, low, his voice strained. "You got the most honest fuckin' face I've ever seen."

He's wrapping me up so tight. One arm gathers my bent legs, another cradles me to his chest. He dusts feather-light kisses all over my face, my lips, and his beard tickles my neck. I squirm, and he tucks me in closer.

And then he gently presses my head to his chest and plays with my hair as he rocks.

"My beautiful girl," he murmurs into my hair. "My brave, beautiful girl."

I look a question up at him.

He raises an eyebrow back at me. "You don't think you my girl? You drivin' my truck."

I don't know what to say.

"Yeah, kinda comes as a surprise to me, too." He shrugs, and then goes back to rocking me, touching me, so gentle I could cry.

And then it hits me like a brick wall. Exhaustion so sudden and deep I know it's my brain taking a break. I felt this way a lot after Jimmy was born. When Dad and Victoria sent me to live with Aunt Felicia, and I couldn't get out of bed to go to school.

When I yawn, Charge sighs, and he puts me on my feet like it's nothing. Then he takes my hand in his work-roughened one and walks me across the parking area and up the metal stairs to my apartment. At my door, he tips my chin up and drops a soft kiss on my lips.

"You got work tomorrow, right?"

I nod.

"I'll drive you. Jimmy go to daycare when you work Saturdays?"

I nod again.

"How 'bout I keep him tomorrow? We can go to the garage. He can watch me Frankenstein that fuckin' Corolla."

"That would be nice."

Charge smiles at me, but his jaw's still clenched. His eyes are still stormy with anger. I know he's angry for me; I've seen the same expression on Sue's face. I've tried to make her feel better, point out how it could have been worse, reassure her that it wasn't her fault. She yelled at me, told me to stop trying to manage her feelings. That she'd feel guilty if she wanted. Anyway, it didn't go well, so I don't say anything to Charge. Don't try to reassure him that it's all really okay when it's not.

"Don't forget the deadbolt," he orders when I slip in the door, careful not to wake Jimmy.

I watch him go down the stairs and take the stairs to Pops' porch in one step. I guess he's sleeping there tonight. A light goes on in the front room. It's still on after I've brushed my teeth and changed into a sleep shirt. Lying in bed, I can see that light from our window. It makes me feel warm inside, knowing he's close.

It also makes me feel warm that he walked me home, kissed me goodnight at my door. Didn't push me for more. Some kind of reassurance I can't give or resolution I don't have.

Jimmy grunts in his sleep and kicks me with one skinny, strong leg. I pull him close and give him a hug. It feels delicate, like an empty eggshell that's still miraculously whole, this thing between Charge and me. I can't think about it too much, or it feels like it'll break, an impossible dream that'll come to its inevitable bad end like everything else in my life so far.

So I drift off instead, bathed in the light of the moon, heart calm from the light in the window next door.

12

CHARGE

I stand in that fuckin' window, staring at the door to Kayla's place, wonderin' how Nickel and Creech and all my other hot-headed brothers handle the fuckin' rage. I know I'm made different than them. The hippie bitch who birthed me gifted me a good dose of mellow in my DNA, and Boots laughs at the good and the bad alike.

What the fuck am I goin' to do with this killin' urge when there's no motherfucker to put down? Maybe if Kayla's shitty excuses for parents did what they were supposed to do at the time, there'd be a name. Leads. But six, seven years on?

Who remembers who all was at a kegger when they was fifteen?

One thing for sure: that fucker who let his little girl out of his sight to walk into trouble and then didn't have her back after? No kind of father at all.

Not all my brothers are stand-up. Bullet, for one, has a bad record when it comes to child support. Dude cannot grasp that givin' his old lady a sack of cash when he wins at the races and then going into arrears when shit gets lean is not acceptable support in the eyes of the state. But there's not a one of them that wouldn't paint the walls with blood if a fucker touched his kid.

My body ain't used to this shit. Muscles bunched to cramping, gut sour, fuckin' fists locked so hard my knuckles look like they gonna bust from the skin. A ride would chill me out, but I ain't movin' from this house. She may not be in my bed, but that girl across the parking pad is mine. Her boy, too.

I don't know when it happened.

And it's strange. I was addicted to Harper. Wild for her classy pussy. Ate shit from my brothers for years for puttin' up with her drama. But I never felt this click. One minute I'm checkin' out a sweet peach of an ass, then click, next minute my soul is fuckin' sick cause I can't go back in time and kill a man. Men.

Fuck.

I need to do something.

That girl and her boy need to be under my roof.

Fuck. I need a god damn roof. And I don't know what I'm thinkin', but an hour later I've got a measuring tape and a hammer, up in the attic, with floorboards pried up, examin' the joists. Checkin' to see if they'd hold a second floor.

"Fuckin' squirrel! Get out of my damn attic!" Pops yells at one point, and I hear a thump, likely from a thrown boot.

"Go back to sleep!" I holler back.

He's been after me—since Harper and I split—to move back in. I didn't want to do that, didn't want to go backwards in my life.

Now, though, one thing I know with some clarity. Bein' with Harper wasn't movin' forwards. Bein' with her demanded nothin' from me. I just had to go along with the good times.

Kayla, though...my girl is work. But she's worth the work.

After exhausting myself with sketchin' out plans for an addition—those joists are solid, but not close enough to support another floor—I get a few hours of sleep before it's time to drive Kayla to work.

She's hidin' when I go up to get her. Her hair's down in her face. Fussin' over Jimmy while he finishes his cereal. All bashful.

I slap her ass so she knows where we stand.

She shrieks and makes a little angry face at me. Her eyes ain't worried no more, though.

I could slap her ass all day if it makes her feel better.

Oh, sweet Lord, now that image is in my head. Kayla bent over my knee, round ass bright red, squirmin' and whimperin', beggin' me to stop and make her feel all better.

I gotta pull it together. Remember where I am. And what my girl's been through. I don't need to be thinkin' shit like that. Besides, I'm spendin' the day with the little guy. I need to focus on that.

"Ready, bud?"

Jimmy nods, grabs his toy tool belt from where he must have set it out on the bed.

"Mama says we're going to fix her car."

"We gonna try. You got your belt?"

Jimmy nods, buckles it around his waist, and says, "I ain't bringing my tools cause they ain't real."

"They're not real," Kayla corrects, grabbin' her shit from the kitchen counter and stuffin' her purse.

"I know, Mama. That's what I said."

Jimmy races out the door ahead of us, and I take advantage, pullin' Kayla close, arm tight around the small of her back so I'm restin' my forearm on that juicy ass. I take a sip from her pretty lips, taste the gloss, groan.

She sighs, soft, like she don't mean to. From that open face of hers, I can tell her brain's been twistin' shit. She ain't totally at ease, like she was when she was tuckin' into that steak last night. But that's part of the work, isn't it? My girl don't understand what it is to belong to a man.

She will.

Once she moves in with me, she ain't workin' no more. Or if she does, it'll be at one of the club's businesses where I know she's taken care of.

It 'bout kills me—after last night—to drive her to General Goods, let her walk past those gates in that ass-ugly, red-collared shirt. But I do. After I drag her into me for a kiss that leaves her shaky and flushed the same color as her shirt.

I can't rush in, make demands, swing my cock around like some brothers do. Not with Kayla. She's young and sweet and the world ain't treated her right.

I got to do this right.

And I have no fuckin' clue how.

"How you doin' bud?" I glance at Jimmy in the rearview. Like his mama, he don't say much. Not unless he's into something like fishin'. He don't talk to hear himself. It's nice.

"Good."

Little dude's added a matchbox car and a small rubber duckie to the soldiers he's got battling in the back seat. No idea where they came from, but the duckie ain't long for the world. He's surrounded, and the soldiers are now mobile.

When we roll up to the garage, Jimmy tucks the soldiers into the pocket of his tool belt.

Scrap is here, and so's Gus and some of the older guys.

They're workin' on a rebuild. Or rather bossin' around some prospects, supervisin' and drinkin' beers. It is a Saturday.

"Charge, what up?" My brothers greet me, not hidin' their curiosity at my little helper. I ain't never had no kid in tow before. "Who's the little dude?"

"This is my man Jimmy. We gonna work on the Corolla. Parts in?"

Scrap nods and leaves off his work to show me where my shit got stored.

Jimmy is all big eyes, checkin' out the lifts and the work-benches. He sticks close to my heels, and it feels strange. Strange but right.

"Shit's still boxed," Scrap points out.

"Ayup." I know what he's hintin' at.

"Easy enough to return. Southwestern is down with us. They'll take it back, no questions."

I shake my head and lift the box onto my shoulder, headin' for the bay with Kayla's car.

Scrap follows. Don't know when he got so interested in other people's business. Actually been keepin' most to himself since his release.

He helps me get the hood up, and I pick Jimmy up and set him on the bumper so he can see better.

"You put that new engine in there, you puttin' lipstick on a pig." Scrap eyes me like I'm dumb or gone crazy.

Jimmy giggles. I guess at the idea of lipstick on a pig.

"Little man, this your mama's car?" Scrap asks.

Jimmy nods.

"She love it, I guess?"

Jimmy shakes his head. "I don't think so. She kicks it sometimes. And she calls it the Crapolla."

Scrap gives me the eye. "What you doin', brother? Throwin' good money after bad on this."

"My money," I point out. Shouldn't have to.

"So put it toward somethin' new. You could almost buy a better used straight out for what you're payin' for parts for this piece of sh—er, crap."

"Cain't just buy a female a car."

"So lease." Scrap shrugs and stalks away, back to his own bay, leaving Jimmy and I staring at a rusted-out hulk with a busted, black-coated engine.

The asshole has a point. I ain't in this for kicks. And my old lady ain't gonna be drivin' a Crapolla.

"Change of plans, little dude. We goin' shoppin'."

He looks a little crestfallen. "I hate shopping."

"For a car."

He perks up a little at that.

And he's a good partner, Jimmy is. We start at the Ford dealer up near Ebensburg, and each time we look under a hood, he stands next to me, arms crossed like mine, stone-faced. Freaks the sales guys out. They try and tousle his hair, offer him a lollipop, but he ain't havin' it. Kid's got a world class poker face.

What was his dad like? A fuckin' rapist, for one.

Second thought, I don't like that fuckin' question. Jimmy don't have a dad yet, but he will, and ain't nobody'll need to be askin' any questions about anythin' after that.

The rage washes through me again, not so bad as last night, but enough that the sales guy backs up a step or two from me.

I make an effort to pull myself out of it.

"Think your mama needs a backup camera?"

Jimmy and I are checkin' out an SUV. Pig Iron's old lady drives this model. So does Grinder's. The bitches like the clearance since they always ridin' over curbs and shit.

"What's that?"

"See this screen here? Shows what's behind the car. So she can see when she's backing up."

"Mama don't need that. She's got eyes there."

"What? Where?" the sales guy asks.

"In the back of her head. That's what she says. 'I have eyes in the back of my head.' So I don't think she needs a camera to see back there."

I don't laugh out loud, but it's close.

In the end, I pick a vehicle with the backup camera, curve control, highest safety rating, heated steering wheel, all of it. I put ten thousand down, makin' a mental note to return the parts and move some funds around.

Then I have a prospect meet me, swap the car seat into the SUV, and send him back to Pops' with my truck. And then, finally, I can get my girl. I pick up three sodas on the way. Jimmy's stoked. Apparently he don't get soda much. Must be a luxury my girl can't afford.

Those times are over now.

Not that she knows it.

She's surprised when I pull up. I walk around to open her door, and a foot away, that vanilla scent hits me, turns me rock hard. I tug her close to hide it, but I want her to feel it, too. Know what this is. I kiss her, no tongue; the kid's awake in the back.

She looks all flustered and confused and in her eyes I can see the heat for me. She don't know what it is, what to do with it. I understand better now why that may be. But that don't stop me from restin' my hands on that lush ass, down low where her boy can't see if he were lookin'—which he ain't cause that duckie is makin' a comeback; somethin' has made that kid hyper. I cup that ass, massage, stoke that heat until I get a sweet whimper.

"Brought you somethin'." I gesture to her new ride.

"What's this?" She likes it. Her eyes sweep from hood to trunk with appreciation. But she's unsure.

I've thought this out. A little bullshit for the sake of takin' it slow. "Loaner. The Corolla's gonna take a little longer than I thought."

"Oh. I guess...that's okay."

"You guess?" I nibble the puffy bottom lip she's been workin' with her teeth. She giggles, and I figure I'm the hottest fuckin' thing in western PA.

"Thank you," she says, soft. And then she glances in the car window. "Did you bring me a soda?" She smiles. The prettiest smile, no fakeness to it, all gentle and toothy and delighted. I mean, fuck, I bought her a car.

But it took a pop to earn that smile.

13

KAYLA

Sue's already made herself comfortable on my bed. She's dip-dyed her long black hair white, and she looks more than ever like a pin-up girl painted on the side of an old airplane. She's playing with Jimmy, mostly letting him build a tall tower with blocks and then ramming into it with a matchbox car until the blocks scatter everywhere. Build, ram, repeat.

I'm fidgeting, packing and unpacking the same blue cardigan in my overnight bag. When Charge gets home from work, he's taking me away for the weekend. On his bike.

Except for Charge taking me on short rides along the river while Jimmy hangs out with Pops and Shirlene, I've never ridden on his bike before. And that's not all I've never done before. Or rather... I push the ugly thoughts away.

Charge and I have talked about it. He understands. I don't have to worry. If I'm in the mood, we'll do it. If I'm not, we don't.

"Leave it, nervous Nelly," Sue orders, tugging the cardigan out of my hands.

I do and sink into a chair, but she's right. I'm a ball of nerves. Charge has been taking me on dates—he calls them dates and makes me call them that when I slip and say we're hanging out—for over a month now. He's taken Jimmy and me bowling, fishing on a boat up on Lake Patonquin, and to a cookout at this guy Dizzy's house.

Dizzy's one of his brothers from the MC. That was an experience. He's married to a crazy biker chick close to my age named Fay-Lee. Well, I think they're married. Fay-Lee wears a vest with a top rocker that reads *property of*, and Dizzy calls her his old lady. She also wears something that looks like a dog collar.

They've got kids, though, two boys a few years older than Jimmy. Dizzy's from a first marriage. Fay-Lee's the step-mom. The kids were as crazy as Fay-Lee, cussin' bold as day, roughhousing, no shirts, no shoes, and elbows and knees all scraped to hell. Jimmy loved every minute playing with them. And they took off with him like he was a long lost brother. I teared up a little at that. No one noticed except Charge. And then Charge looked mad as hell until I smiled at him.

Charge gets worried when I frown. He always wants to know what's wrong so he can fix it. I usually make up something around the house, a loose floorboard or a window that sticks in the frame. He feels better once he makes it right.

I don't tell him it's usually black thoughts. Wondering that gets me nowhere. Regrets.

I have a lot, and they're stubborn suckers.

Now, though, I have something good besides Jimmy. I've got a boyfriend. And to my complete surprise, he's sweet as hell.

After each *date*, Charge walks Jimmy and me up the steps to our place, kisses me gently—sometimes on my forehead, sometimes my cheek, sometimes the quickest brush across my lips—and then he reminds me about the dead-bolt and goes back to Pops'.

He's been staying at Pops' most nights. When he isn't there, I know he's at his work site. He gets home early in the morning, mud-caked and exhausted, with worry wrinkling his eyes. They have a problem with trespassers, and I can tell it frustrates him. He shakes it off real easy though once his boots are off. I don't think the man has an uptight bone in his body.

Me, though. I'm wound tight.

Every week, every respectful kiss, the anticipation grows. We're going to have to do it at some point. And I want to.

I'm scared, but I'm ready. I think.

"You have Charge's cell phone number, right?" I check with Sue. Again.

"Yes. And yours. Charge texted me where you'll be staying and the phone number there."

"Where are we staying?"

I've tried to worm the information out of Sue a few times already, but she's keeping mum. She came with us fishing on Lake Patonquin, and even though she wouldn't cast a line and played RPGs on her phone the whole time, she had fun. She says Charge is the first guy in a man bun she thought she couldn't take in a fight.

"And you know all of Jimmy's emergency numbers are on the fridge. Pediatrician. Dentist. Poison Control."

"Your mom thinks we're gonna be having way more fun than we actually are," Sue tells Jimmy and winks.

That's when I hear the engine to Charge's bike and my nerves go truly bonkers. I flush hot, sweat breaks out behind my knees, and I grab the cardigan and shove it back in my bag like it's a life preserver.

Sue sits up, one smooth movement—damn her rock-solid abs—and she grins, her eyes full of love.

"You're gonna have fun, Kayla-cakes. Breathe."

I can't. My throat is parched.

I'm going off on a weekend away with a biker who's probably been with hundreds of women, and I have no idea what I'm doing, and what if I freak out in the middle of it, and am I really going to leave Jimmy to have sex with some guy? What if he falls and breaks an arm? Doesn't that make me the worst mother on the planet?

Sue narrows her eyes and reads my mind.

"Jimmy and I are going to spend the next two days eating junk food, going to the arcade, eating more junk food, going to see a superhero double feature, getting ice cream, and then we're going to go to Municipal Park and run around with no shoes on."

Jimmy brightens up. He loves his Aunt Sue. He knows she's serious. She's a big-time spoiler. And kind of a nut.

"And you know what else? If you don't go on this well-deserved little getaway with Hottie McManBun, Jimmy and I won't get to spend all this quality time together."

I nod. I appreciate her trying to talk me down.

"No, Kayla. I'm serious. Jimmy's my godson. Loving on him is a gift. Don't crap on my gift with your garbage-culture induced mom-guilt."

My eyes mist. "Don't let him run around in Municipal Park with no shoes. There's goose poop all over the place."

"Okay," Sue says, pulling me to her by the back of my head to plant a loud, wet kiss on my forehead. "Now kiss Jimmy and go ride off into the sunset with McManBun."

"Could you make him sound less hot?"

"Kayla, nothing on the planet could make that man less hot. Enjoy. For all of womankind, honey. Go."

~

"THAT'S A CHAMPAGNE GLASS BATHTUB."

Charge grins, sniffs, and stomps his boots in the entryway. "Ayup. It's a whirlpool."

I don't know what to say. I don't know what I expected, but I don't think any twenty-one-year-old would expect a suite done in pinks and reds with a champagne glass bathtub. And a heart-shaped jacuzzi?

"And a fireplace?" My jaw has permanently dropped open. It's the set of a cheesy porno. From the eighties.

Charge grins wider. There's a fire already crackling, and next to it, a plate of chocolate dipped strawberries and a bottle of wine in a silver ice bucket.

Charge drops the helmet he got for me onto a table, and he shrugs off his cut, hanging it in a closet.

Must be civilized, of course. Use a hanger. In the bow-chicka-wow-wow suite.

And that's what this is. It's one of those couple's resorts in the mountains. I saw the signs on the drive here—and it was such a gorgeous drive, the air mellow and earthy-smelling like it gets in spring. I thought the signs were funny. Hokey. The pictures of Barbie and Ken doll couples in two-story, foaming champagne glass bathtubs.

I guess I thought we were gonna go camping. Or to a cabin.

But no. We're at a resort where people go to fuck.

My chest is getting a little tight, and I'm sweating under my new leather jacket. I mean, I knew we were coming here to fuck. But this—this is very obvious.

I shrug my jacket off and hang it next to Charge's cut. He bought me the jacket. Said I needed protection. And then he'd said, "Speaking of, you on the pill?"

I said I was, and then he changed the subject to what kind of *leather* I should get. So I shouldn't be surprised that his choice of getaway is...not subtle.

I'm not gonna lie. It's disorienting. I'm Jimmy's mom, for heaven's sake. I keep my head down, work hard, don't give people a reason to talk. I'm not the type who goes to hotels to do it on fake silk sheets. Or real silk sheets? How do you even begin to know the difference?

While I'm dithering, Charge has climbed the stairs to the loft where you enter the champagne glass tub. He leans over the rail and grins at me. The man looks like the cat that ate the canary.

I'm one more weird-shaped tub away from a panic attack.

Does he bring all his women here?

Does he expect me to know what to do in these tubs?

My hands clutch the back of a velvet chair, and I try really, really hard not to run. Or throw up. Or throw up while I run.

"Peaches?"

"Uh huh," I mumble, not looking at him, not looking at anything. This whole suite is embarrassing.

"Eyes up here."

I look up.

He does have a way of bossing me. Weird that I don't really mind. It doesn't feel ugly like control, but safe. Like he's coaching me. I want what he wants, but I also want a push. Cause I'm a little scared. Not of him. But...of it.

"You here with me, baby?"

He's still in the loft, close enough so I can see the serious in his blue eyes, but not so near that he's in my space at all.

I nod.

"We're gonna have sex," he says.

We are?

I mean, yeah, I know, but it's not like I'd thought about it very specifically—except for replaying those moments in his truck—because...because I've got some hang-ups.

Which is one way to put it. Another would be that I'm damaged goods. Broken. I don't even masturbate well. I can't. I try, but nine times out of ten, I give up frustrated. There's always this disconnect.

Charge stares down at me like he can read all of this on my face. We've talked about the masturbation thing once. I'd had two beers on his porch one night after Jimmy was in bed, so maybe he does know what I'm thinking? He seems to get me pretty easy. Which can be embarrassing.

"When you're ready," he adds. "Until then, we're gonna put on our bathing suits, drink sparkling white wine, and play in the bubble bath."

I giggle. I can't help it. Charge in a champagne glass bubble bath?

"This place is ridiculous." I gesture to the circular bed. I mean...why a circle? Are circles sexy? Oh, and there's a mirror above it.

Yikes. I don't want to see myself in bed in a mirror. I know my boobs flatten under my arm pits when I lay on my back. I don't want to see that. I'll never get to sleep.

Hell, my nerves are so taut, I'll never get to sleep anyway.

"Go to the bathroom, Kayla. Put on your bathing suit. You wanna do the champagne glass or the hot tub first?"

Well. Since we're here. And for some reason, I'm not having a full-blown panic attack yet. "Champagne glass. Obviously."

Charge grins again. "That's my girl."

I change quickly into my two-piece. It's red gingham, a

classic cut with boy shorts and a halter top that nearly reaches my belly button. Sue lent it to me.

I can't help wrapping my arms around my middle when I go up to meet Charge at the tub. He's filled it and turned the jets on, and I'm kind of grateful for all the foam and swirling. He won't be able to see me when my suit gets wet and clings to my little belly pudge.

He's already in, but he reaches a hand up to help me to a bench across from him. His hair is loose, and there's a bit of foam clinging to the tip of his beard.

He looks chill. Content.

He takes a swig and then passes me the open bottle of champagne.

"No glasses?" I ask.

"Seemed like overkill. Considerin' what we're sittin' in."

A giggle sails from my mouth. I didn't even feel it coming. And then Charge is laughing, and I'm laughing so hard my belly aches, and I can't catch my breath.

This place is ridiculous. I swat the bubbles, and a mound flies up in Charge's face, sticking in his beard and sliding down his upper chest.

He doesn't have a shirt on.

Of course he doesn't. But I'm just now noticing. I was so worried about my belly, I missed his broad, cut chest with dabs of foam caught in dark, wet hairs. Now I can't drag my eyes away. He's so pretty. So perfect.

"Oh yeah? That how it's gonna be?" Charge growls, teasing, scooping up a handful of bubble and dolloping it on top of my head.

My giggles trail off, and Charge drifts toward me, guiding me onto his lap, and he doesn't have a swimsuit on.

I can feel him, hard, pressed into my butt cheek.

He takes a little foam and boops it on my nose. "There. Now you're perfect."

I roll my eyes. Tense a little. I know I'm not pretty. Nowhere near perfect. I'm so not in his league—looks-wise —it's not even funny.

"You don't think so?" He frowns.

I shrug.

Charge leans closer, his lips skimming the shell of my ear, and he whispers, "Perfect."

Despite the hot water, a shiver runs down my spine, all the way to my toes.

Then he tugs my scrunchie loose and runs his hands through my wind-mussed hair, scritching my scalp with his fingertips, sending even more shivers dancing down my arms and back. He buries his nose in my hair, and then he murmurs, "Perfect."

I shift, restless, hot. Not sure what to do with my hands. Not sure what to say.

He strokes my back, soothing me. Going slow. And then he unties my halter, peels the front down until my boobs are totally exposed.

The air is chill enough so that despite the hot water, my nipples are hard and achy. Raised nubs like the erasers of those big pencils kids learn to write with. Too big.

I raise my hands to cover them, and Charge bats them away. Then he cups me, brushing his rough thumbs over my nipples, and I'm squirming, not from nerves but because between my legs is throbbing now. Pulsing.

I whimper, and he growls low in his throat.

"So perfect."

He bends down and captures a breast in his mouth, sucking and drawing the nipple in deep, and I'm turning and climbing him now, straddling him, arching my back, pressing him to me by the back of his head, because I want more, I want him to keep doing this and...I want him to do more.

I grind down, chasing the feeling that's lighting up the nerves between my legs.

"You like that, baby?"

"Shhh." I hush him.

I can't believe I hushed him.

But it feels like I have something in my sights, I'm so close, and I don't want to lose focus, not for a second.

He laughs. "Okay, baby." And he slides his soapy hands up my back and then cups my neck, holding me still while he plunders my mouth, thrusting up where I ride him. I press down to meet him, and each roll of my hips stokes the want swirling in my belly.

I'm losing my breath. I think I'm losing my mind. Shouldn't I be scared? Triggered? I reach into my head, but for once, there's really nothing there but a greedy, demanding little voice. Get it. He has it; he wants to give it to you. Get it.

"Charge," I gasp.

"Humm?" He nips at my lower lip and then squeezes my ass, rocking his erection harder against the seam of my bikini bottom. The legs are too tight for me to push them aside, and I want to.

He takes my mouth again, and I want to scream in frustration.

I think he could do this all day.

But I want more. I want there to be nothing between him and me.

I draw back, suck in a ragged breath. I try to tug his arms so he knows I want to go further. Do what's next.

He raises his arms from cupping my ass to wrap gently

around my middle. He sweetens the kiss, brushing lightly over my swollen lips.

That's not what I want. That's not more.

I groan, try pulling at his arms again.

He drops them to the bench and nuzzles my nose with his. He eases his thrusts, and it hurts, honestly *hurts* between my legs to lose the pressure.

This is not going in the direction I want.

I think a moment. Check in with myself. Still not freaking out.

So I push back, stand up, water sluicing down my sensitive skin, and Charge gives me a look of total, blinking surprise.

"What's wrong, baby?" His blue eyes darken with worry.

"Nothing," I pant. I grab his hand, and drag him to the steps. I don't know how to do this—I sure as hell don't know how to do this in a whirlpool tub. I'm not thinking too clearly, but I've got it in my head that to get what I want, what I crave, we need a bed. And I know where I can find a big ol' circular one.

Charge finally gets what I'm doing, and he lets out the most amazed, amused chuckle I've ever heard from him.

"You want it now, baby?"

I don't bother answering. He knows. He's leading me now, down the stairs to the bed by the fireplace. He unties my bikini bottom, peels my top all the way off, and I'm trying to get closer to him, hide my pudge and touch him at the same time.

I'm so distracted, I can't say which impulse is stronger: modesty or getting some of this amazingness that's all mine. His skin is hot from the tub, damp, and when I touch him, his pecs and abs jump like with a jolt of static electricity. He's murmuring, telling me I'm perfect, asking me if I'm sure, grabbing my ass with both hands and massaging the cheeks, lifting and circling, totally erasing the remaining ache in the small of my back from the long ride on his bike.

"Oh damn, it's like fuckin' Christmas," he pants into my mouth. "You're amazing. You want this bad, baby, don't you?" The question sounds oddly *not* rhetorical. Does he really not know? Is he worried, like I am, that the past will rise up and turn all this beautiful ugly?

"Yes," I breathe as I reach down, stroke his hot length as it twitches, insistent against my palm. "I want you so, so bad." I'm not afraid. I'm here in this moment, with Charge, and I can't stop smiling.

I push him onto the bed, and he falls, pulling me with him until I'm straddling him, naked as a jaybird, and he's huge beneath me, his broad shoulders and thick thighs and massive hardness that nestles up the cleft of my ass.

He's raking his eyes up and down my front. Taking in all of me. I flush hot. Squirm. I don't like this. He can see everything. My stretch marks. The sag I got from carrying Jimmy. My smile falls.

Charge notices right away. "You don't want to be on top, baby?"

I shake my head. No.

He doesn't argue or ask why. He rolls me onto my back, and rests his cock against my hip bone. He takes my lips, gently, nibbling and tugging the top, then bottom, smoothing my hair.

I love how he kisses. Like it's a destination; he has nowhere else to go.

"I love how you make me feel, baby," he murmurs. "You're so soft. So fuckin' perfect for me."

He's so big, he covers all my flaws. I look up into the mirror on the ceiling, and all I can see is his ripped shoulders, his carved ass, flexing as he rocks against me, and the long muscles on the backs of his thighs. And I can see my face when he moves down to lick my breasts again, and I'm flushed, drunk-looking, my lips swollen.

I look young, I think. And happy.

I guess I am.

I don't usually realize it.

I feel heat pooling between my legs with every stroke of Charge's tongue on my skin. He nibbles my sides, my tummy. I shriek, giggle, and he uses the moment to slide his shoulders between my legs.

I'm open to him now. My throat dries. I'm nervous again. Scared. Excited.

I look down. I don't know what he's doing. I tap on his head, and he raises it, blue eyes twinkling.

"I told you what I was going to do to this peach. Didn't I?"

I can't answer. I just blink.

I guess Sue was wrong about at least one guy with a man bun.

I think he's going to...go to town. But he doesn't. He rolls to his side, next to my hip, and pushes my knee up and out. Then he grabs a pillow and tucks it under my butt.

"Look up," he says.

I can't. But I do anyway. And in the mirror, I can see...me. The pillow has canted my hips, and Charge has urged my knees so wide that my pussy is on display. And, oh Lord, he's looking up, too. At me. In the mirror.

"See how pretty you are," he says, spreading my lips. On instinct, I try to close my knees, but he has an arm wrapped around the one closest to him. He easily nudges them apart again.

"Look at how wet you are for me. A perfect peach." He

strokes his fingers down my folds, all the way from my clit to my asshole. He circles it, and I hold my breath. I'm not ready for...that. He chuckles, a sound that promises "later," and dips a finger into my wet channel instead. I whimper.

And then he bends forward and takes my clit in his mouth, sucking, and in the mirror I can see his head, the bunching muscles in his shoulders, and a red flush creeps over my whole chest.

I squirm. I can't help it. It tickles, and it makes me ache at the same time. I'm begging, complaining really, and Charge responds by flicking at my clit with his tongue, circling it, pumping a finger inside me, making the most embarrassing, wet noise.

I don't know if I can take it any longer, the intensity, the realness. But this is Charge. It's okay. He's okay. And then there's the gathering want in my belly, the emptiness deep up between my legs. I want him. Need him.

"Charge," I mewl.

"Do you want it, baby?" he pants, lifting his head. My juices are in his beard.

"Y-yeah," I stutter. "Yes."

He smiles, so wide, and wipes his face on the sheet.

"You tell me if you freak out, okay, baby? I'll stop. Don't matter when." He's staring at me so intent, so serious. I know he means it.

"Okay," I agree, and I look down while he lines his cock up with the place that aches so much it's pulsing with need.

He's big. Reddish purple. A vein juts down from the head which glistens with pre-cum.

I'm glad I didn't really check it out until now. If I had, I'd have lost it. No doubt. It's huge.

"Still okay?" he checks in.

I nod.

"Give me the words, baby," he grunts, pushed up on his arms, his biceps straining.

"Still okay."

And he sinks into me, splitting me, slow but steady, and I try to breathe through it, in and out. I stiffen a little, and then he's seated in me, all the way. There's no space between his pelvis and mine. He's inside me, to the hilt.

My eyes fly up to his. And he's smiling down at me. He's bracing himself on his elbows now, so he's closer. I can feel his beard tickle my neck.

"Hi," he says. And suddenly it really is totally okay.

"Hi," I reply, wiggling. I feel pinned, like a bug, and also full. It doesn't hurt, but there's pressure. Definitely pressure. I guess it feels good?

I can't really think about it feeling good. My whole attention is on Charge, how he seems zeroed in on my eyes, reading me so closely I want to cover my face with my hands.

"Talk to me, baby," he says.

"About what?" I bite my bottom lip, and his gaze darts down. He's missing nothing.

"You feel good? Ready for me to move?"

Oh. Moving. Yeah. I guess that's part of it.

I nod.

He sighs, brushes kisses across my lips. "Words, baby."

"I'm ready," I say.

He groans—it sounds like relief—and then he's stroking into me, slow but deep, and he's worked his hand between us so he can circle my clit with a calloused finger. The achy heat is building again now, and inside me, he's dragging against a place, high and deep, and each time he hits it, it feels so good. And I get wetter.

Like really wet. Too wet.

Gushing.

Oh dear Lord no. I'm not peeing myself. Not now. No, no, no.

I pee sometimes when I sneeze; the doctor says that's not uncommon after having a baby. I should do Kegels.

But I don't do Kegels. Why haven't I been doing Kegels? This is the worst moment of my life. I want to heave Charge off me. Run and hide and never, ever come out.

"Oh, fuck yeah baby," Charge grunts. "I should have known my Peaches would be a squirter."

A squirter? What is that? I've really stiffened up, and if not for the flood between my legs, I think Charge would have a hard time getting inside.

He's staring down at me, his lips turned down, a question on his face. He strokes my hair, molding his hand to my cheek, as he rocks into me in that slow, deep rhythm.

"You don't know, do you baby?"

I shake my head, my chin firm in his rough palm. I'm not sure what he's talking about, but I don't know hardly anything. I was a kid, and then I was a mom, and I never learned shit about sex or men or what to do when your vagina malfunctions in the middle of doing it. My eyes well up, and his lips turn down sharper.

"It's okay, baby. I hit a sweet spot. That's all. You're squirting on my dick. Totally normal." He thinks a second. "Not totally common, but normal. Hot. Do you know how good it feels for you to soak my cock, baby?"

I don't.

"I'm going to show you, baby. I'm going to cum all up inside you. Hard. And you'll feel how good it is. Okay, baby?"

I nod.

"And you're going to come with me. So get out of that

pretty little head of yours. Look up in the mirror. Watch me fuck this perfect pussy."

He reaches down again, circling my clit, and then he pinches it, light and quick, and a surge plumps the lips stretched around his cock even more, a gnawing need returning to the small spot where he's playing, strumming. I buck my hips into him, wanting more, and his cock finds that place again, and I clench him without even meaning to.

Warm, wetness floods down, and Charge shouts, pistoning into me now, harder and faster. I couldn't be in my head if I wanted. The world has narrowed to what I want that Charge can give me, and I buck up to meet him every thrust, and he pinches my clit again and orders, "Cum for me, Peaches. Right now."

And I do. My belly and my pussy clenches and a wave of pure delight crashes through me, cresting hard, wringing me out, sending little after-shocks racing down my arms and legs, into my fingers and toes. I'm hot and limp and all the skin pressed against Charge feels raw. But good.

I'm drowsy and freakin' amazed. I had no idea my body could do that. Charge strokes my cheek, my side, runs his hands everywhere, like he's checking to make sure I didn't break anything. I didn't. Just my brain.

Then he kisses my nose and rolls, striding to the bathroom as if his world didn't just rock on its axis. I couldn't sit up if you paid me.

"You wanna go see the comedian tonight, Peaches?" he calls from the bathroom.

"There's a comedian?"

"Yeah. And then a live band."

He comes back, grinning like a dope, and he kneels beside me to wipe between my legs with a towel he's snagged. Then he lays on his side, cradles me to him, and strokes my back.

I yawn. "No. I wanna take a nap. And then I want to do that again."

Charge laughs. He presses a kiss to my shoulder. Then another.

I open one eye. Just a slit. "I just have to ask. A couples resort? With a champagne glass tub?"

Charge shrugs, and keeps stroking my arms, my hips, my belly. It's like he wants to pet all of me smooth. I'm too exhausted to suck anything in or move to my back so my chub is less obvious. So I let him. And after a little while, it works.

"Didn't know where to take you. I asked some brothers where they take their old ladies for a good time. Big George said the El-Car Motel off the interstate. Eighty said his dick. Pig Iron said this place."

I giggle. I've driven past the El-Car Motel. They've got free cable, but I've got to say, this place is better.

And then it occurs to me. "Old lady?"

Charge twirls a piece of my hair around his finger, passes it over his lips. "Uh huh."

"I'm your old lady?"

I've watched TV. I know this is something more than a girlfriend. Definitely more than a casual lay.

"Don't you have to ask me?" I tease. I don't know much about it, but it's Charge. I want to be his old lady.

"Nope," he answers. "You're my old lady."

"Just like that?"

"Just like that."

We're quiet a few minutes, breathing together, drowsing. And then a thought comes to me, and it's out of my mouth before I can think better of it.

"I wish you were my first."

He doesn't say anything for a long moment, and then he rolls me gently onto my back, hitching one of my legs over his hip. He pierces me with those blue, blue eyes and brushes a kiss across my lips.

"I am, baby." He kisses me again, harder, demanding that I open, and twines his tongue with mine. "Say it baby. I'm your first."

"You're my first," I breathe on an exhale.

"Now I want you to squirt all over my dick again. All right, Peaches?"

"All right," I agree. And I feel lighter than air. As if anything can be true because Charge says so. Because I am young. And happy. Like the reflection in the mirror says.

Too bad I forgot. Young and happy is the recipe for dumb as dirt.

IT'S BEEN A MONTH, and I'm Charge's old lady for sure. He got me a vest and a T-shirt that says "Property of Charge." I don't have to wear it all the time like those biker babes on TV. Steel Bones isn't one percent, though from what I gather, they used to be. As Charge tells it, their businesses are more-or-less legitimate, his brothers are more-or-less law-abiding, and the women who hang around the club can do what they want. More or less.

Sue thinks the whole "old lady" thing is male supremacist bullshit, but for some reason, it gets my motor going. I made sure to wear the vest when Charge took me for a quick ride while Shirlene watched Jimmy. We rode up to the El-Car motel and did it like crazy bunnies for an hour before we had to come back to put Jimmy to bed.

It's kind of hard balancing work, a kid, and doing it like bunnies. Math plays hell with time just like it does with money. There's never enough.

I love the evenings Charge spends with Jimmy and me though—mostly hanging with Pops on the pier or going to town for ice cream. And I only feel a little guilty that I'm crazy for alone time with Charge. I know he feels the same. He's been wanting me to come by the clubhouse, meet his brothers. Check out his bunk.

I feel bad taking advantage of Shirlene, though. She has her hands full with Pops and the other guys she checks up on. She's a real cool lady. She was an emergency room nurse. She met her old man on the job. He'd laid down his bike, and she patched him up. She said after that, she'd had to go out with him so he stopped coming by the hospital and giving the squares a coronary.

Anyway, Shirlene loves Jimmy, and she won't take any money for watching him, so I feel bad asking her to babysit. Which is why I'm stoked when Charge tells me about the cookout at the clubhouse. It's a family thing; kids are included. Charge says it won't get crazy till dusk, and we'll be out of there well before.

Even though they cuss a blue streak, all the guys I've met from the MC have been very respectful, really nice. Except this angry dude named Nickel who rolled up one day when Charge and I were rocking on the swing. He'd sneered at me. Seriously sneered. Charge says he's an asshole, but harmless. And then he'd snorted. So I'm not sure what that means.

I'm feeling pretty okay when Jimmy, Charge, and I roll up at the clubhouse. Jimmy is excited he finally gets to see Pops' leg. I'm not sure what I was expecting, but the place looks like a huge garage from back in the fifties, the kind with an arched roof. There's an addition on the back with a spiral stair that goes up to what looks like apartments. There's a chain link fence surrounding the yard which stretches a few acres back from the road, dotted with outbuildings and a bonfire pit. There's a wooden stage at the way back and metal barbeque grills under a huge maple tree, and a smoker going a few feet from the addition.

You can tell these guys like meat.

A few older ladies are grilling burgers under the maple, fussing over a picnic table full of salads and chips and bowls heaping full of watermelon. Jimmy's eyes get wide.

"Go on," I tell him, following close behind. It smells amazing.

As we walk, guys are calling out to Charge, bumping fists. A few come in for a half hug and a back slap. I recognize some, and Charge introduces me to the others. They all have crazy names. Fat Gus. Hobs. Boomhauer.

They are scary looking dudes, some more so than others, but I'm not intimidated. Shy, yes. But I feel safe with Charge. And Jimmy...he's totally unfazed. As soon as he gets to the picnic table, he's filling up a paper plate.

"Can I have two slices?" he asks, and all the older ladies smile.

"Of course, sugar," one of them answers. "And try this brownie here. Has protein in it, Mama. It'll put hair on his chest."

The lady has silver, feathered hair like Shirlene. She's wearing dangling Native American-style earrings and a dream catcher necklace. Her vest reads "Property of Trip." She has a serenity to her, the kind that underlines her pretty, making her beautiful.

Charge kisses her, and even her giggle is warm and earthy.

I thank her and fill a plate of my own, and I'm so distracted that I don't see them coming.

Descending.

Like sashaying locusts on high heels.

It starts with a blonde, tall and leggy, a little older than Charge. She's way confident in a way I've never been. Her belly shirt shows off the bottom of her boobs, and she's not wearing a bra. Her cut-offs are so short I can attest she's not wearing panties either. She can carry the look off though. Easy.

She gives Charge an enormous, full body hug, and then she turns to me. Smiles.

"I'm Danielle," she says. She offers me her hand, and I take it, but her fingers are weirdly limp. Like maybe she didn't really mean to shake.

I feel stupid. Off balance. She ignores me soon enough, though. She's talking to Charge about some run, whatever that is. I'm lost.

Charge keeps his hand on the small of my back, and Jimmy sticks to my side, but he's elbow deep in watermelon. I feel like I stick out like a sore thumb.

From that moment on, they just keep coming. Kissing Charge hello. On the lips. Dangling off him. Giggling. Tilting their beers into his mouth.

Tousling Jimmy's hair and making over him while making eyes at Charge.

Talking about poker runs and shows and biker nights and all kinds of things I don't know about.

My face is burning. Charge keeps glancing down, checking on me, and that makes it worse.

I don't know what Jimmy's thinking. A quick inspection, and he's still focused on his plate. He's not paying attention to this at all.

And...is it really so weird?

Charge has a lot of friends. He's a friendly guy.

And he's gorgeous. I've noticed waitresses and check-out girls and ladies at the gas station eyeing him up. Slipping him their number. He smiles and walks away. Back to me. And the couple times he was slipped a number, he handed it to me. I have to admit—two of the times, I hadn't even noticed he'd gotten a number so he could've kept it if he'd had a mind to.

I was a little thrown, a little amused. But not hard-core jealous.

Maybe sometimes I'd have a long moment wondering what he sees in me, the butter-faced single mom, but I'd shake it off. At the end of the day, Charge walks me to my door. Bumps fists with my boy. Texts me if he's working late.

This never-ending stream of hot biker chicks, though... I'm feeling queasy.

Cause they obviously know Charge. Well. They feel totally comfortable copping a feel. And they're all more than me. Taller, prettier, thinner, firmer, blonder, bigger-boobed, bolder. They look like a lot more fun.

This is starting to suck.

Charge is frowning, trying to discourage the ladies, not in a harsh way, but in his mellow, man-of-few-words way. They think it's funny.

"Danielle. Stop."

"Stop what? What am I doin'?"

She's plastering herself to his side, tickling his middle.

"Makin' yourself look stupid." Charge steps away, but she's on him like a wet towel. He must be miserable. He's really ticklish on his sides.

Maybe I should say something?

But I'm not getting into some catfight in front of Jimmy. Hell no.

"Danielle." Charge's voice is low. A warning.

"That's my name. You gonna wear it out." She giggles, and it ends on a hiccup. Oh. She must be a little tipsy.

"But you can wear me out all you want." She whispers it to Charge, but it's a tipsy whisper. I think all the ladies at the picnic table could hear her. They're definitely shooting her dirty looks.

Thanks for the solidarity, older biker ladies.

I need to get Jimmy away from this. He's not curious yet, the food and all the cool stuff like the bonfire and all the bikes parked in a row is holding his attention. But he's not dumb. He's going to realize this isn't the usual boring adult conversation sooner or later.

I can't think of a thing to say to get out of this massively awkward suck-fest, though. So I stand there, blushing like crazy and tugging at my shirt. I didn't wear my vest. I was too shy, and Charge didn't push it. He'd raised his eyebrows though and asked if I was sure.

I had been, but I wasn't now. Would the ladies have backed off a little if I were wearing the vest?

I'm starting to cycle through some really dumb ideas— maybe I should stick my hand in his back pocket like the girls used to do in high school to mark their territory?—but before I can make a move, Danielle is peeled off, and there's Fay-Lee and her boys.

Jimmy pops up, plate forgotten, and almost before I can say okay, he and Dizzy's boys are running off to some enormous, half-buried tires, climbing and swinging, and in the case of Dizzy's boys, shouting and hooting like wild things at the top of their lungs.

"I need to borrow your old lady," Fay-Lee tells Charge,

and she grabs my hand and tugs me toward the clubhouse. I don't say a word. I'm so grateful I could kiss her on the lips. I don't want to mark my territory. I'd so much rather hide.

I really don't want to see Charge's face when he gets a good look at me standing next to Danielle or Jo-Beth or any of the others and realizes he brought the female equivalent of the napkins to the picnic. No one gets excited when the person bringing the napkins shows up.

I'd rather hang out with Fay-Lee. She's my age, and she doesn't see the need to hang all over my man.

"Looked like you needed a rescue." Fay-Lee waggles her eyebrows and tugs me down onto a couch. "Beer us!" she yells at a woman—our age, maybe younger—who's working behind the bar running the length of the building. It's a wood bar, old and weathered, and there's elaborate brands burned in every few feet. The Petty's Ironworks logo. The wood must be from the mill when they tore it down.

The woman teeters over on high, high heels, passes us the beers, then sinks to the arm of the couch. She snaps her gum and shakes out her long, white-blonde hair. Those must be extensions. No one has hair that big outside the pageant circuit.

"You Charge's old lady?" she asks.

I nod.

"You're pretty," she says. She seems sincere. Also a little more wide-eyed than the other ladies.

"Thanks. I'm Kayla."

"Story," she says, wiggling her fingers at me.

"That's a cool name." It is. Unique. Like her look. She reminds me of a super-sexy fairy. Her boobs and hips are huge, her waist is teeny tiny, and her blue eyes are so big and round, they almost seem unreal.

"Thanks." She nudges Fay-Lee for a sip of her beer, then

hands it back. "You see She Who Must Not Be Named is here?"

"Shh-iii-t." Fay-Lee draws the word out so it has at least three syllables.

"Who's She Who Must Not Be Named?"

"Oh, she don't know?" Story wrinkles her perfect up-turned nose like she smells something bad. "Charge's ex."

His ex.

This party keeps getting better and better.

I don't know a lot about her, but what I know makes me want to never, ever meet her. Her name's Harper. She's the daughter of the old club president and the sister of the present one, so she's been around the club—and Charge—her whole life. She's a lawyer. She lives in their old house in Gracy's Corner. And apparently, she loved anal.

I'm inferring that last part. Charge put his finger there when we did it at the motel, talked about how good he'd make me feel, how he'd go slow until I got used to it, and then I'd want it all the time. It sounded like he spoke from experience.

Sue loves anal, so I know some women do, and that's cool and all. But anal kind of feels like going straight for the top of the mountain when I've only gone down the bunny slope twice.

Anyway, what I know about the ex: she has more money, more education, and more butt sex than I do. I don't want to meet this lady. Especially when my self-esteem is very, very not-healthy from watching a good half-dozen women hit on my out-of-my-league hot biker boyfriend.

"Is there, like, a getaway car around here?"

Fay-Lee snorts, and I realize I said that out loud.

"No. There's noooo escape. You must face your fears to

defeat them," Fay-Lee moans in a cheesy ghost voice. "Find the whore. The whore crutches?"

"Horcruxes," Story supplies.

"And you can vaaaanquish her!" Fay-Lee finishes with flair, sinking back into the couch and slapping my knee.

"She really that bad?" I ask.

Both Fay-Lee and Story nod, totally fake-serious.

"I'll put it this way," Fay-Lee says. "You know how there are sweetbutts and old ladies?"

I nod. Charge explained it. The sweetbutts are women who hang around the club. Party with different guys. Come and go a lot. The old ladies are like the girlfriends and wives.

"Yeah, well, at Steel Bones, we got a third type of female." Fay-Lee sticks up her thumb, then her index finger, then the middle. "Sweetbutt. Old lady. Bitch lawyer."

"Bitch lawyer?"

"Yeah. What Harper wants, Harper gets. She wanted the prettiest man, so she got Charge. Now she wants the richest so she's got Des Wade. She wants a sweetbutt gone, she's gone. She got a beef against an old lady, she's gone. Bitches ain't supposed to be in club business, but Harper's a shot-caller. Cause she's an attorney."

"It's fucked up." Story shakes her head. "She ran Claudette out because she said Grinder is a bad lay. He is a bad lay."

Fay-Lee nods in agreement. "Best you can do is keep your head down."

"She ain't gonna like Charge makin' you his old lady. Not so soon." Story gave me a look of condolence. What the fuck? Charge could have warned me.

"Hell, maybe you should take pretty boy home," Story suggests. "Bail before she sees him."

"You know bitch can sniff her property a half mile away.

Best you can do is punch her in the face straight off. You might be able to take her with, like, the element of surprise." Fay-Lee looks totally serious.

"You cannot be serious."

And then Fay-Lee and Story both crack up, falling out of their seats.

Fay-Lee hiccups, pounds her beer, and then hugs my shoulder. "Seriously, though. You pop her, I'll jump in. You just say."

"Not me," Story stands up, hands raised. "That bitch'll fuck up my dental work. And I ain't paid it off yet."

"You need to get yourself an old man, Story." Fay-Lee shakes her head. "Get them bills paid."

"I got an old man," Story says, tugging her micro-mini down, straightening her back.

"Bullshit," Fay-Lee laughs, waving her back to the bar. "You got a delusion. Tell Crista to keep 'em coming."

Crista must be the tomboyish woman behind the bar, super busy with tapping kegs and pouring drinks. She has a hoodie on, sleeves pushed up, and a ball cap. She must be really hot. It's a mild day.

I sigh. "I gotta check on Jimmy," I say, going to stand.

Fay-Lee grabs my hand, suddenly totally for-real. "You know, don't you, that there's no man or woman in this club who would let a child get hurt? Right?"

I nod. I've gotten that sense.

"You go check on him, Mama, but know he's safer here than at school. Every kid here is his brother. They might scrap, but ain't none of 'em sayin' shit about his daddy or his mama or any other bullshit."

How does she know?

But then I think. And look around. There's older guys here with long grey beards and big ol' guts, bellied up to the bar next to girls my age, laughing, joking. I can hear the kids outside, shrieking. Behind the bar, in the kitchen, the older women are clinking pots, chatting. Hollering out the window to the pack of kids when they race past.

I think about how Fay-Lee is being a mother to two boys not young enough to be her own. About Shirlene, taking care of old, grizzled men who aren't hers. I think about Charge's mom, gone since he was little, and Pops taking care of him alone. Like I'm trying to do for Jimmy.

My heart warms a touch.

And I start to see, a little, how there's *safe*, and then there's safe.

There's Dad and Victoria in their gated community with church on Sunday and Saturday night dinner at the club. Knowing the *right* people, avoiding the *wrong* ones. Like that'll keep you safe.

Didn't do much for me.

And then there's this feeling. That no one is going to look at Jimmy and see less than. No one is going to look at me and see a fuck-up.

It's a good feeling. New. Strange. But good.

The dread and the little green monster ease up for a little. Long enough for me to sit with Fay-Lee as she finishes her beer, laugh some together, laugh more when her old man Dizzy drags her off upstairs, and then to go check on Jimmy and find Charge out by the bonfire. Where he's talking to the most stunning woman I've ever seen in real life.

They look like a magazine spread, standing together.

She's almost as tall as he is, and she's leaning into him. Her hand is on his forearm.

I can imagine romantic music swelling in the background and a camera swooping to capture every perfect expression on their two perfect faces. In slow motion.

Like every meet-cute in every romance movie ever.

My stomach turns.

I stop in my tracks about four feet away. Subtle.

I can feel my face flame.

The woman turns to me, a smile pasted on her model-perfect face. It's gotta be Harper. She's so pretty. So long and lean. She's wearing palazzo pants, and her ass and hips look amazing. I don't know anyone who can wear palazzo pants. Even Sue, with all her cardio, can't. She doesn't have the height.

Harper's wearing a belly shirt, too, with a high collar and elbow length sleeves. So it's classy. And her abs. Tanned. Ripped. A little rib showing.

I feel like a little kid. And a fat dumpling. And like I really, really don't belong.

Charge smiles at me, and it's warm, but his eyes don't quite match his mouth.

"Baby," he says, grabbing my arm, pulling me to his side. He kisses me. Quick. Perfunctory. "Where did you get to?"

"I was hanging out. With Fay-Lee," I answer, but I can't take my eyes off Harper. It's instinctive. Like you wouldn't turn your back on a tiger.

"This must be Kayla." Harper almost purrs when she talks. She tucks a lock of her perfect hair behind her ear. She's wearing a messy bun, but she doesn't have a single frizz or fly away.

The humidity was so bad today, I had to use a handful of mousse and pull my hair back tight in a ponytail. I still have pieces sprung out all over my head. Not sexy locks to tuck behind my ears, but weird sprouts sticking straight up from the mousse that's supposed to hold them down.

I try really hard not to smooth down my hair. And I don't. It's a freakin' huge victory.

"Hi," I say.

"Harper," she says, taking my hand, shaking it. Her fingers aren't limp. She clearly does this all the time. "You're cute." She gives me a once over. I can feel the pudge puffing over my jeans. And how one of my boobs is sticking out of its bra cup and you can see it through my shirt.

"Um," I say. Then, after way too long a pause. "Thanks."

"I'm so excited to meet the woman Mark has made his old lady after...what's it been? A month? I would've held out for a ring, but you know, that's old-fashioned, isn't it? Holding out."

There's a lot of mean to unpack there, but my brain clings to one word.

"Mark?"

Harper raises an exaggerated, perfectly-sculpted eyebrow. Smiles all polite. Like she's definitely not trying to suggest I'm an idiot. "That's Charge's real name. Charge, you didn't tell your old lady your government name yet?"

Charge isn't smiling at me now. His face is cold. Blank. His body's stiff.

I had no idea Charge was a nickname.

Harper answers the question I didn't ask. "You know. Cause of all the charges. His rap sheet. Isn't just his dick that's long." And she smiles at me. Her first genuine smile.

It's evil as shit.

She calls out to a bald biker hanging out on a log by the bonfire. His head's tattooed, and he has a young blonde sitting on his lap.

"Creech! Who's got a longer rap sheet? You or Charge?"

The bald man leans back, smirks. "Charge got more

arrests. I done more time, though. I ain't got that pretty face to get me off."

The blonde whispers in his ear, and he snorts. "Good one, babe."

I blink, look down at my feet. I don't know what to say. I can't act like I knew. And I should have really known. People like me. What did I think that meant?

It meant criminals. Ex-cons.

Holy Lord. I brought Jimmy to a cookout with a guy whose rap sheet is so long, they named him after it. I thought he was in construction.

"Aren't you in construction?" I ask so quiet, I don't know if he hears me.

I feel so stupid. So naïve.

Charge puts his hand on the small of my back, but his face is stone. I don't want to make a scene, but I can't think of anything to say to this woman. I'm too busy trying to sort through the thoughts flying around my head.

What did he go to jail for?

What if Dad and Victoria find out?

What if Jimmy finds out?

I've been reckless. Again. Walked blind and dumb into trouble.

"Don't worry." Harper pats my hand. "He's been flying straight awhile now. At least since you graduated high school."

"Harper." Charge growls a warning.

Harper tosses a shoulder, rolls her eyes.

And that's when Jimmy comes running up, panting, the biggest grin on his face. He knocks into me, and I grab him, tight, and I hold on.

"Mama. They got snowballs. Can I have one?"

"Have," I mumble. My brain's slow. It takes me a minute

to register what he's asking, so I focus on the grammar. "They have snowballs."

"And who are you?" Harper leans over, her hands on her knees. She must know damn well.

I tug Jimmy to my front, my arm across his chest.

"Is this your brother?" Harper cocks her head, bares her teeth at me. "Stuck babysitting?"

And then *snap*. I've got this.

I don't know what to do with a perfect ex-girlfriend or a mean girl or a bitch-lawyer-biker-chick-princess. But I sure as hell know what to do with someone who's a threat to my kid.

"Jimmy, you can get a snowball, baby," I say, ignoring her.

"Thanks, Mama," he calls and he's off quicker than a flash. Thank the Lord.

Harper makes a mock expression of surprise at Charge, raising both eyebrows. "My, my, my. Playing daddy? That's a new one."

And I wonder if Fay-Lee's suggestion to punch her in the face is really the worst idea ever. Probably. Because she's a lawyer. And surrounded by her friends and family. Who are badass bikers.

I think for a second about what Sue would do, but I don't have the vocabulary or nerve or imagination that Sue does.

So I do what Kayla would do.

"I'm going for a snowball," I tell Charge.

And I don't say bye to the bitch, and I don't look back. I shove my hands in my pockets, so if they shake, no one can tell.

I don't care what Charge thinks or does or who he owns a house and a dog with. I don't care who rubs up on him, who he's in the habit of sharing a beer bottle with, or whether he's so totally chill and laid back that he lets a woman grab his jock before he tells her off.

I've got other priorities.

Snowballs with my son. Followed as soon as possible by getting the fuck out of here.

Jimmy gets cherry, and I get grape.

I can't get any of it down past the lump in my throat or the pit in my stomach. I take up one of Fay-Lee's boys when he offers to eat it for me.

Definitely the suckiest party ever.

14

CHARGE

"What the fuck are you doing messing around with a child?"

Harper rounds on me before I can open my mouth.

I'm so pissed, I'm seeing red. I can feel my girl's hurt, see it plain as day on her face, and I'm so pissed I can't even say shit. I've never lost it before. I can't lose it now; Jimmy's right over there, flashin' me looks. Like I fucked up.

Hell, boy, I know I did.

I should have walked Kayla away as soon as the sweet-butts came over. But I figured they're harmless, and the sooner Kayla sees ain't none of 'em have a hold on me, the sooner she'll relax and treat 'em like the other old ladies do. Guests, more or less. Sometimes the help.

Harper never minded the sweetbutts.

And that's my first mistake. Thinkin' Kayla and Harper would see anything the same. Harper's as hard-bitten as they come. Kayla's...she's a tender peach. Ripe. Has to be handled gentle.

And that's my second mistake. I know this about my girl. I should have walked away as soon as Harper showed up.

But I'm the chill one, right? It's all good. No beefs. No grudges. Boots' kid. The one who'll take the charge, smooth shit over.

"You don't know what the fuck you're talking about." I cross my arms.

I don't want to keep this goin', but Harper ain't done, and I know her well enough that if I walk, she'll follow. And I am real clear now that she goes nowhere near my girl.

Kayla's sittin' at a picnic table across the yard, chippin' at a snowball with a plastic spoon. Her face is so fuckin' sad. And I'm here, not where I'm supposed to be, cause this bitch, the one I picked, the one I backed all those years, she's a viper. And if I don't let her unleash her venom on me, she's gonna go after my girl.

If she didn't just ruin shit with her mouth, she can always make it hard for Kayla, stir the women up against her. Try to run her out. I've seen her do it before. To sweet-butts who rubbed her the wrong way or an old lady she thought was gunnin' for her seat at the table. I always figured it wasn't my concern.

How much of my chill is just that? Thinkin' nothin' much is my concern? Now I got concerns, my chill don't seem so solid.

Harper sees where I'm lookin', over at my woman and my boy, and she grabs me by the chin. Narrows her eyes.

"What are you going to do? Be that kid's daddy?" She raises her eyebrows. "I had to tell you when to take the dog out. Every damn time."

Untrue. She's a control freak. She'd fuckin' *remind* me when I already had the leash in my hand.

"Ain't your business, Harper."

She laughs. "Well, damn, Charge. I knew you were broke up over us, but I didn't think you'd take advantage of some desperate little teen mom to make you feel all big again. I just thought you'd let Jo-Beth blow you or something."

It takes a lot not to wince. One thing I can say about her, Harper's aim is true.

"Why do you care, Harper? You walked away."

She laughs. Bitter. And her eyes go a little blank. "Yeah. I did. I'd do it again if I had to. You, more than anyone, should understand that."

What is she talkin' about?

"Oh, you don't know the whole story, do you? Didn't Heavy tell you yet?" She sighs. "Bet you didn't bother talking to him. Easy's always been easy enough for you, hasn't it?"

"What do you mean, Harper?"

She leaves me hangin' for a long minute, then she says, "Never mind. You don't have to think too hard, Charge. Just go along, get along. Pick up the first easy pussy that walks by. Little girl who'll look up at you like you're a big, big man. Pay her bills. Throw a ball with her kid. I bet she thinks you're a boss. Really something."

Fuck. That stings. Wasn't that what I was thinkin' just a few weeks back?

"Why you so mad, Harper? Jealous?"

"Cause single mom gets to fuck you for rent money?" She laughs. "Dick wasn't that good."

"Done here." And I am. Past done. I feel dirty, low. Like I brought something bad down on someone good.

I walk toward Kayla, and Harper waits until I'm almost there. Until Kayla's looking up at me, sad and hopeful and lost-as-fuck and pretty as a damn picture.

Then Harper yells, "Just make sure her ID's legit. I can't get you off for statutory."

Everyone looks. That asshole Creech laughs. He's gonna fuckin' pay with his teeth later.

And Jimmy squints up. Confused. His mouth stained red from the snowball.

He's askin' me a question with his eyes.

I can't even look at my girl because I can't handle whatever's on her face.

I grab Jimmy's hand. "You done, buddy?"

He nods.

"Want to see Boots' leg before we go?"

And he forgets everything, he's so stoked. I grab Kayla's upper arm, and I thank the Lord she comes along.

But she's so quiet. When I take her to the church to see the leg, when I say goodbye to the brothers, all the car ride home. She shakes me off every time I try to touch her.

"Baby," I try when we've gone a few miles.

She shakes her head.

"Please."

"I don't want to in front of Jimmy."

So I shut up.

And I can't help thinkin' about a line after you lose a fish. Limp and still. Slippin' back under the water, and you can yank all you want, but that fish is gone.

And I'm pissed. Fire in the gut, jaw clenched shut, have to force myself to ease off the gas I'm so full with it.

This ain't me.

The man I see in the rearview, eyes hard, white knuckles. He ain't me. And I'm afraid cause I don't know what this man'll do. I thought I'd lost it all before, but I had nothin' then. Not anythin' worth cryin' over. Now I got the entire world in this truck, and what am I goin' to do if I lose it?

A wave of rage takes me over again, and Kayla sucks in a breath.

She's eyein' me, scared.

I grab the wheel tighter.

"It's gonna be fine, baby," I tell her, turnin' on the radio.

But her face says it ain't. And my sayin' can't make it so.

I 'm really glad that statutory is four syllables. There's no way Jimmy's going to remember it.

All the car ride home, I think about what I can tell him, if he asks what Harper yelled.

Stationary.

Supervisory.

Sanitary?

I'm thinking about this because if I think about the rest of it, I'll cry. Or I'll scream at Charge. Or yell at him to make it not true.

Or yell at myself.

I should have known. He's a biker, for Christ's sake. A badass with a cut and a patch. Did I think it was just a look? A weekend thing? I watch TV.

I thought cause he didn't have that one percent patch they talk about, he wasn't that bad. I'm an idiot.

I took Jimmy to a biker party with an ex-con. Where there's people like *her*.

The good news is, I'm totally over the fact that the ex is prettier and smarter than me. I couldn't care less. She talked shit like that in front of my kid. She's trash. Pure and simple. And she's not coming near either me or Jimmy ever again.

Which shouldn't be a problem since we're never going near that clubhouse again. And Charge...

My heart hurts. My stomach hurts.

Charge.

I blink real hard to keep tears back.

I can hardly look at him. He's obviously pissed. His face is...stormy. His whole body is bunched up, the kind of hard and tight that men get before they rage. My dad mostly bullies and steamrolls you, but he's lost his temper on occasion. I know what it looks like.

I'm more scared now than when he came bounding up the steps that first day.

Then, I didn't know what he was capable of. Now, I thought I knew, but it turns out I had no idea. He's never raised his voice to me. Never did or said anything that made me think he's the kind of man who'd raise his hand to me. But what do I know?

You don't go to jail for being upstanding and even-tempered.

I want to trust myself—Charge would never hurt me or Jimmy—but how can I?

My judgment landed me in the dirt behind that pool. In a dead-end job, living in a place with a busted fridge and a slum lord. It lost me Jimmy.

I need to think. I need some time, snuggled up with my boy, watching Robo Rangers. Peace and quiet. Space. I have to sort it out.

But that's not going to happen.

When we pull up at the apartment, there's a silver Buick in the drive. Dad and Victoria.

It takes me a second to see where they're standing. In front of Pops' house, talking to Pops and Shirlene.

My dad's doing his *boss* thing where he stands wide and leans back, hands in his pockets. Victoria has her arms folded, and she darts disapproving glances down at the gravel she's standing on, the river, Pops, Shirlene's ratty old *Appetite for Destruction* T-shirt with the sleeves ripped off, all while keeping a fake smile plastered on her face.

This isn't good.

"Mama?" Jimmy calls softly from the back seat. He's caught sight of them. There's worry in his voice.

I hate that there's also worry flooding my gut.

"It's okay, buddy. I'm sure they just dropped by for a visit."

"Your folks?" Charge asks, turning off the truck. I nod. This day is the worst.

He squeezes the steering wheel hard once more before he gets out to open my door. While I'm waiting, Jimmy leaps from the back, skirts Victoria, and hops up the steps to stand next to Pops.

"Saw your leg," I hear Jimmy say as I hurry to join them.

Victoria drops the smile and looks fit to be tied. I don't know if it's what Jimmy said, the fact he ignored her to go to Pops, or the general not-Gracy's-Corner quality of my new digs.

"Hi!" I interject before this can get even more awkward. "What are you guys doing here?" I hear, don't see, Charge coming up behind me. He stands close. Real close.

I can't help but stiffen. I'm still mad, hurt. Freaked out. And this is not how I imagined meeting the folks would go.

I hadn't imagined that at all. In fact, it gave me heartburn to think about it. There's no way a guy like my dad was going to approve of a guy who looks like Charge.

"And who is this?" Victoria's fake smile is back.

"Um. Charge. This is Charge." I step to the side so they can see him. He walks forward, offering his hand. Even now, more uptight than I've ever seen him, he moves with total confidence. I'm too chicken to look at his face, but I can tell he meets my dad's eye. His shake is firm.

"Vern Tunstall," my dad says. Oh, guess I forgot that part. "This is my wife, Victoria."

Victoria jumps in, her voice high and giggly. "Did you all have a nice time at the picnic? Miss Shirlene and Mr. Boots here were telling us that you were on an outing."

I guess they're going to be the ones asking the questions here.

Also, I highly doubt either Miss Shirlene or Mr. Boots have said the word *outing* once in their entire lives.

"We played on tires!" Jimmy answers. "And there was watermelon and snowballs!"

"Tires!" Victoria repeats, fake-impressed, widening her eyes and raising her eyebrows at me. I guess playing on tires isn't appropriate. I wonder if she knows I had a tire swing growing up.

"And I saw Pops' leg! It was hanging in the clubhouse, just like he said!"

"Pops?" Victoria cocks her head at me. "You mean Mr. Boots?"

"Yeah. Pops' leg is a conversation piece."

"As are some of my other appendages," Pops tacks on, grinning from ear to ear. I can't be mad; the man can't help himself.

Shirlene forces down a smile.

Jimmy looks confused.

Everyone else looks like they're smelling something nasty and trying to be polite about it.

"What's an appendage?" Jimmy asks.

"Somethin' that's attached to your body," Pops answers.

"Like your ears?"

"Nope."

"How come?"

"Good question, my friend," Pops says, and Jimmy leans on the arm of his wheelchair and rests his head on Pops' shoulder, satisfied.

Through all my icky feelings, I can't help but notice the difference. Jimmy sees my dad, and he worries. Steers clear. He sees Pops, and he's bursting to tell him about his day. And inside me, there's not just a ball of sad because of how things are with my dad. There's also a little ray of grateful Jimmy has this with Pops, even if it maybe can't last.

And it can't. Can it?

I can't have an ex-con around my kid, can I? A guy with enough arrests that it's not a one-time mistake but the basis of a nickname?

My eyes are drawn to my dad's face. Despite this new side of Charge I'm learning about, Dad's still the biggest threat. He's the one who's stolen from me.

His eyes are narrow. Determined. The kind of determined that I'm smart enough to be terrified of now.

Victoria's eyes promise a reckoning, too.

And worse, there's excitement there. She thinks I've fucked up. She's been waiting for me to fuck up again for years now.

Have I fucked up?

Obviously, yes. But how bad? Enough for them to try and take Jimmy again?

The blood rushes from my head, my body goes sweaty and shaky, and I can't follow the conversation. My dad is talking to Charge about the river, I think. Small talk.

Charge must sense something. Even though his mood is as dark as mine, he rests his hand on my back, reassuring like, and even though I want to lean into it, take the comfort he's offering, I can't. Not with Dad staring at me like a dare. I step off so quick my ankle turns a bit. Charge gets real still, but I can't worry about that.

I need to get Dad and Victoria out of here. My mind's casting for words, a way to distract them, make them leave. But my panic has caught my tongue.

"So you live here, too, Charge?" Victoria asks.

Charge shakes his head. "Between places at the moment."

"Oh," Victoria says. "Well, it's nice to have family that'll help out in a pinch." She flashes a fake smile at Pops and Shirlene.

Shirlene's face doesn't crack.

"Where's the Corolla?" my dad asks suddenly. "Figured you were out in it. But I see you were..." He trails off, as if *in a man's truck* is too unseemly to say.

"In the shop," I say. It's been awhile now. Every time I ask Charge about it, he says the garage is really busy, and since I like my loaner, would I mind them putting my work off? I don't mind. At all. I love my SUV, and it's gonna kill me when I have to give it back.

My dad's jaw tightens like I just told him I totaled it. If we were alone, he'd ask what I did to it. Nothing ever breaks, after all. I break things. Like things are never fucked up. I must have fucked them up.

"That's going to cost," he says instead. "Any repair isn't going to be cheap. And once a car that old starts to break down, it can't be considered reliable anymore."

I don't know how my dad can manage to make *your car's*

unreliable into a personal criticism, but by his tone, he does. It's one of his talents.

"Don't worry," Jimmy pipes up. "Charge and I bought Mama a new car."

I shake my head, ready to correct him.

"You did?" my dad asks, screwing Charge with a look, half disgust, half disbelief.

I expect Charge to deny it.

Instead he says, "Yeah."

That's it. Yeah.

"You're 'between homes,' and you bought my daughter a car?" There's even more contempt in my dad's voice now.

"Ayup." It's one word, but somehow, Charge makes it hold as much contempt. Maybe more.

"Kayla has a family that is fully capable of taking care of her." My dad eyes Charge up. If he were the sort to spit, he would, but he's too civilized for that.

"She does now." Charge's voice is low, lower than I've ever heard, and there's a challenge in it, a core of rage there I've only seen hints of before. That night on the porch. A few other times we talked about my past.

The hairs on the back of my neck prickle.

I've never been the center of attention like this. Not since that day in ninth grade when I was taken to the hospital. Surrounded by the nurse and my pediatrician and a lady police officer and Dad and Victoria. And just like then, I'm at sea, unsure of who to trust. What I should say. How to fix it and make it go away. So I stand there, my throat dry and my tongue thick in my mouth.

"How old are you, son?" My dad's not scared. He's not the type. The world does what he wants. I've never seen him back down.

"Ain't your son."

My dad raises an eyebrow. "Right. That you aren't. You do know, my daughter's twenty-one. And my grandson's six."

"Dad." I know it's useless, but I beg him to leave off with my eyes anyway.

"So how does a—what—thirty? Thirty-five-year-old man 'between homes' buy my daughter a car? You got a job, son?"

"Vern," Victoria murmurs, pinching his sleeve. "This is not the time nor place." She glances meaningfully at Jimmy. He's stone-faced, shoulder-to-shoulder with Pops.

Oh my goodness, he's holding Pops' hand.

Tears threaten, and I speak up. "Dad. Please."

He ignores me. Turns to Victoria. "See? Her judgment has always been like this. It was only a matter of time until someone took advantage again."

Charge makes a sound, a choked off snarl, and he steps forward.

I put a hand out. Stop him.

Keep my eyes on Jimmy.

And like earlier at the picnic, Jimmy has a way of making my way forward really simple. I might be frozen on the inside, but I can't afford to be. My boy doesn't need to hear this.

I take a deep breath. "Dad. Stop. Okay? Victoria...I'm sorry we weren't here when you got here. We've been out all day, though, and Jimmy's tired. He needs a bath and dinner."

I stare at Jimmy, willing my little dude not to bust me. He's eaten hot dogs, hamburgers, cold salads, deviled eggs, brownies, chips, and snowballs all day. No way he's hungry for dinner.

After a second, he gives the biggest, fakest yawn. Then he says, "I'm real hungry, Ma."

I love my guy.

My dad's face is bright red. Shirlene and Pops are silent, taking some kind of cue from Charge. Victoria, as always, steps up to pretend everything's not totally jacked up.

"Of course. We just dropped by to see how the fridge was working out for you. We were on our way to Harrisburg for dinner with Angela and Bob, so we thought we'd pop in. We should have called first. Lesson learned." She trills a hollow laugh.

My dad sniffs, nods bluntly at everyone, and after Victoria demands a hug and kiss from Jimmy, they leave.

I feel fifty pounds lighter.

"That where you get your elastic pants from, girlie?" Pops asks me as they drive off up the cul-de-sac.

My...oh yeah. My hand-me-downs. "Yeah."

"Good thing you don't get much else from 'em," Pops mutters, and then he waves at Jimmy. "Come over tomorrow, boy, and we'll cast a line or two. If your Mama says okay."

A smile cracks Jimmy's somber expression, and my heart cracks open wider. How am I going to take this away from him?

But I know that Victoria's on the internet right now. If not, she will be later tonight. Or Dad'll be on the phone with his buddy Hank Armitage, the deputy sheriff. They won't let this lie. If they wouldn't allow their own daughter to be around Jimmy, there's no way they'll see a biker with him and let it go.

A biker with a record.

Dread seizes my chest.

And then Charge grabs my arm. I send Jimmy up to the apartment, and after a long look—a touch confused, a touch worried—he goes. Pops and Shirlene go back inside, so there's no one to see me yank my arm away.

"Wait a minute, Peaches."

And finally, we're alone. At the foot of my stairs. The sun is resting on the horizon like a ping-pong ball on a table, small but bright. There's enough light left to see by, but the crickets are getting louder and a few fireflies are out.

I don't know where to start.

"What did you do?" I ask, finally bringing my eyes up.

Charge's face, still dark with rage, jaw tight, eyes stormy, goes hard. "What do you mean?"

"Your arrests. What were they for?"

He runs a hand through his hair, leaving pieces pulled loose to get whipped around in the evening breeze. "That's what you want to talk about?"

He glances up, like he's praying for patience, and paces off a few steps. He shakes his head like he's remembering something messed up, and he says, "That was just shit talk. About statutory. I ain't never gone down for nothin' like that."

"What have you gone down for?" If he doesn't tell me, I know Dad and Victoria will. Soon. Maybe with their close, personal friend Denise Edgerton from the Department of Child Services.

I feel sick. If my stomach weren't empty, I'd really be afraid I'd puke.

I can't do this again. I can't be this terrified of losing my child. Never, ever again.

Charge is shaking his head. "I don't know, babe. A lot of resisting. Simple assault. Drunk and disorderly."

"Simple assault?"

"Yeah. Third degree."

"What does that mean?" I put up a hand. "No. Wait. I don't need to know."

"I'll tell you anything, baby."

"Like about Harper?"

"I didn't know she would—"

"I don't need to know." I raise my voice. Somewhere in all the fear, anger's swirling up. "I'm so stupid. You warned me, didn't you? About people like you?"

"You judgin' me, Kayla?"

"Yeah, I'm judging you. You think you get a free pass for some reason?" I think a second. "But you kind of do, don't you? People judge you, they think you're some badass. You get a badass nickname and a hundred girls hanging on you. People judge me, you know what I get?"

Charge is looking at me blank. Like I've lost my mind.

"I get sent away. I get my kid taken. Cause I'm a bad mother. Unfit. I can't have that, Charge. I won't."

"What are you talking about? Can you just—just slow the fuck down for a second?"

I can't. My mind's going like a blender.

"I can't do this," I say. Not now. I need to calm down. Call Sue. Talk it through.

"You can't do this?" Charge's face freezes. "You can't do this? After—after—" It's like he's stuck on a skip.

His eyes go wild; his grimace is bitter as hell. He balls his fists, and in that moment, he's every inch a thug, a badass biker with a rap sheet a mile long. My breath gets quick and shallow. I take a step back and my heel hits the bottom step. I curl my hand around the bannister.

Turning to the wall, he pulls a fist back, a small movement, almost the jerk of instinct, and then he stops, throwing his head back. His Adam's apple juts from his corded neck. He forces his fingers apart. Dragging in breath. Shakes his shoulders out.

"Yeah. Fuck. Whatever," he says.

And then he stalks off to his bike, revs the engine, and races up the cul-de-sac, skittering gravel, sending it flying.

My heart goes flying into pieces, too.

I sink to sit on the stair, and I fold in half, tears flooding, my whole body shaking.

I give myself to the count of ten. Then twenty.

At fifty, I pull myself together. Wipe the tears on the shoulder of my shirt. Ignore the knot in my stomach. The cold that's settled in my chest. I need to make Jimmy dinner and give him a bath.

I don't get to drive off.

I don't get to say yeah, fuck, whatever.

16

CHARGE

I'm an asshole.

I pull off my ride at the overlook on the bluffs, walk the boulders at the edge, try to calm my ass down to the point where I can go back and talk sense to my woman, but I can't shake the ugly.

Kayla's face when Harper rubbed her face in my record.

Her jerkin' away from me in front of her father. Vern. Exactly the puffed-up asshole I thought he'd be.

I can't do this.

Same words Harper said when she put me out. Because I wasn't the man she needed. I was a bitch. A leech. A stooge.

Doesn't escape me that Vern pretty much thinks the same thing. How does a grown man "between homes" buy my daughter a car? Like that shit's gonna get repossessed. Like I don't know how to take care of a family.

And shit...I don't know. All I know about family is what I know from Pops and the club. Loyalty. Bustin' your ass for your brothers. Bein' there. The logistics? Nothin'. Nada.

How am I gonna keep a woman? And a kid? What have I

got, really? A patch, a bike. Stuff I didn't buy, in a house I didn't pick, that I don't live in no more anyway.

I'm workin' myself up to a real fuckin' shit fit when my phone goes off. Not Prince's "Peach," although my pulse spikes anyway. The Hollies. "He Ain't Heavy, He's My Brother."

"Speak." I sound angrier than I mean to.

"You with your girl?" Heavy booms, speaking over brothers laughing, females shrieking. He must still be at the cookout. I didn't see him there; he must've rolled up late.

"Nah, man."

"Good. Meet me at The White Van. ASAP."

"Heavy. Dude. Not in the mood. Besides, it's Sunday. They're closed."

The party sounds fade on Heavy's end, and I hear his bike rev. "Cue called. There was a break-in."

"Shit."

"You believe in coincidences?" Heavy asks.

"Sure as shit don't. Be there in twenty." I mount up and tear off, grateful for the speed and the wind and the reason to stop thinking for a minute about the grand mess I've fuckin' made with Kayla.

When I pull up at the club, four bikes are already lined up at the door. And shit. The Rebel Raiders' tag drips from the fake, tufted leather front door.

Cue's gonna be pissed. He commissioned that door from some dude in Philly.

"'Sup!" I call out as I go in, not wanting to set off Nickel's hair trigger. Saw his Street out front. Looks like a bitch's bike next to the Softails.

"In back!"

The place is destroyed. Torn curtains, glass everywhere. It reeks of liquor and no wonder. The top shelf of the bar is empty, but some asshole took the bottom shelf shit and shattered it against the mirror.

I make my way through overturned tables and past the stage, back through the short hall to the dressing room and Cue's glass-walled office. He's got a view of both the dressing room and the stage from his swivel chair, the perv.

Heavy and Cue are leaned over the CCTV feed, and Forty's standin' in the doorway, chin up, chest out as always.

"At ease, dude." I slap his shoulder as I make my way past. It's tight back here.

Nickel has popped a squat on a bench in the dressing room, and he's bouncing a tennis ball against the lockers. Smart man. Ain't none of us small men, so it's ass-to-jock in Cue's office. Besides, Nickel's not really the figurin' shit out type. He's more the execution. And sometimes, the executioner.

"There." Heavy directs Cue to zoom in on a grainy image on a monitor.

I get closer and check it out. There are three mother-fuckers on screen, black hoodies, neoprene half-masks. One's clearly young, bouncing around like he's on a pogo stick—and meth—spray can in hand. One's packing, standing look out by the door, and the third is pitching liquor bottles, throwin' his head back, raisin' his arms wide, and howlin' at each explosion of glass and booze.

Smash. Head back. Arms wide. The young one bounces, tippin' tables, taggin' the walls, while his buddy throws discus. Smash. Arms up. Head back.

"Stop."

Cue hits pause.

"Ho-ly shit." Cue squints, his bald forehead wrinkling, and Forty steps closer.

"Good eyes, Charge." Heavy claps my back.

"Mother. Fucker." It takes me a second to place him, but then...I knew it. I knew there was somethin' I hated about that guy.

Paused, in blotchy grey and black, is asshole Dan. From Garvis. The dude with the initialed forms. Des Wade's "man Dan."

"You know him?" Heavy asks.

"He's Garvis. One of Des Wade's."

"Well that's fuckin' intriguing." Heavy exhales and sinks onto a round-seated, girly chair next to Cue's desk. I can only think of fuckin' King Kong crushin' shit into sticks. The chair wobbles, but it holds.

Heavy closes his eyes and leans his head back, resting it on the wall. Cue's got it papered with old headshots of the big-time strippers that used to come through back in the day. Blaze Starr and Satan's Angel.

If you didn't know Heavy, maybe you'd laugh. This enormous hairy motherfucker, takin' a nap against a wall plastered with pics of tassled tits. Maybe you'd think he's some giant moron, in over his head. But then you wouldn't know Heavy.

"He thinkin'?" Nickel's come and joined us in the office.

"Ayup." I nod at the screen. "You seen him around here?" Nickel heads security at The White Van when we ain't aimin' him at somethin' and firin'.

"Nah. He looks like a bitch." Nickel cracks his neck, and he gets that dark look, the one he's got more often than not these days, the detached, nothin' look that only breaks when his fists fly and blood sprays.

At least it's not like when we was kids. Back then, he'd pop off for nothin'. And more than a few times, it seemed he was lookin' to get his own blood spilled.

Heavy sniffs, shakes his great bearded head, and sits up.

"Here's the plan," he says. "Charge, take Nickel and find this fuck."

"Do him?" Nickel asks.

Heavy groans. "God damn, Nickel. How many times I got to tell you. We ain't one percent. We businessmen."

"Beat the shit out of him then?"

"Yes. I want to know who the other two are. And I want to know everything about the Rebel Raiders. Where they hangin' now, date and time of church, every-fuckin'-thing. We even know for sure if Book Daugherty's still president?"

"You thinkin' change of leadership?" I eye Heavy. I don't follow this shit like he does, but I been around long enough to know how shit usually goes. Some asshole makes a play for head of table, he often gotta make his name off someone else's ass.

"Would explain the change in tactics." Heavy stares down the hall to the mess. "This is petty shit. Like the break-in at Patonquin. Tryin' to get a rise. They want us to take the bait."

"So we gon' take the increase in the insurance premium then instead? Might as well start takin' it up the ass, too." Cue's pissed. This place is his old lady, baby girl, side piece, all in one.

"Yes to the insurance premiums. And to the other, I don't judge no man. 'Cept if that's your thing, your choice of décor and profession's a bit bafflin'." Heavy strokes the side of a black-and-white tassled tit on the wall behind him and waggles his bushy-ass eyebrows.

"You talk like you got a dick up your ass right now," Cue grumbles.

Heavy laughs, hauling his Hagrid-size bulk to his feet, and he lays a huge paw on Cue's shoulder. "I'll send some prospects over to put this place back to rights. Don't let the girls in 'til it's set to rights. No need to freak them out. Charge and Nickel, take care of Dan the Vandal. Forty, I want you on background. What the fuck's goin' on with the Raiders? Why now? When we know what we're dealin' with, then we move. We ain't all stupid." Heavy cuffs the back of Cue's bald head.

We all stand, make to move, but Forty speaks before we can shuffle out. "And Des Wade? We gonna ignore the fact that Dan is apparently his guy?"

Forty don't talk much, and never against Heavy. His words rend the room like a record scratch.

Heavy's lips thin, and for a second, I think he's pissed at Forty. But then I see the unholy light, the pure rage turnin' his brown eyes black as sin and cold as death. This is the rage reserved for the shit that cannot be changed, that cannot be made right. The past. Hobs' brains dripping off a Rebel Raider's baseball bat. Crista Holt's broken body curled, knees to chin, to keep her insides from leakin' out.

"Leave Des Wade to me." Heavy says.

"This ain't about you alone, brother," Forty pushes.

Heavy's shoulders square, and I take a step forward, in between him and his VP. All of a sudden, this small office feels veal-pen tight. Fists fly, ain't none of us comin' out unscathed.

Nickel slips to stand at Heavy's back, and I inch forward to block both men from havin' a clear shot.

How did shit go so quick to hell? My girl, my brothers. Like someone took the world and shook it like a snow globe filled with bullshit and bad news.

"No, it ain't. It's about Steel Bones. Our paychecks. The future. And Crista and Hobs, and yes, makin' wrongs right, but also the shit we're building. It's about you trustin' me. You all trustin' me."

There's a long pause, a weighty silence, while we wait for whatever's goin' on behind Forty's hard, still face.

For me, for Nickel—Heavy don't need to ask for trust. That'd be like him askin' for his own arm. Forty, though. The time he did overseas put a thing between him and us. A thing he's gotta negotiate every once in a while. A few minutes for him to remember we're his brothers, too. First and always.

"Trust," Forty says, and he nods. "Can we get the fuck out of here? It smells like stripper sweat and whatever wax Cue uses on his head."

"And nut sack," Cue volunteers, cackling.

We file out of the office, and Cue heads for the utility closet to get started on the clean-up, cussin' and bitchin' the whole way.

Nickel and Forty head for the door. I'm right on their tails, but Heavy stops me. I raise an eyebrow.

"This gonna be okay with that new little girl of yours? You leavin' at a moment's notice?"

"Can't fuck things up worse."

Heavy chuckled. "Creech told me I missed the catfight."

I shake my head. "Not a catfight. Me handlin' shit poorly."

Heavy's brow furrows. "You know, man, Harper—"

"Ain't about Harper," I interrupt. "Not really. I mean, Harper didn't help shit, but...I don't think it's gonna work out."

"She can't handle the lifestyle?"

I shrug. That's not it exactly. The lifestyle ain't exactly what it was when I was twenty. Back then, it was rot gut and runnin' trains and stints in county. Now, it's mostly beers and babes flashin' tits on a Saturday night.

"She's got a kid. He comes first. I ain't exactly daddy material."

Heavy snorts. Damn. He didn't need to agree so easy.

"Besides, she got rich parents all up in her business. I don't think they approve."

"Cause of the club?"

"The club. My record. My long-ass hippie hair. Take your pick."

"So you're her walk on the wild side? Not a bad way to rebound." Heavy grins, but it doesn't reach his eyes. He's studyin' me in that way he has. Like I'm a clock and he's got my pieces laid out on a table.

Steaks at Broyce's. A weekend at a couples' resort. Yeah. Not a walk on the wild side.

My heart takes a blow with each memory. Her silly smile when I got her stuffed on filet and then ordered the chocolate cake. Her hazy brown eyes when she led me from the champagne tub to the bed, too dopey with need to fuss with all those worries she carries all the damn time.

And now my stomach is aching, too, sour with knowing I'm not enough.

She can't do this.

With all the shit weighing her down, with all the shit she's jugglin', I'm fuckin' worse than useless to her. I'm another fuckin' problem.

And I thought I could be somethin' to her boy?

Hell, if she was mine, I wouldn't want her and her kid around an ex-con loser like me either.

I didn't think I could feel lower than when Harper kicked me to the curb. But I guess I'm an optimist after all, cause damn if there ain't a way to feel a hell of a lot worse.

I realize Heavy's starin' at me, waiting. "Man, I just need to get my head straight."

"You need a long ride." Heavy strokes his beard. "And a strategy."

Despite the suck, my lip sneaks up. Heavy talks about strategy like some brothers talk about God and pussy.

I hug the huge motherfucker and slap his back. "Don't need no strategy. Need a fuckin' miracle."

"We goin' to find Dan the douchebag or what?" Nickel hollers from out front, and he revs that Street. For a pussy bike, it's got a righteous purr.

I'm right behind him, now, strappin' my helmet on. We peel out together, side-by-side, crouching low and burnin' through the gears.

Nickel is a brother to me, closer than he could be if we were blood, but I ain't never really understood him before. Never felt like the world was total shit and nothin' good could ever come of anything.

When we take the turn to Dolchester Road so fast and low I can hear gravel ping off my half shell, well, I start to get it.

The man I am ain't what my woman and her boy need.

The world is total shit.

17

KAYLA

"He said what?"

Sue brings me a soda from her fridge. Jimmy's in her bedroom, playing video games. He's stoked. We don't have a console, so as soon as we get to Sue's, he's all over her to play racing games. She always gets him the newest ones and hides them around the apartment for him to find. Keeps him busy for hours.

"Yeah. Fuck. Whatever."

"Yeah, fuck, whatever?"

I nod, cracking open the pop.

"He's real articulate, isn't he?"

I crack a smile. My first in six days.

"And he texted you what on Monday?"

"Out of town this week. Business. Talk this weekend."

"Nothing else?"

Nope. I've checked my phone every fifteen minutes since —except at General Goods in the warehouse where I don't get service—and that was it. I wrote a dozen replies, and I deleted them all.

Mostly because I don't want to say what I think I have to say. Don't bother. It's over.

Tomorrow's my day off, and I can't bear thinking about a talk. I don't want to talk.

I don't want to hear the nice, chill biker version of *this isn't working for me*. You're too much work. You can't hang. You're not down; we clearly come from two different worlds.

I've imagined Charge dumping me so many times by Friday, that when Sue invited Jimmy and me to her place for a sleepover, I was more than ready for a break from the strain of waiting for the blow to strike. Knowing that if the blow didn't come, I'd have to deal it myself. Right?

Sue and I had talked Sunday night, but the connection hadn't been the best. She'd been out of town at a convention. She said the company she worked for was using her as a *booth babe*, and that even though it's sexist, it pays time-and-a-half, and who's she to judge any kind of sex work after all?

She brought Jimmy back a bunch of T-shirts, lanyards, and key chains. I'm going to accidentally leave them at her place when we go.

"So did you hear from the parents of the year?" Sue wrinkles her nose.

I did. First thing Monday morning.

"My dad called. Said he was very concerned about the influences I'm allowing around Jimmy. That I need to seriously consider my choices and the possible repercussions. And I'd better remember that I agreed to certain conditions, and he is obligated to make sure I adhere to them."

"Does he always talk like an asshole lawyer from a cable TV drama?"

"Yeah. Pretty much."

"He shake you up?"

I jerk a nod. I spent the day on the verge of a panic attack. I kept thinking that I should get Jimmy from school, pack everything, leave town. But when I picked Jimmy up from school, he reminded me I promised him tacos for dinner. And I remembered I'm not a helpless kid anymore. I'm a grown woman. With taco night obligations.

Sue shoots me a sympathetic look. "So you take me up on the sleepover so you can hide from the boyfriend? Avoid having the talk?"

I shrug. "A little?"

"Do you want to make the break-up official?"

No. Really, really no. My heart twinges thinking about it. A for-real, physical twinge. Like what might show up on an EKG.

"It's not about what I want," I say, grabbing one of Sue's tasseled throw pillows and hugging it to my chest. Putting pressure on the ache.

"Then what's it about?"

"Jimmy," I say.

"And Charge is bad for Jimmy?"

"No." I don't even have to think. And then I pause. "I mean...I don't know."

"So let's start there. What's good for Jimmy?"

"Safety. Food, shelter, toys. Fresh air, sunshine. Good role models. Love." I smile. "Vegetables."

"Is Charge unsafe?"

I think about him before he rode off angry. His fists. His whole body tight. How he'd been that tight for hours. When Harper called him a perv. When I iced him out on the ride home. When my dad called him a loser and a user. Then, when I told him I couldn't do it, I thought he was going to punch a wall, but he'd walked away. Well, rode away.

And I think about Charge putting Jimmy's seat into the

new SUV, and then taking it out again, unsatisfied with the fit. Twice. A third time. Until I made him let me do it. I remember Charge stopping at Outdoor World before we went boating on Lake Patonquin. He bought Jimmy a life jacket because *the ones they rent with the boats ain't worth shit.*

I think about the many times, in a little more than two months, that Jimmy has let an easy catch get away, dropped his utensils, spilled his milk, tracked mud into Charge's truck, kicked the back of Charge's seat, grabbed him with dirty hands, shouted indoors, slammed Pops' screen doors, run through the house...and never once has Charge yelled at him. Or ground his teeth and shot Jimmy a dirty look. Or asked me whether I had rules at my house or if I just let Jimmy run wild.

"So that's a no?" Sue asks, poking my foot. She has an L-shaped sofa, and she's laying on her stomach across the seat cushions. I'm sitting cross-legged on the chaise lounge part. There's a big bowl of popcorn between us, and a movie on for cover so Jimmy can't overhear.

"Maybe? He's never done anything, but there's his record."

"Ah, yes. The infamous charges. Let's make an informed decision." Sue reaches down and scoops her laptop off the floor. "How do you spell his last name?"

"D-e-n-n-e-y."

"First name?"

"Mark."

"Not nearly so badass as Charge, is it?"

I guess not. I was mad at first that I didn't know his real name, but over the week I got to thinking. I don't know Pops' real name. And I'm guessing Dizzy, Heavy, Nickel...none of those are the names on the guys' birth certificates. And wasn't I really pissed that Harper was the one who told me? I'm not so proud that I can't admit it to myself.

Sue's click-clacking on her keyboard.

"Are you hacking something?"

Sue snorts. "This information is public record, Kayla-cakes. Three clicks. Voila. Dirty laundry. It's a brave new world."

"Don't tell me if it's bad, okay? Just say 'it's really bad.' And then get me a glass of wine."

"Nothing doing, Kayla-cakes. You can face anything with your best girl backing you up." Sue stops typing for a second and screws me with her weird, piercing green eyes. Her glasses make them look as big as half dollars. "What does your gut say? About this guy?"

My gut loves him.

Shit.

I want to unthink it, but I can't. It's true.

My gut loves him, and my brain thinks he's a good man who takes good care of us. Who's rough around the edges, who might have a past, but who also drove to the twenty-four-hour hardware store in Harrisburg at ten at night, after working a full day, to buy a length of chain, wood, and rubber tubing to make a swing for Jimmy in the willow tree. All because Jimmy'd off-handedly asked him if there'd been a swing when he was a boy. Charge went so late because he didn't want to leave until I went to bed, didn't want to miss time with me, listening to the ball game on the radio out on the pier.

My stomach aches so bad.

"I can't listen to my gut," I say to Sue. "I've got a stupid gut."

"Fair enough," she says, scanning the screen, speed read-ing. She chuckles a few times. "All right. Ready?"

I guess. Please don't let there be something really bad.

"Ready."

Sue draws in a deep breath. "Failure to show license on command, driving vehicle on highway at speed exceeding limit, failure to comply with a lawful order, disorderly conduct, disturbing the peace—apparently those are different things? Huh—another failure to comply, illegal entry of a park facility, false statement to an officer, disorderly conduct, oooh—"

"Oooh?"

"Assault, third degree."

"Is that the worst kind?

"No, it's not like golf. The higher the number, the less bad the offense."

"Golf?"

"You wanna nitpick my analogies or hear about your boyfriend's dirty, dirty deeds?"

"Dirty deeds," I mutter. Like she has to ask.

"Looks like he did thirty days for the assault. So maybe a bar fight or something?"

"What else?"

"Okay...where was I...failure to comply, and another disorderly conduct. Malicious destruction of property. Assault, third degree. He did another month for that one. False statement to a peace officer. Disturbing the peace. Failure to comply. Malicious destruction of property. Violation of probation... Kayla?"

"Yeah."

"There are like two more pages of this. Do you want me to read them all or sum it up?"

My throat burns from the acid churning in my stomach. My heart's sunk so low it's pinning me where I sit. "Sum it up."

"No drugs. No theft. No domestics that I can tell. Pretty much the worst are the third-degree assaults. There are a handful of them. Altogether, he did about a year and a half of jail time spread over six or seven years. And Kayla?"

"Yeah?" A year and a half in jail. I can't have him around Jimmy. What kind of mother would I be if I ignored that? I'd be the kind of mother my dad and Victoria think I am. Only worried about myself. Thoughtless. Irresponsible.

"The last charge is when he's twenty-five. Nothing for the past six years."

Nothing? He just...turned it around?

Or that's when he hooked up with Harper. Moved to Gracy's Corner and became her live-in boy toy.

"What are you thinking, Kayla-cakes?"

"That I'm so stupid. It's not like he lied to me. He warned me off. Did you know that? He said I should stay away from people like him. Instead I—"

I can't find the words. Stuck my head in the sand? Followed my heart and not my head?

Put my child at risk because of my bad judgment?

Sue rolls her eyes. "Went on a date to a steakhouse? Took the kid fishing? Had normal vanilla sex in a champagne room?"

My lips twitch. I can't help it. "It was a champagne glass hot tub. Not a champagne room."

"Go to a picnic at a biker clubhouse?" Sue's presses on. "Where apparently the wildest drama was some fancy bitch acting like she was still in high school? Very disappointed by that, by the way. I was hoping for nudity, at the least."

"Jimmy was there!"

"Exactly. Which means you felt safe. You'd never put that boy in danger—"

I make a sound to interrupt, but Sue mashes her finger against my lips.

"No. I get to finish. I know you're thinking about when they shipped you off to Aunt Felicia's—'for your own good'—and somehow convinced you that being a rape survivor with post-partum depression and the shittiest parents on the planet made you a bad mother—"

"Sue—" My face burns, and my heart drops. I glance at the door, reassure myself that Jimmy's not listening. He can never hear this.

"Nope. I'm going to finish." Sue grabs my hands in both of hers and squeezes tight. "A rape survivor with a shitty best friend who left her alone and got her hurt. And who couldn't help her when things proceeded to get worse. But I can at least tell you the truth now. Because your dad and Victoria and your own baggage have got it all twisted. I see through the bullshit, though. 'Cause I'm your best friend."

"And you know me." I sniffle.

"Down to your damn socks, I know you."

I've lost it now. I'm bawling, silent, streaky tears. Sue gathers my hands to her chest.

We don't talk about this, Sue and I. We talk around it. Mostly, though, we leave it in the past. She feels guilty; I feel like I let everyone I love down in the worst possible way. It's weird, but carrying that weight is kind of the glue that keeps us tight.

Sue's crying too, now, and she never cries. There's a sheen over her eyes, but no drops. I bet her tear ducts don't know what's going on.

"And here's the truth." Sue firms her wobbly chin. "You didn't do anything wrong. You had Jimmy when that was literally the hardest thing to do, and you loved that little grub from day one."

"I stayed in bed and let Victoria bottle feed him."

"You took care of him as best you could, but you were fifteen, Kayla. And yeah, some days you couldn't get out of bed. Because you were healing from a horrible trauma and sleep-deprived and Vern and Victoria, the victim-blamers— the people who were supposed to be taking care of you— had completely washed their hands of their own child. Because Victoria saw her chance to finally play Mommy."

"He got a rash because I didn't change his diaper often enough."

"You were fifteen, and you had no mental health support. No meds. No therapy."

"I slept through it when he was screaming for a bottle."

The shame, heavy and dark, settles on my shoulders. Scratches and makes my skin crawl.

I was a terrible mother before they took Jimmy away. I cried all the time. I wouldn't take showers. I'd stare at him, and instead of loving him, I'd wonder how much he looked like the person who'd done this to me.

A sob racks my chest.

Sue grabs the back of my head, presses her forehead to mine.

"Not done. After they sent you away, you took yourself to the guidance counselor. You made me honk in Aunt Felicia's driveway until you got your ass out of bed and to school. You walked all the way to Gracy's Corner every day to see that baby, no matter what they said and did, and you didn't stop going until they let you move back home. And then you didn't stop until they let you move out with your little boy."

"He's my little boy," I whisper. It took me a year after I had him to get my head straight, but once I did, I got on the right path. And I've been on it ever since.

'Til now.

Now I feel like I don't know what's right and what's wrong.

I know what my dad and Victoria would think. And maybe everyone else would see Charge and his bike, see that rap sheet, and think I'm stupid and selfish for being even a little mixed-up about breaking things off.

But my heart breaks when I think about taking Charge and Pops and Shirlene away from Jimmy. They've gotten more smiles, more belly laughs, more words from my boy in a few months than I've heard his whole life.

The guilt bears down even harder.

Another way I've messed up. Letting my boy get attached. Letting myself get attached.

"I'm not losing Jimmy again," I tell Sue.

She leans back, gives me a sad smile. "Why do you have to lose anyone? People make mistakes. People change. You know, good people make good in the world. And bad people make misery. What does Charge make?"

What does he make? He makes me happy.

But it's not about me.

"How'd you get to be so wise, Sue Malone?"

"It's the systems engineering. You should try it sometime."

"Not interested in the least."

I dig my cold toes under Sue's thigh and turn to watch the movie. We're quiet awhile. I'm half-watching the movie, half-listening to Jimmy's video game in the other room. I almost don't hear Sue whisper.

"I'm so fucking sorry, Kayla Tunstall."

She's said it before. And I've told her she doesn't have to be. A few years ago, I realized that she's not looking for forgiveness. It's not about regrets or wishing we could rewind time to that party, stick together, or hell, stay home and listen to music and do our nails all night instead like we had a hundred times before.

It's about love. When she says sorry, she's saying she loves me, and she hurts, too.

"I love you, too, Sue."

She sticks her tongue out at me and passes me the bowl of popcorn. On the screen, the guy runs to the girl in the rain. It's the most depressing thing ever.

"Sue?"

"Yeah, Kayla-cakes."

"Why isn't Charge calling? Has he already bailed on me?"

"I don't know. Maybe he thinks you've bailed on him."

Have I?

On the screen, the guy lifts the girl and spins her. They kiss while the rain tapers off.

It's sad as hell.

18

CHARGE

Kayla and Jimmy ain't home when I finally get back from the wild goose chase Saturday night. Turned over every stone in the tri-state and no douchebag Dan. Couldn't find a single Rebel Raider, neither. They've gone to ground.

I sit on the bottom step in front Kayla's place until it gets dark. She came home now, I'd tell her I get it. I ain't what she and her boy need.

The whole time we was shakin' down Rebel Raider hanger-ons and combin' through road houses and traps, I kept thinkin' about all the time I wasted.

This whole time I was coastin', I could've been buildin' somethin'. For her. Prettiest, sweetest thing I ever held in my arms. When I fell into bed at a shitty Motel Six, I tortured myself thinkin' about when we're alone—not enough, not like I could ever get enough—and she curls up into me, wriggling, those cheeks flushed and those brown eyes sparklin' like it's fourth of July.

There just ain't nothin' as sweet in the world. 'Cept maybe drivin' home after dark, Jimmy snorin' soft in the back, Kayla up front, head on my shoulder, makin' those little sleep noises. That peace.

Feelin' it gone rips me up inside. Tears me down. Ain't never felt a low this low.

I gotta say spendin' a week with Nickel didn't help. Heavy said I needed a strategy. After this bullshit week, I need anti-fuckin-depressants.

I ain't got no pride left. No hope, no nothin'.

Hell, she came home right now, I'd beg her to take me back. On my knees. Swear I'd get the moon for her and Jimmy. I would, too.

But she ain't here.

Pops is out, too. A brother probably came by to take him to the clubhouse. I might as well join him.

I should call Kayla. Shit, I should've called her days ago. But whatever she's got to say, I don't want to hear. Definitely don't want to hear it sober.

The clubhouse it is.

When I get there, a bonfire is in full swing. Tits are out, the music's loud, and brothers are gathered around out back, layin' money down on a fight. Scrap and some hang-around. Trey. Ray. Somethin' like that.

Nice to see Scrap out of the garage. I'd say he must be doin' better, but by his face, it looks like he's already lost a few bouts tonight.

I skip the action, go inside to the bar. Pops is bellied up, alone except for Wall, an enormous motherfucker who looks like one of those lumberjacks who competes throwin' telephone poles.

Wall must've put Pops up on a stool. Cain't see his chair nowhere. It better be safe in a closet, or I'm gonna be goin' a few rounds with the asshole who thinks he's funny. Found a prospect usin' it to race a sweetbutt on roller skates once.

Crista's tendin' bar. Long sleeves. Hoodie up. Like always.

"Your boy's out there gettin' his bell rung." I like needlin' Crista. She don't think I'm shit, and she blushes too. Like Kayla, but not as pretty.

"Ain't my boy."

"Brother does time for you, he's yours." Don't know why I'm pushin' this. Maybe cause I can't push the girl I want to.

"Didn't ask him to."

I shrug.

"What you doin' here, boy?" Pops finally noticed me sittin' next to him. He's clearly several drinks in. I'm hopin' Crista has the sense to start waterin' his shit down soon.

"What's it look like?"

"You hidin' from your woman like a bitch."

Crista cracks a smile. Wall snorts.

I can't say shit cause he ain't wrong. "She ain't home."

"She was all week. You call her?"

I shrug again.

Pops tries to crack me upside the head and misses. Oh, yeah. He's had a few.

"You let that civilian get in your head, boy? Fuck him and his *between homes* bullshit. He come around, talk like that with Jimmy standin' there again, I'll beat his ass."

"You'd need to get in line, old man."

"So why you here and not with our girl. She's not been smilin' this week, you know."

Crista slides me a beer and a shot, and I shoot the whiskey quick.

"Keep 'em comin'," I say.

Wall wanders off toward the john, and Pops and I sit together in silence, awhile. A minor miracle for Pops. Finally, the quiet wears me down.

"Vern wasn't wrong, Pops. What am I doin'? Kids...kids need a house. Stuff. Lessons and shit. I don't know...structure. A man who they can look up to."

"You look up to me?"

"Naw, Pops. You're like half my height in that chair."

Pops lets loose his hand again, and this time he makes contact. I duck away, chuckling.

"Kids don't need all that. They need food, a roof. Mostly they need you to stand up."

"Well, you ain't never been much good at that. Even when you had the one leg. Wobbly son-of-a-bitch."

Pops cackles, raps the bar for another. "Smart ass."

When Crista brings him a refill, I give her a look. Encourage her to get busy at the other end of the bar. Slow him down. He don't get to the clubhouse much these days, so he goes a little wild when he's let off the chain. Can't be good for his condition.

"What do you mean, Pops?" I try to distract him. "Stand up how?"

"You know. Sign the paper. Give the kid your last name. Stick around. You actin' like it's more complicated than it is. These days, man...you all make it harder than it needs to be."

"What are you talkin' about, Pops?"

He's slurrin' a little and makin' a little less sense than usual. Which means hardly none.

"You know, when Mandy came to me, I didn't ask no questions. I didn't mope around like no bitch. I stood up."

Shit. He brings this up now?

It's kinda known that at least a half dozen brothers could be my real daddy, but it ain't somethin' Pops and I talk about. It's kind of settled business, past-is-past shit.

"Pops? We really gonna get into this?"

He shrugs. "Seems topical," he says, takin' a swig. "I mean, by how you turned out, looks an' all, I'm guessin' I weren't the one, but I was up in that, too. Didn't have no who's-the-daddy,   find-out-when-we-come-back-from-this-commercial-break in those days. She said it was mine, ain't nobody else spoke up, so I said okay."

"You didn't have to."

"No, I did not," Pops agrees. "But a man knows when somethin' is his. Felt that way about my first Shovelhead. Felt that way about you."

Ain't gonna lie. My eyes mist a little.

Pops slaps my arm. "And you is mine. I raised you, didn't I? Besides, if you ain't really mine, you one of my brothers', and that's the same as."

"It ain't never bothered you?"

"Why would it? That's my point, boy. You was mine, so I did the best for you I could. I know we didn't have much, but you didn't go hungry. And if I'd got it all twisted like you doin' now, you wouldn't have had no daddy. Figure even some fuck-up who gives a shit is better than no daddy at all."

I lean back. Sip long on my beer. "I guess you got a point."

Pops rotates his hips, turning his stool toward me so he can look me full in the face. His bleary eyes are dead serious. "Jimmy needs a daddy who gives a shit about him. You care about that kid?"

I do.

At first, truth is, it was about Kayla. But over the past few months, it's become about Jimmy, too. The kid's a tough customer. He understands a hell of a lot more than Kayla thinks. Hurts more, too. The other kids at Gracy Elementary ain't easy on him. He's from the wrong side of town, and he don't suffer fools. Not a recipe for an easy time of it.

He was mine, I'd transfer him to Petty's Mill where Dizzy's youngest goes.

He was mine, he'd have a good enough right hook he wouldn't need to worry about other kids, no how.

He was mine, I wouldn't let his mama run me off. I'd show her I was serious. Let her know I can take care of her and him.

Shit.

I'm dog tired, I miss my girl, and now I got to sober up cause I have shit to do. I pound the rest of my beer, slam Pops' back a good one, and I make for the door.

And it really ain't my fuckin' week, cause before I can bail to get some fresh air out the back and do some thinkin', there's Harper. Sittin' on a sofa, vodka on the rocks in one hand, her phone in the other. She's starin' me down. Smirkin'.

She pats the empty seat next to her.

I consider walkin' past, but I ain't never been one to hold a grudge. Kayla's gonna be mine, Harper ain't goin' nowhere, so the sooner we have this out, the better.

Don't mean I need to make it easy.

I sit, silent 'til she sighs, all aggravated, setting her drink down with a clink.

"You really gonna make me apologize?" She rolls her eyes.

I shrug. I know how stubborn she is, but I'm a patient man.

She huffs. Drums her shiny nails on the arm of the couch. "You remember that summer you and Heavy rehabbed that Bobber?"

Hell, yeah, I remember. It was my first bike, even if I had to share with Heavy and neither of us was legal drivin' age. It fell apart by Halloween, but that summer...it was the best.

"Great bike."

Harper rolls her eyes. "Remember how I came home with that flamingo pink Cabriolet?"

I snort. That car was ugly as shit. "Yeah, you blew all those tips you made at Johnny Burger, and you looked like you was drivin' somethin' Barbie shat out."

Harper purses her lips, but I see a smile in there. First in many, many months. Since long before we split.

"I've never made good choices when I'm jealous, Charge."

"Jealous?" I don't get it. I don't get her. Not really. "You put me out, Harper."

She nods. Sighs. Then she uncrosses her long legs, stands so graceful she could be a dancer, and drops her phone into her purse.

"You're welcome," she says and winks over her shoulder as she struts away like she owns the joint.

19

KAYLA

It's over.

On Sunday morning, Charge texted me. *Busy. Hit you up soon.*

By Sunday evening, I figured *soon* wasn't, well, gonna be anytime soon.

Sue says it's called the *slow fade*. Like ghosting, but the guy doesn't totally disappear. He just backs away like you're a rabid raccoon.

I could call him. Have it out.

But it's all I can do to keep my face okay for Jimmy. It doesn't help that Pops has picked this day to clean his lawn out. Three young guys without patches on their cuts, *prospects* Charge calls them, are there all day, hauling away the old car on cinder blocks and some of the other junk out back.

The noise is grating, and all the action means I have to keep Jimmy inside. Which does not go over well in a studio apartment.

It doesn't help that Jimmy's getting antsy about where Charge has been. I told him he's been away at work, but I think that excuse is wearing thin.

I decide to call Charge tomorrow, after work, before I pick Jimmy up from daycare. Dump Charge. Or get dumped. Then, I'm going to have to have the world's shortest breakdown in the sweet SUV that I'm going to have to return. There's not any of this that doesn't totally suck.

The worst is that I miss him.

I miss his beard.

I miss him drawling *Peaches*, blue eyes twinkling, looking at me like sin on a stick when we're hanging out on the pier, me knowing exactly what he's thinking, and him knowing that I know. I miss him taking Jimmy to check my tire pressure or fill up my gas tank or top off my windshield wiper fluid. How Jimmy's shoulders straighten and he walks like a man, imitating Charge's swagger.

All the missing, though, is mixed-up with the hurt and the anger and the disappointment. About the women at the picnic. His nasty ex. His past. The fact that he's doing the slow fade on my little boy.

But I have to keep my game face on, pack lunches, drop Jimmy off at the babysitter, and then work eight hours in the dark, creepy cavern of junk that is the General Goods Warehouse.

All Monday long at work, I play the conversation in my head.

Charge, it's cool. I need to break it off anyway. No big deal. We can still be friends.

Charge, I can't keep seeing you. It's not you; it's my folks. They'll use any excuse to take my kid from me.

And variations thereof.

By the time I clock out and clear loss management, my stomach is a knot. When I dig my phone out of my purse, my hands are shaking so bad, I don't enter my passcode right the first time.

And then it's every mother's worst nightmare.

Ten missed calls and five voicemails.

From Gracy Elementary. And Victoria. And my dad.

Oh, God. Oh, God. Oh, God.

I pray as hard as I can while I go to voicemail, running toward my car as I listen.

"Ms. Tunstall. This is Mrs. Devany. The assistant principal from Gracy Elementary. Everything's fine—"

I can breathe again. I slow to a trot.

"—but we need you to come and get Jimmy. There was an...incident. With Jimmy and another boy. A physical altercation. It's not our policy to suspend students Jimmy's age, but you are going to have to come get him until we can process this and take steps to deal with this situation in a restorative way."

Mrs. Devany left her number. That was at nine-thirty in the morning.

Did Jimmy get into a fight the second he stepped off the bus?

My heart's beating a mile a minute, and I half-listen to the next message, also from Mrs. Devany. Also asking me to call and come get Jimmy.

There's one more voicemail from Mrs. Devany. She says she's calling the next person on Jimmy's contact list. Victoria Tunstall.

Oh shit, oh shit, oh shit.

Why did Mrs. Devany not call my work number? The school has used it before. The nurse called when Jimmy had a fever and another time to let me know he got a good scrape falling off the jungle gym.

The fourth voicemail is Victoria. Telling me the school

called her. She's getting Jimmy. I need to call her as soon as possible.

And then there are three missed calls from Victoria.

The last voicemail is from my dad. Thick with sarcasm.

"I don't know if you're at work, Kayla, or out gallivanting with that biker, but when you're ready to take care of your responsibilities, call me. Not Victoria. We need to discuss what we're going to do going forward. Do not come to the house. We have Jimmy. He's fine, if you care. Call before seven. If you call after his bedtime, we will not be answering."

Click.

The air is sucked from my lungs like a vacuum.

My body's half in the car, and I'm frozen. What do I do?

I try to think, but I can't. I can only remember.

Coming home from grocery shopping with my dad. Part of me had known something weird was up. Dad didn't do the grocery shopping, and it was an odd day for it. A Tuesday. But he'd bullied me into the car. Said I had to start pulling my weight again.

When we came home, Aunt Felicia's car had been in the drive. Victoria was standing on the front porch with my aunt and another matronly looking woman in a teal pantsuit. My packed bags were at their feet. No Jimmy.

I'd bust past them, run to the nursery, looked in every room. His things were there, but he was gone.

And then all my breath was gone too, like a cannonball had slammed into my gut, and I was a cartoon character because for some strange reason, I was still standing. Not blown into pieces.

I should have been blown into bits.

Dad had dragged me by the arm, sat me on the sofa. The woman in the pantsuit, his personal friend Denise Edgerton from the Department of Child Services, explained Jimmy was at a friend of Victoria's. I was not able to meet his needs. There were concerns that my negligence would pose a danger to his safety. There could be a case file opened, an investigation, maybe even court, but wouldn't it be better to handle it within the family?

I'd go stay with Aunt Felicia. Get better.

Victoria and my dad would take care of Jimmy.

It was temporary.

I said I wanted my baby.

Dad asked if I wanted to bring the police into the matter.

I remembered the hospital room, the officer in her polyester blue uniform, gun and taser and nightstick, and the pity and judgment in her eyes. Poor, stupid girl. What a bad situation she got herself into.

I went with Aunt Felicia.

And then the next day, when I asked to come see Jimmy, they told me it wasn't a good time. He needed to *adjust to the new normal.*

After that. My breasts aching with milk. Light hurting my eyes. How it took the energy of a thousand men to sit up, swing my legs off the bed, and walk to the bathroom. All my thoughts fuzzy, one biting the tail of the next until I was paralyzed into inaction.

One day, waking up to Sue dragging me out of bed by my ankle.

"Damn it, Kayla. They stole your baby. Fuckin' baby thieves. You got to get it together so we can go rescue Jimmy from growing up listening to Air Supply and drinking unflavored seltzer. That shit ends with us, Kayla-cakes. Get up!"

I blink. It's not then. It's now. I'm sitting with the car door open, my phone on my lap, key in the ignition.

I was sixteen when they took him. Powerless. But I had a

friend, and as it turned out, a lot more stubborn in me than I'd have guessed.

I still do.

I take a deep breath. Swipe the memories out like I'm mopping up after a flood.

I call Sue. I always call Sue.

It goes to voicemail.

My hands start to shake. I don't know what to do. I can't go to my dad's alone. He knows people. And I'm holding on by the tiniest thread. I want to speed off to Gracy's Corner, break down their door, take my baby back.

And it's so strong, I can smell it. A lake of fire bubbling under the surface of the fear and inadequacy, rage so hot I have to turn my head from it.

That's what is underneath.

I could beat them until they give me my baby back. I could kill them. I could.

It's in me. It was put there at that party, behind that pool, and it is so big, if I look, if I let it...it will burn me alive.

I force myself to picture Jimmy's face. His old man eyes. His stiff chin.

Nope. Not going to happen.

I am not losing it now.

I need back up. I need help.

Charge.

If I call, he'll come running.

I know this, bone deep, and like the hate, it still surprises the hell out of me.

I *do* have back up.

The messed-up picnic, the hard words, the slow fade. Still, he will pick up the phone. There is no doubt in my mind.

I don't know what smacks me harder. The rage which

feels years late? The fact that I have someone big and bad with a dozen big and bad friends in my corner?

Or the trust. That I *can*, after everything. That I *do*, despite it all.

I drag a deep breath in, and I say, "Call Charge."

"Calling Charge," the robot-lady Bluetooth replies.

He picks up on the first ring.

"Peaches."

His voice is rough, guarded, sorry, and relieved. And I have missed it so, so much. It breaks me. A full-throated sob wrenches from deep in my chest.

"Th-they took J-J-Jimmy!"

He hisses a breath, then he's all business. "Where are you?"

"G-General Goods."

"I'm at the clubhouse. I'll be there in twenty. Hold tight. What happened?"

"Jimmy got into a fight at school. They couldn't get ahold of me so they called Victoria. Now my dad says don't come get him. He says 'we need to discuss what we're going to do going forward.' Charge, I'm not letting them—this is not happening."

"Bet your ass it's not. Now, baby, you okay if I hang up? I'm gonna call—I'm gonna get us some help. I'll be there soon, baby. Don't worry. Calm down. Ain't no one takin' your boy."

No one's taking my boy.

I force my hands to grip the steering wheel. To stop shaking. That's right. No one is going to take my boy.

"Peaches? I gotta hear you're okay."

"I'm good."

"Okay."

I spend the next twenty minutes breathing deep, in and

out, fingers wrapped tight around the steering wheel, my knuckles bulging as I hold my shit together.

Only to lose it again when Charge rolls up on his bike, his hair loose and shoved down the back of his cut. He pulls it out after he dismounts, and before he finishes, I'm on him, and he wraps me up in his thick arms, and I smoosh my face into his hard chest, let the smell of leather with a hint of gasoline hit me like a drug.

It's okay. He's here. I'm not alone.

Charge whispers in my ear, smoothing my back. "It'll be okay, baby. You don't have to worry none now. It's okay."

"I don't know how this happened."

He tilts my chin up. Frowns at my tear-streaked face.

"Cause you so sweet. People don't know."

"Don't know what?"

"You got backbone. And back-up." He smiles at me, that killer smile, and as always, I wonder at how beautiful a man can be. "Ready to get Jimmy?"

I nod, and he guides me to the passenger seat, hands me up. "Buckle up, Mama," he says.

Getting going triggers my nerves. Was this the right move?

"Charge? I—I—I don't want Jimmy to be scared."

"I get that, baby. I got a plan."

"What's the plan?"

"Have a reasonable conversation between reasonable men."

"You're a reasonable man?"

"Ever known me not to be?"

And no. No, I have not.

Charge stops a minute, hand on the emergency breaks, and he turns to me, speaks hard words, but softly.

"Baby, you need to decide if you trust me. You don't...I

already made some calls. I'll make some more, do what I can for you. I'll back off. But you got to know I ain't never gonna hurt our boy. Ain't gonna let him get hurt, neither."

I used to think trust felt like taking a leap with your eyes closed. But I think now that's probably wishing.

Trust doesn't feel like leaping. It's like sinking back, knowing in your soul that what's beneath you is solid.

Charge is solid.

"I trust you." I unclench my fisted hands and reach up. Tuck Charge's hair behind his ear so I can see all of his beautiful face, now hard and tight with worry for me and Jimmy. "I knew you'd pick up. I knew."

"Okay, then. Let's go get our boy. After we can go to Finnigan's for ice cream."

"Charge, he got sent home from school for fighting."

"Right." Charge grins at me then rests his big hand on my knee. "We'll let him get the sundae with sprinkles."

By THE TIME we reach the gates at Gracy's Corner, my stomach is a riot of nerves again. How are we getting through the gate? What are we going to do when my dad refuses to hand Jimmy over? What if he calls the cops? With Charge's rap sheet, they all must know him. Petty's Mill is a small town.

Dread and panic tear up my insides.

"Hey, Charge, my man. What up?" The guard at the gate is all smiles.

"Not much, Lucian."

"Surprised you back. Pickin' up some stuff?"

"Somethin' like that." Charge gives him a nod of thanks as he raises the gate and waves him through.

I'd forgotten Charge lived here.

"How long did you live here with...her?"

"Her? That's another thing we're gonna talk about when we got this shit straight." He flashes me a look that promises later. "Lived here six, seven years."

"We were neighbors then."

"Ayup. Shoulda come borrow a cup of sugar."

I snort, but thinking about something else is calming me down. That calm flies out the window when we pull up at Dad and Victoria's.

There's a car out front. Not the Buick. An old Civic with cat paw bumper stickers.

My hands are shaking; a band is squeezing my chest. But somehow I have to make my legs move. Talk my way out of this with sandpaper in my mouth and that new anger licking up inside me.

Charge isn't having the problems I am. He gets out with his usual grace, saunters around, opens my door. Takes my hand. Without hesitating, he bounds up the front steps, and ignoring the doorbell, bangs on the front door three times.

Then he steps back.

"You trust me," he murmurs as there's a shuffling behind the door. I do. Do I trust myself?

My dad only takes a minute to answer and step out to the porch. Behind him is a woman I'd recognize anywhere. She's wearing a pink blazer and pleated slacks now, but her expression hasn't changed in five years. Narrow eyes, pursed lips. Dad's personal friend, Denise Edgerton from the Department of Child Services.

Instantly, I'm fifteen-years-old again.

Charge squeezes my hand.

"I told you not to come to the house." My dad's face is

beet red. His hair's thinning on top so it looks like his whole head is sunburned.

I open my mouth to speak, words I can't even put in the right order, not sure if I want to beg or curse, but Charge beats me to it.

"Go get Jimmy and his backpack. We're taking him home." His voice is strong, even. Kind of weirdly laid back.

"And you are?" Denise Edgerton narrows her eyes even more, which I wouldn't have thought possible. Her eyes remind me of a raccoon's when you catch them in flashlight beam. Beady and mean and not going to give up the trash she's dug from your garbage can.

"Charge Denney."

"Oh, yes. The biker boyfriend with the criminal record." Denise turns those beady eyes on me. "Kayla." Her voice oozes insincere disappointment. "You had all the resources and support to make good choices. Do you know how many of my clients would kill for the opportunities you have had?"

"Kayla has never cared about taking advantage of her opportunities. She throws them away." Dad's talking to Denise like I'm not here.

Panic scrabbles up in my chest. They're standing between me and my boy. I want to push past them, scream his name.

But Charge has my hand.

"Get Jimmy now," I say. Why is my voice so breathy? I try again. "Now." That's better.

"Yeah, you two gonna hafta finish doing your Dursley impersonation once we've gone." Charge clicks his cheek. "Go get Jimmy now. And his backpack."

Oh my goodness. Was that a Harry Potter reference?

Charge looks down at me. "What?" he says. "Your dad's name is Vern. Shit comes to mind."

"I didn't know you were a fan."

"I'm a total Hufflepuff." He grins, and it's like a sunbath. The panic eases away; the rage ebbs.

"Yeah, you are."

"You're a Gryffindor."

He thinks I'm a Gryffindor.

It's true. I totally am. I'm doing this, and at the moment, I'm in one piece. I grin. In the middle of all of this, I grin.

"Are they high?" Denise Edgerton stage whispers to my dad.

"No." I answer quick, but then the question makes me mad. "You know, I've never done drugs. I never drank underage. I never had a boyfriend until now. I was good at school. I was a good kid." Tears are threatening.

"Now Kayla—" my dad starts, and everyone can hear the *we all know better* in the words.

"No. You stopped caring about anything I did when Mom died. You probably do believe I was some messed up, crazy, drug-addled teenager cause how would you know different? You never talked to me. You never even looked at me."

"You're blaming me and your mother's death for your poor choices? Very predictable, Kayla. You're the one bringing this...poor caliber of person around your child now. Putting Jimmy in danger to get your own needs met. I suppose that's my fault as well?"

I go to answer, a thousand truths and as many curse words bubbling up, but Charge tugs my hand, steps a bit in front of me.

"A conversation for another day, I think. For now, we're gonna need you to go get Jimmy."

I don't know how he's staying so calm. Every moment

my dad keeps stalling, the volcano in my middle burbles higher and higher, burning up my throat.

"That's not going to happen. Mr. Denney, was it?" Denise Edgerton crosses her arms. "When Vern and Victoria agreed to allow Jimmy to be placed back with his mother, she agreed to certain conditions to ensure the boy's well-being. Did you not?"

"I did." I would have agreed to let them cut off my arm to get Jimmy back. I still would. I ball my fists.

"And one stipulation was that Kayla was to always be available to her son when he needed her. It's my understanding that today, you were not available. And Jimmy was hurt."

I suck in a breath. Mrs. Devany had made it sound like a tussle. A shoving match maybe.

"Is he okay?" I step to the side and forward, trying to get closer to the door, get a peek through the sidelight, but Dad and Denise aren't budging.

"You would know that if you'd answered your phone," my dad interjects.

"I don't get service in the warehouse. The school didn't call my work number." Even to my ears, they sound like excuses. Jimmy needed me, and I wasn't there. I am a shitty mother. Shame dampens the fury, crushes me like it always has.

"Well, she's here now," Charge says. "Go get 'im."

Denise Edgerton shakes her head. "That's not going to happen, Mr. Denney. I suggest you take Kayla home, and call, like Mr. Tunstall asked, to set up a meeting to talk about steps going forward."

I'm not sure what I'm expecting Charge to do, but it's not get on his phone.

"Nope," he says, not to Denise Edgerton but to whoever's

on the phone. "Can you come over? All right." It's a very quick conversation, and then he hangs up.

"I hope you're not calling your biker gang to somehow back you up." Denise Edgerton takes a small step back. "First, this is a gated community, and secondly, that's exactly the sort of behavior that makes the Tunstalls leery about their grandson's safety when in Kayla's custody."

Did he call the MC?

That's not what I want. A scene. More ugliness. Jimmy scared.

I tug Charge's hand. Mine slips a little, my palm slick with sweat from nerves.

"Trust me, baby." He ignores Denise and speaks directly to my father. "You sure you don't want to end this now? Go get the boy. We drive away. You get to be a good father for once. For a change, you know."

"What do you know about being a good father?" The vein in my dad's neck is bulging at his collar.

"Dunno. I had one, comin' up. Still do. Anyone lay a finger on me, that person would not have a hand. And maybe he couldn't give me all this—" Charge gestures to the huge houses on the tiny lots all around us. "—But he ain't never looked to take from me what's mine."

There's a silence, a strange one, and it's only broken eventually by a clip-clop ringing in the early evening air.

It's the clack of high heels on pavement.

My stomach turns as a woman rounds the corner from Bolt Court. Sue used to live up that way when we were kids, but this woman isn't a short, toned nerd with funky glasses. She's a sex goddess from a hot teacher music video.

Harper's wearing a tailored suit, black, tight and totally unwrinkled, with a shiny white blouse and a Prada messenger bag sporting the silver triangle emblem so everyone knows how much she paid. Her hair is pulled back in a low bun, flawless, and even though she's just trudged up a hill in six-inch black heels, she's smiling.

A shark's smile.

"You called her?" I whisper to Charge.

"How you think I got through the gate? She called ahead for me."

Harper's in front of us now, and she glides up the porch steps, her hand stuck out toward my dad. His manners—and his shock—make him take it.

"Vern Tunstall," he says.

Harper doesn't offer Denise Edgerton her hand.

"Harper Ruth. Esquire." She cocks her head as if this is all very cute and entertaining. "Vern. You must be Kayla's dad. Love to meet new neighbors. I'm over on Bolt."

"I'm sorry, Ms. Ruth." Denise Edgerton flicks her glassy eyes over Harper. "I'm not sure what you're doing here."

"See, that's funny. Because from what my client tells me, I'm not sure what you're doing here."

"Your client?" My dad's getting over his pretty-girl-struck-dumb moment.

"Yes. Steel Bones MC, and its affiliated businesses, charities, and associations are my client. Your girl Kayla here is an association. And I believe you have her son. So first thing, let's talk about where the young man is. Currently."

"My wife has him. In the house."

"Good, good." Harper hasn't dropped her perfect, plastered on smile for a second. "Well, let's produce the boy, shall we? So I can get back to enjoying our little slice of heaven. Eh?"

"You got a lawyer?" There's mostly disbelief in Dad's voice, but also confusion. And it strikes me again...he really believes that I'm a bad person and a terrible mother. It would be easier if he only wanted to give Victoria the baby she always wanted, but that's not the root of this. He honestly thinks I don't care about my child.

My dad didn't believe me back then. And he doesn't believe in me now.

It's weird how many times the same thing can break your heart.

It's funny how many times you let it happen.

"She got a lawyer, and she's got forty men behind her," Charge says. "She ain't on her own no more. Go get her boy."

"We will not be intimidated," Denise sniffs. "If you were interested in the well-being of this child, you, Kayla Tunstall, would have abided by the agreement you entered into when you took Jimmy from this home—"

"Pardon." Harper has taken out a small notepad and clicked a pen. "Can I have a copy of that agreement?"

Crickets.

Literal crickets. The sun is heading down, and even here in the development, you can hear them in the houseless lots.

"It was a verbal agreement."

"Oh." Harper's smile widens. "As a lawyer, I love me a good verbal agreement. And, sorry, what is your name?" Harper eyes Denise Edgerton with the same disdain she showed me at the picnic. I can't say I mind it now.

"Denise Edgerton."

"And you're with..."

"The Department of Child Services."

"Oh, you work for Bob! Bob Angelsea! You have to tell Bob I said hi. I do pro bono for him sometimes."

Denise Edgerton turns a bizarre shade of purple. I'm guessing Bob is her boss.

Harper takes her phone out of her fancy purse and starts scrolling. Does she have this guy in her contacts?

"And what's the case number on this?" Harper seems to finish her scrolling, looks up, and blinks, her eyebrows so high that on another woman, the effect would be either insane or clownish. Harper Ruth, though, looks magnificent and terrifying.

We all listen to the crickets again, the chorus swelling and receding.

"There's no case number. This is unofficial. Helping a friend and his family in crisis." Now, the raccoon is cornered, and those beady eyes dart up to my dad. My dad's fixed on Harper, though.

"Verbal agreement. No case number. Unofficial. Oh, my!" Harper winks at Charge. "If only you were this easy as a client."

I've been staring stupidly, watching this go down, but the reminder puts my hackles up. Harper hasn't even acknowledged my existence. What does that matter though? If she can get them to give me Jimmy, I don't care what she says or doesn't say to me.

"So, I'll break this down for you." Harper finally turns to me, pinning me with her slightly up-turned cat eyes. "You listening, little girl?"

I nod. Swallow my pride and the fury her words stir back to life. If she's helping, I don't care what she calls me.

"Number one, verbal agreements aren't worth shit in court. Number two, no case number and unofficial blah blah is something we like to call misuse of authority—"

Denise Edgerton makes to interrupt, but Harper holds up a hand, dripping with a few carats of diamond. "I'm conferring with my client, Ms. Edgerton. If you'll hold your horses." She purses her naturally red lips. "Where was I?

Misuse of authority! Now, my friend Bob Angelsea might be interested that one of his people is running around, interfering in private family matters, not following proper procedures."

Denise Edgerton says nothing.

"Now, wait a minute. Denise is a family friend. Here at my invitation. You can't threaten her!" My dad's getting really pissed. You can tell because his red face and head are developing a sheen of sweat. "This is a private family matter, and you have no business here! You will all get off my porch, or I'll be calling Hank Armitage. The sheriff's deputy."

Harper yawns. Yawns. "While this truly toxic little family drama is the slightest bit entertaining, I have a thing tonight I have to get ready for. So I'll cut to the chase. Produce my client's son, and I won't call my personal friend. Doug Baker. The sheriff."

My dad gapes like a fish. He doesn't know what to say. I don't think I've ever seen him at a loss. He usually just declares the discussion over. And everyone—me mostly—goes along with it.

"It's a small town, Vern," Harper says. "Everyone knows everyone. Some people know sheriff's deputies. Some people know sheriffs. Some people know it's fucked up to keep a kid from his mother."

My dad opens his mouth to respond, but whatever he's going to say is lost in a scuffle behind the closed door. I hear Jimmy's voice, too high, close to a wail, like those rare times when he's about to bust out in a full-on meltdown.

That's it.

I'm not pushing anything down anymore. And I'm not waiting one more second.

These fuckers took my kid from me.

They aren't family. And they aren't in charge.

I'm the mother. And that is my child.

I drop Charge's hand, and I ram my shoulder into Denise Edgerton, hard, dropping my weight low like I'm inching a heavy piece of furniture across the floor, and I hiss, "Get the fuck out of my way!"

She loses her footing, stumbling a little, and my dad moves to steady her. That's all the room I need. I throw the door open.

"Jimmy!"

Even in the dim foyer, it doesn't take me any time to find him. He's trying to tug away from Victoria. I open my arms, dragging myself forward despite the grip someone has on the strap of my purse, and then Jimmy gives the hardest yank he can and he's there and I scoop him up, tucking his head into the crook of my neck while I look for something, anything hard or metal because if they think they're going to keep him from me ever again, they are wrong, wrong, wrong.

And then Charge's arms are wrapping around us both, and he's gently urging me back out to the porch, murmuring, "It's all right, baby. It's all right, you guys. Breathe, Mama. I got you."

I'm panting, and there's a red tinge to everything, so I do the only thing I can. I hold tight to Jimmy, and Charge holds us both in his arms, one hand stroking my arm as I press Jimmy to me, the other hand resting on Jimmy's back.

It takes a minute to realize the lava has receded and to really see what I'm seeing.

Victoria has slipped out the door, and she's standing with my father. His shirt is half-untucked from his pants.

Denise Edgerton has backed off several feet, and she has her glasses off, rubbing them with the sleeve of her jacket. She seems out of breath.

Harper is the only one who seems unfazed, unmoved. She pastes an even wider fake smile on her face.

"That's assault," Denise Edgerton huffs.

"Oh, please. I've gotten shoved harder in the beer line at Heinz Field." Harper rolls her eyes and then she approaches us, her hands raised slightly, saying she means no harm. "Well, here's the little guy we've been talking about. Let's see you."

Jimmy keeps his head buried in my neck, his skinny arms digging into my ribs, his legs around my waist like a monkey. I hold tight and rock. He smells so good. He feels so warm.

"It's okay, baby. It's okay." My vision blurs a little, but I hold the tears back. I can feel my boy shaking, and it hurts.

"Kayla?" Harper cocks her head, and for the first time, her expression isn't hard. It's not soft either, but there's a seriousness to it that's new. "We need to check out Jimmy. Make sure he's not hurt. Then you can go home. Okay?"

I nod. "Just gonna put you down for a second, baby."

Jimmy tightens his grip.

"Just for a second, okay?"

He slides down me, turns, and stands there, his head down. My poor little guy. I'm never, never letting this happen ever again.

"Look up, baby," I say.

He does. He has a small bruise by his eye.

I can't help it. The tears start dripping down my cheeks. "What happened?"

"Cal Porter ran his mouth again. So I said something, he hit me in the face, and I punched him in the stomach. Then Mr. Evans the janitor broke it up."

"Oh, Jimmy. You can't hit people because they say something. What did he say?"

"He said I don't know who my daddy is cause my mom's a slut. But you're not a slut!" Jimmy's shout is so loud; it startles me. How does a six-year-old know the word *slut*?

"Cal Porter is a shithead," Charge says, and before I can say anything, Jimmy looks up, his forehead un-crinkling and his worried eyes brightening just a tad.

Jimmy nods. "Yeah, he is."

I can hear Victoria hiss at the curse words.

Kind of feels to me like cursing isn't the worst thing happening at this house today.

Harper catches my eye again. "Looks like the bruise is the only injury, and I think we're all agreed that Cal Porter's to blame for that one? Ms. Edgerton? Vern?"

They keep their mouths shut.

Then Harper does something strange. She reaches out, as if to tousle Jimmy's hair, but she seems to think better of it halfway. Instead, she goes down to her knees, so she can look him in the eye.

"I don't know about daddies, little man, but I do know what your mama is. She's Steel Bones. And that means so are you. So you've got dozens of brothers. And a mean sister who's a lawyer. Cal Porter talks shit again, punch him in the face. Charge has my number."

Then she stands, as graceful as a ballet dancer on those high, high heels, nods to Charge, and sets off down the sidewalk, like a model down a runway.

I don't wait for my dad to get out from under the spell she cast. Charge is thinking the same thing as me. I take Jimmy's hand, and Charge guides us in front of him to the car. I buckle Jimmy in, dropping kisses on his forehead, and he doesn't even wipe them off.

I don't know if he remembers the year I was gone. He shouldn't; he was so little. But I know he remembers some of living in the house after they let me come home, the strain, the walking on eggshells. I wasn't fun back then. I was trying so hard not to screw anything up.

"All good, baby?" Charge asks me, backing out of the driveway.

"All good," I say as the house I grew up in fades in the rearview.

I stare out the window, thinking about it all, and when we crest the hill before Route 12 becomes Main Street, a roar and a rumble breaks the quiet. Heading toward us is a line of bikes, black and shining in the late afternoon sun, huge men straddling leather seats, feet cocked out on metal pedals.

At the head is a mountain of a man, hair in a wild brown braid whipping back and forth in the wind. On the side of his helmet is a skull with two hammers intersected underneath. Steel Bones.

He raises a hand to Charge as we pass.

Charge chuckles, and he says, "Call Heavy." A ring echoes in the car.

"Ayup." A man answers. There's a lot of static on the line. Wind.

"You comin' for us?" Charge speaks loud and slow. The man must have Bluetooth in his helmet. Still must be hard to hear.

"We was. Now I guess we're headin' to the Headless Horseman for some brews. Since we mustered an' mounted an' all."

As each biker passes us in perfect formation, he raises his hand and nods.

"Harper call you?" Charge asks.

"Naw," the man laughs, gravelly and full. "Boots. Said some fuckin' accountant was tryin' to steal his grandson.

Dude just kind of comes up with kin out of thin air, don't he?"

"You really need forty men?"

"Probably, no. But that's how many showed up when the call went out."

"Put the first round on my tab," Charge says and then presses the end button.

I watch the line of bikes disappear in the rearview, riding into a hazy orange sunset, and I can't help marveling.

I know I've lost a father and a stepmother today. Whatever they're going to be to Jimmy now—and I'd never take anyone he loves from him, ever—they've proven they're nothing to me.

But isn't the world a strange, strange place because damn if in the same day, it didn't show me that family can be more than I ever thought it could be.

By the time we pass the gate to Gracy's Corner, Jimmy's conked out in the back. His bruise looks like a dirt smudge. I have that mom-itch to wipe it off.

My heart aches, thinking how I didn't know it'd gotten bad at school. He hadn't told me.

When I asked about his day, he told me about the new hamster. Playing with a parachute in gym class. Getting papier-mâché in his hair in art.

When I asked who he played with, he said the boys. And I didn't dig deeper.

He was keeping the hard stuff bottled in.

I know where he gets that from.

Charge makes a quick call. Asking someone named Wash to go pick up his bike from General Goods and take it to Pops' house.

Then he rests his hand on my thigh.

Not hard. No pressure.

When he goes to shift, he lifts it, then sets it back. Other than that, he's quiet.

"So, Harper, eh?" I say after a while. It weirdly feels like the safest topic of conversation.

"Yeah. Didn't figure you'd like me callin' her. But I figured if it worked out, you wouldn't hold no grudge."

"I hated her at the picnic."

"She was bein' a real bitch." He snorts. "Ain't gonna lie. She is a real bitch."

"You didn't say anything. And all those women hanging on you. You didn't say anything."

Charge shrugs. "I was with you. They saw that."

"Didn't seem to faze them."

Charge shoots me a look. Not an ounce of guilt on his too handsome face. His eyes are crinkled with amusement. "Baby, you just don't know the life. None of 'em flashed tit or cupped my jock. They was...fazed."

"I didn't like it." Understatement of the year.

Charge's lip twitches. "It's kind of our way, baby. But you say hands off, hands off." His face gets serious again. Guarded. "You said you can't do this no more. You mean that?"

I did? Oh, I did. "I meant that night. I can't do it anymore that night. I heard about your record...I got scared. You can see why."

Charge's face gets somber again.

"Baby, you don't get it. But you will. You're my old lady. I ain't gonna let anything hurt you or Jimmy. Sure as hell not my past. You two are my future."

"We are?"

"Yes, baby." There's a tinge of exasperation in his voice. "And don't tell me you can't do it no more. I'll do it for both of us. All three of us. I don't wanna hear that shit again."

My beat-up heart swoons a little. Then I remember the slow fade. "Why didn't you call this week? Come by?"

Charge sniffs. "I was drivin' around the tri-state on a wild goose chase for most of it. Club business. And I was bein' a pussy. I didn't want to hear you tell me it's over."

"I wasn't gonna say that," I say softly.

"No?"

"Probably not?" I sigh. "I was afraid of what would happen if my dad and Victoria found out about your record."

"Somethin' like what just happened?"

"Yeah." Exactly like what just happened, but without a bitch lawyer rolling in on stilettos to save the day.

"You mean you kickin' ass, Mama Bear?"

Me kickin'... Was that what I did?

"Yeah," I say slowly. "Me kickin' ass."

"That's my girl. But anyway, you missed your chance."

I look him a question.

"Cause it ain't ever gonna be over, baby. You're mine. Jimmy's mine. I might not have what you need now, but I'm gonna get it."

"What do you mean?" Until this moment, it never occurred to me that beautiful, sexy, gainfully employed Charge Denney might think he didn't have what we need.

I mean, damn, he bought me a car.

"We're buildin' an addition to Pops' house. A room for Jimmy. A bigger one for us. Add an accessible bathroom to Pops' room. That'll leave a third room for the future. Figure the part of town is rough, but Jimmy loves the river. Gonna convince Irvin Gunder-what-the-fuck-ever to sell your building to Steel Bones, rent it out to some of our girls from The White Van. Class up our part of the neighborhood. Heavy's already on board."

"Isn't The White Van a strip club?" I whisper, in case Jimmy's not all the way asleep.

"Yeah." Charge grins. "A classy one. The girls are clean. Sweet, too. They'll look out for Pops when we're not around."

"Where will we be?"

"I don't know. Some boat. Somewhere."

"Fishing?" Jimmy's drowsy voice pipes up from the back.

"Yeah, little man. Fishin'."

WHEN WE GET HOME, I rouse Jimmy back up and head for the stairs to our place. Charge grabs my hand, tugs me toward Pops' instead.

"Not tonight. The sofa's a pull-out. Jimmy can sleep there. You're sleepin' in my bed."

"Your bed?"

"Yeah. Still maybe got Star Wars sheets from when I was a kid, but there's room for a lil' peach next to me."

"But..." I nod at Jimmy.

"My woman and my kid ain't sleepin' another night under a different roof."

"But it's not, you know...appropriate."

Charge shakes his head. "Mamas and Daddies share bedrooms, Kayla. That's normal as shit."

I don't know why I'm arguing. My whole body wants to curl up on Pops' couch, feet in Charge's lap, while Jimmy plays Legos on the carpet. It's my brain that's slow to come along.

Jimmy's already up on Pops' porch, gazing back at me expectantly.

"Come on, Mama. Sleep over."

"You trust me, remember?" Charge cups my neck with his big palm, nudges me forward.

"I trust you."

"You just gonna have to come to understand that we're a family now. I'm Papa Bear. You Mama Bear. Mama Bear does what Papa Bear says. An' she best git inside an' git me a beer."

"Oh, yeah?"

Charge's voice has gotten gravelly, and it's doing something to my insides.

He growls, soft and playful. Lunges, snaps his teeth, and slaps my ass. I shriek and hurry up the stairs. "I'm going. I'm going!"

Later that night, after we order pizza, and after we have a long, teary talk with Jimmy about Cal Porter and smack-talking and keeping your temper, and after I nod off on the sofa while Pops and Jimmy watch *Spaceballs* while Charge goes to my place to get pajamas and toothbrushes...after that we tuck an exhausted, smiling Jimmy into bed. Charge leads me to his old bedroom, posters of Mustangs and motorcycles still hanging on the wall, and a set of dumb-bells in the corner.

It smells like decades-old Axe body spray and fresh cotton sheets.

"This where the magic happened?"

Charge grins at me while he sits on the edge of the bed to unlace his boots. The sheets aren't Star Wars. They're dark green plaid. Faded from washing, but clean.

"Nah. Didn't bring girls here. When I was a young buck, I was more the climb-in-her-bedroom-window type. Once I prospected, the clubhouse was always closer."

I close the door, lean back against it, and it strikes me.

This man is beautiful.

I'm still in my work clothes, clutching my pajamas—a tank top and boy shorts—to my chest. I can't wait to get out of these khakis, but I wait. And watch.

Charge is so big on that bed. After kicking off his boots and peeling of his socks, he unbuttons the flannel he's wearing, shrugs it off his broad shoulders. The straps of his undershirt rest in the divot at the top of his delts. He's so cut, when he moves to take off his watch, little muscles jump and ripple.

I can't believe this man is mine.

This is my life. Kayla Marie Tunstall. The girl who gets dealt a crap hand every time.

I freakin' won the man lottery. A hunger begins to gnaw in my belly.

"You gonna stand there all night?" Charge grins.

"Maybe," I say. And then, I don't know where it comes from, maybe the leftover adrenaline from the day, but the devil gets in me.

I grab the hem of my ugly, red General Goods shirt over my head and pull it off, tossing it to the floor. Then I tug the scrunchie from my hair and shake it out like a lady in a shampoo commercial.

"Yeah?" Charge's grin grows impossibly wider. "That's how we're gonna play it tonight?"

I shiver. I've never stripped for him before, and it's chilly in here. But the way his blue eyes are eating me up? It's hot, too.

I take tiny, deliberate steps across the room to the bed, and I stop about a foot from him, standing not quite between his knees

"What else you got, Peaches?"

I crinkle my nose like I'm thinking, and then I reach behind and unclasp my bra, letting it fall down my arms.

The chill air puckers my already hard nipples, and Charge groans, reaching for me.

"Uh, uh, uh." I hold up a finger. "I'm not done yet."

"All right, Peaches. Whatever you say."

"Yeah. Whatever I say." The thrum between my legs turns into a throb.

Charge leans back on his hands, grinning like the cat who ate the canary, and for once, I'm not trying to hold in my stomach or twist a little to the side to narrow my profile. I just want to wipe that smile off my man's face and make him go absolutely crazy.

I know I can, and the idea makes me punch drunk.

I pop a button, lower a zipper, and kick off my pants.

"You gonna show me, baby?" There's an edge to Charge's voice now. He's not smiling so much.

"When I'm ready."

"Okay, baby. You're in charge."

I am. And for a second, a cold wind from the past sends goosebumps down my arms, but it's not strong enough to dampen the heat that Charge's gaze is stoking in my core.

I hook my thumbs in my panties, and I slowly slide them down, stepping out of them. Charge holds out a hand. I pause. Make him wait. Then I drop them into his waiting palm. His fingers close them in his fist.

"Oh, Lord, baby. They're soaking. You wet for me?" His voice is an octave deeper now, at least. Nothing's funny now.

"You want to see?" I don't know where this is coming from, and it doesn't feel quite like me, but I can't stop. I'm riding a wave, and it feels amazing.

"Hell, yeah."

I think a beat, and then I lift a leg and prop it on Charge's thigh, opening myself to him. He could reach me if he wanted, but he keeps his palms flat on the bed and caresses me with his eyes. The blue is dark now, and it's like he can't settle on where to look: my face, my breasts, my pussy.

I slip my hand between my legs and part my lips for him, so he can see what he does to me.

He moans. A full-out, tormented moan. "Oh, let me touch, baby. Please."

I shake my head no, and he groans.

"Then you touch it, baby. Run your fingers over that sweet clit and give me a taste. Come on." He's almost panting.

So am I.

"I do what I want," I say.

"Come on, Peaches. Please."

So I take pity on him. And myself. I swipe my fingers through my cream, sending delicious little spasms zinging through my belly, and as soon as I lift my hand, he's taking each finger in his mouth, sucking them clean, pulling me to straddle him with one hand while he unbuttons his jeans with the other.

"You like teasin' me, Peaches?" he murmurs, fevered, while he adjusts me over his angry red cock which strains toward me as if it has a mind of its own.

"Yeah." I giggle. "I guess so."

"You guess so," he mutters, thrusting up at the same moment I sink down, allowing him in all the way to the root, steadying myself with a hand on his shoulder while I exhale to take every last hot inch.

It feels so good.

And that's before he leans over and takes one of my stiff nipples in his mouth. His beard rasps the sensitive skin, and he uses his tongue, laving, and his teeth, scraping lightly as he sucks. I'm so wet now it makes a slurping sound when he strokes into me, over and over. I'm going to fly apart.

He takes a break, moves to my other nipple.

"Lift it for me, baby. Offer it to me."

I do, not sure exactly when he took charge, but not caring either, and he licks and sucks, squeezing me, and I'm so tender and swollen, I arch my back, trying to get away or get more, I'm not even sure myself. The coil in my belly is getting tighter and tighter.

Charge strums my other nipple with his calloused thumb, letting go of the one in his mouth with a pop. He leans forward, rests his forehead on mine, and rocks into me slower and slower until he has my full, undivided attention.

"Not now, but when you're ready, I'm gonna put a baby in your belly," he says. "A little brother or sister for Jimmy. And these tits are gonna swell up so fuckin' pretty."

He obviously doesn't know what happens to boobs when you're pregnant. But the idea of a baby? One day?

It makes me feel raw. But good. Like how a spring day is raw. Looking forward when you've been just getting by...it's a hopeful feeling, but there's hurt in it, too. Sadness for the past that can't be changed.

Charge notices that I've lost focus so he strokes harder, gripping my hips so there's no give, no space between us when he's all the way inside me. I had been so close, but the orgasm's danced off now, and I groan in frustration.

"Where'd you go, baby? Come back here. With me." He takes my chin and lifts it for a kiss. A soft one, despite his bristly beard.

I reach up, ring my arms around his neck.

"Hold on, baby. Okay?"

"Okay," I moan into his shoulder, and he does this thing...he lifts himself from the bed, half bounces me, filling me deeper than ever, and he turns to lay me on my back on the bed. I hook my legs around him, and he rocks, then thrusts, slow and steady, as if he has nowhere else to ever be. I'm just hanging on for the slow, sweet ride.

He uses his free hand to brush a piece of hair from my eyes, and he drops kiss after kiss on my forehead, my nose.

He moves a hand to push my knee higher so he can hit deeper, so deep inside me that there's a twinge of pain and the hunger-stoking sensation of him nailing that spot, and he knows it, so he goes to work, slamming it over and over until a wet, hot gush of fluids soaks his cock and trickles down between my ass cheeks, pooling on the sheets.

"That's it baby. Squirt all over me. You know how I love it when you get me all wet."

Even though I've flooded the bed, he's not stopping, going double-time instead, murmuring encouragement. "Now cum on my cock, baby. Let go. Let go."

I'm crying, moaning into his chest. I have enough brain still working to know I can't make too much noise, but it's hard. I'm so close, I've been close for hours now, and I want it so bad, I'm desperate.

"Charge," I whine. "It's so close."

He slips a hand between us and goes for my clit, circling the edges with the light touch he's learned I like.

"I got you, baby," he murmurs in my ear, and then the orgasm is right there, and all I need is Charge, whispering, "You're so fuckin' beautiful when you cum for me. My pretty peach. I'm gonna make you feel good every night, baby. Just like this. Just like this."

He cums, hard, his body seizing, muscles bunching, and I can feel a rush of hot wetness fill me up while my insides clench and flutter, my own orgasm racing through me, cresting in waves one bigger than the next, making me gasp for air.

After, he props me in a chair while he changes the sheets. Then he sneaks out to the bathroom in his boxers to bring me a warm washcloth. He sinks to his knees in front of me, props a leg on his shoulder, and with gentle swipes, cleans between my legs.

I don't have the strength to be embarrassed.

He bends over and plants a kiss in the curls above my slit.

"Next, I'm gonna taste this peach again."

I want that, but I also want to sleep for one million hours. And I have work tomorrow. Plus I have to go up to the school, find out what's going on with Cal Porter. Give them a piece of my mind for not calling my work number. Make some changes to the emergency contact list.

Oh, crap. My mellow is gone.

Charge can tell.

He scoops me up, clicks off the overhead light, takes me to the bed, and lays me between his legs as he leans against the headboard. A one bulb lamp casts a tiny glow from the bedside table.

"First order of business, we gonna need to do it on towels from here on out. I ain't gonna do a load of laundry a day cause my girl's a squirter."

I slap his chest, play-mad. Then I think twice. "You're gonna do the laundry?"

"Did you want to?" he asks.

No. No, I did not.

"Now tell me what turned that dopey grin I worked so hard for upside down just now."

I sigh. My grin probably was totally dopey. "Work.

Jimmy's school. What to do about Dad and Victoria. My dad knows people. He's not going to drop this."

"Oh, yes he is. Baby, you know people, too. One of those people is the long-time side-piece of the principal at Petty's Mill Elementary. I say we talk to Jimmy. There's only a week or two left, but if he's down with switchin' schools, next year, we move him. So he can be with his brothers. That's where Dizzy's youngest goes. You have to drive him, but you'll have time."

"Not if I want to get to work on time."

"Lucky you, your new boss is flexible."

"My new boss?"

"Uh, huh. Ain't at all like your old boss. This one's sexy as shit."

I give him the side eye. "I'm going to work construction?"

"Nah. Inventory. Pig Iron says he can use you at the businesses. The garage, The White Van, the warehouse where we keep the tools and shit. Doin' inventory mostly. Same wage as General Goods. You pick your hours. Figured that'd do until I can convince you to quit."

"I'm not going to quit working."

I might be stupid in love, but I'm not full-blown stupid. I'd love to stay home, but not 'til I have a ring on my finger. And some bucks in a bank account with my name on it.

"I figured, baby." Charge wraps his thick arms around my middle, nuzzles the crook of my neck with his beard. A good, warm tired settles over me like a thick blanket.

"Hey, Charge?" The words keep coming, although I'm drifting off.

"Yeah, baby?"

"What do you inventory at a strip club?"

He chuckles. "Don't know, babe. The excitement's in the findin' out, I guess."

We lay there a little longer, me curled on top, him stroking my skin, whatever he can reach, fussing with my hair and dusting me all over with kisses. I'm on the verge of passing out, but I don't let go, instead I hover at the edge, not wanting this moment to end.

The window is cracked open a sliver, enough to let in the night sounds: the crickets and the river lapping its banks. An owl in the distance and the shushing of tires on pavement up the street.

"Peaches?" Charge murmurs.

"Uh huh?"

"Do you love me?" His voice is a little too deep. A touch uncertain.

I smile, lifting the cheek plastered to his chest. How can he not know? He's so deep in my head and my heart, I figured he'd read it all there already.

"I love you," I say.

"I love you and Jimmy, too."

"You didn't make me ask." I squirm, freeing my arms to wrap around his neck.

"You'll never have to ask, baby. You and our boy will always know. My job is to show you every day. Okay?"

"Okay."

And it was.

For the first time.

It was all okay.

EPILOGUE
NICKEL

My cell rings at three in the morning. It's Heavy. He says gear up. We ride.

My brain's a little slow to start, but my adrenaline's on board. It shouts *fuck yeah*.

Rebel Raiders are at the Patonquin site. A Garvis guy raised the alarm. Dude was cryin' so hard Charge said he couldn't make out much about the situation.

I roll over, hop over a club whore lying half across my bed. Jo-Beth? Angel? I dunno. I was wasted when I crashed. I guess the girl must've been worse off than me. She didn't make it all the way on the bed.

I toss my blanket over her, and then I pull on pants and grab my piece from the night table.

Heavy, Forty, and I meet out front. Creech and Wall stumble up lookin' rough. Bitchin' about it bein' late and all.

I ain't sayin' shit. My mind is in fuckin' knots, worryin' shit to death like it always does, but to my body? This is Christmas Day, man. The adrenaline hits my veins, purer than any high, and I draw in a deep breath of crisp night air.

This next little bit? I got a cravin' for it, a jones, and like any addict, I'm running on one part shame to two parts unholy glee I don't have to hold shit in, hold shit back. All the fuckin' ugly that squats in me like a raving lunatic can go where it wants, do what it wants. Wreck anything or wreck it all.

I kick start my ride and shout into the night over the roar of the engine cause the monster in me ain't a quiet one.

Damn, I wish every night was fuck-some-shit-up night.

A thick fog has rolled up from the river, and the light from the full moon is streamin' down and turnin' the world into a funhouse mirror. More brothers meet us as we clear town limits; we hear 'em before we see 'em, the roar of their engines distorted in the fog.

Charge, Bullet, Dizzy, and Cue pull into formation first. Then the old-timers. Pig Iron, Gus, Big George. Grinder and that dumbass boy of his, Bucky. No Scrap. Heavy must not have given him the call. Scrap's done his time on this shit. He'll be pissed as hell when he finds out we left his ass behind, though.

Our engines echo between the hills. The dark is dark. Ain't nobody on the roads tonight. The night air burns my chest, and I swear, my dick gets a little hard.

I'm about to get loose of my chains and ain't no one gonna try and stop me. The fear is there. Heart in my throat and hands shakin'. Is this the time I go too far? The ugliness roars, "Hell, yes. What do we got to lose?"

For an instant, wide blue eyes and long blonde hair flash into my mind, but I shut that shit down.

Nothin'. I got nothin' to lose and never did.

When we take the exit for the Patonquin site, the fog lifts into swirls hovering a few feet above the ground. There should be a gate, a guard. But all's I can see is chain link on the ground.

We back our rides into a line, headlights on, aimed at the site. I check my piece, make sure the safety's off, and then I take a good look around. My pulse races triple time. Someone has not only plowed down the wire fence at the gate, but beyond...

It's a fuckin' rally. An easy thirty or forty bikes. Headlights on, facin' us. They've rode all over the foundation, torn shit up. Somethin' is on fire—a pallet of plywood?—lightin' the scene like a horror movie version of hell.

"Motherfuckers." I'm off my bike and sprintin' toward them, drawing my piece, a half-dozen paces away when Forty catches up to me.

"Think," he barks, hookin' his arm around my middle, usin' his shoulder to push me back. I keep goin'—I ain't easy to stop—so he defensive-linemans my ass back ten feet.

"Use your fuckin' brain." He slaps both sides of my head.

"Ain't my strong suit," I snarl. And it really ain't.

He's right, though. I got to ease up. Pull back. Remember I got brothers, and we got a chain of command. This is Heavy's play. I ain't got nothin' stoppin' me, but Dizzy, Charge, the old timers...they got old ladies and kids at home.

I shake it out. Force the ugly down. Go stand next to my president.

"What's the play?" I ask.

Heavy's at the center of our line, stance wide, his chest is risin' and fallin' quick. That's the only way I know he understands as well as I do how totally fucked we are. Outnumbered two-to-one at least.

This is gonna be insane. I can't stop the grin.

I love insane.

Heavy spits. Sniffs. "YOLO, my brothers," he finally answers, voice low and calm. "What other play we got?"

Then he strides forward, to the edge of the foundation, and cups his hands around his mouth.

"All right, limp dicks. You got our attention. What the fuck do you want?"

For a long moment, there's silence, broken only with the growl of engines. All the Raiders seem to be looking up, not at us, but higher. At the moon? And then a lighter flares in the dark, and we see him.

On a column in the middle of the site. At least two stories in the air. Sitting with his legs dangling over the edge. A mad man. A ghost.

"Heavy," the ghost cackles. Not a care in the world. "You look old as shit." Then he takes a drag, the butt lightin' up a mouth full of gold fronts. His raises his pasty-white face and the moonlight catches it. In an instant, I'm thrown back in time.

Ten years old. Hidin' from the shit at home at the club-house garage. This motherfucker pullin' up in a Willie G. special, blacked-out engine and that badass rear wheel made entirely of aluminum. Hair dyed bright green, hand in the back pocket of a club whore wearin' a tube top that didn't cover her nips.

Fuckin' Knocker Johnson. Legend. Convict. Son of a Steel Bones founding member. And now, apparently, a fuckin' Rebel Raider.

His hair's jet black now. His nose looks like it got broke a dozen times. But it's him. In the flesh.

"I thought you were upstate," Heavy shouts, his voice echoing back to us from the hills.

"Got early release. Good behavior." Knocker gestures at the Rebel Raiders around him. "As you can see."

"I see a man who's got the wrong idea."

Knocker flicks his cigarette and leaps to his feet. He

sways. "Fall, motherfucker," I mutter. Don't care what he was. He been out bad since he blacked-out his Steel Bones ink. Heard about that from Scrap many years past. Knocker wanted no parts of the club when he was upstate.

"I don't think you see at all, prez." Knocker grins and those fronts gleam. With his sunken sockets he looks like one of those Mexican skulls with jewels for eyes. "I'm a free man. Paid your daddy's debt to society." He sweeps his hand like the ringmaster at a circus. "I see you been busy. Makin' bank with Des Wade?"

"We should talk, brother." There's a note in Heavy's voice. A weight. Jagged. What the fuck is happenin' here? Why's Heavy not callin' this shit? This don't seem to be shapin' up into a free-for-all. The ugly in me screams in rage, and all my muscles bunch. The ugly don't like disappointment.

Knocker keeps runnin' his mouth. "Your daddy set up me and mine to take a fall. Then you got in bed with the motherfucker who put him up to it. We ain't got nothin' to talk about, *brother*."

"That's old beef." Toward the back of the site, a stuttering pop draws everyone's eyes. Ain't a gunshot. Sounds like fireworks. Heavy reaches the hand that was on his hip toward the gun tucked into the back of his pants anyway. "The business between Stone and the MC is settled."

"You got eighteen years in that back pocket you reachin' for?"

Heavy's hand freezes.

"Cause if you don't, ain't nothin' settled. My father didn't settle nothin' with you. He lost his mind. You took two sons from him."

"Two pieces of shit!" Pig Iron yells. Damn. He's shakin' worse than me. Poor bastard. Don't know how he's not takin' a shot at that fucker, but Wall is right up on him, ready to shut him down if he gets froggy.

Feels weird for once not bein' the motherfucker everyone is eyein' all wary.

"No parley?" Heavy calls, and squares his shoulders. I recognize the signal. It's go time.

"No parley." Knocker spits.

Heavy moves quick, the kind of quick no one expects a man his size to have, and as he draws we're all with him, at his back, a line of men ready to go against an army, for him, for each other.

It all happens so fast, I can only squeeze off a half dozen shots before a bullet kicks up the dirt inches in front of me, and I dive for my bike.

While bullets are flying, Knocker drops down the column, swingin' from some rope, and the bikes in front of us roar to life. They ride, all over, figure eights and donuts, and added to the noise is fire, flashing into the dark, ropes of flame kickin' up in their wake.

Knocker laughs and hops behind a Raider, ridin' bitch up and out of the site that now crackles and smokes. And then—

Boom!

Dirt explodes, rains down in thick clumps, and then again—boom!

Dark smoke and fire fill the air, and explosion after explosion rocks the ground. The column Knocker was sitting on lists, then crumbles, hunks of concrete piling up, sending grey dust billowing in every direction.

They've rigged the place. And as they drive off into the night, the roar of engines mingling with the rebel yells, I can see clear as day in the light of the fires they set.

Past ain't past no more.

Heavy's weird calm is gone. He stands on a rise, hair wild in the wind, emptying his chamber into the air behind that last Rebel Rider out of the site. His eyes are blown out, and rage has made his face monstrous. I've never felt closer to my brother than in this moment.

My body fiends for blood, and I laugh into the chaos. This is war.

I was made for this.

THE STORY CONTINUES in Nickel's Story, book two of the Steel Bones MC series.

ABOUT THE AUTHOR

Cate C. Wells indulges herself in everything from motorcycle club to small town to mafia to paranormal romance. Whatever the subgenre, readers can expect character-driven stories that are raw, real, and emotionally satisfying. Cate's into messy love, flaws, long roads to redemption, grace, and happy ever after, in books and in life.

Along with stories, she's collected a husband and three children along the way. She lives in Baltimore when she's not exploring the world with the family.

I love to hear from readers! Let's chat.
Facebook: @catecwells
Twitter: @CateCWells1
Bookbub: @catecwells

For a FREE NOVELLA and updates, sign up for my newsletter at www.catecwells.com.

Printed in Great Britain
by Amazon